Chronically Dolores

Chronically Dolores

Maya Van Wagenen

DUTTON BOOKS

DUTTON BOOKS

An imprint of Penguin Random House LLC, New York

First published in the United States of America by Dutton Books,
an imprint of Penguin Random House LLC, 2024

Dutton is a registered trademark of Penguin Random House LLC.
The Penguin colophon is a registered trademark of Penguin Books Limited.

Visit us online at PenguinRandomHouse.com.

Library of Congress Cataloging-in-Publication Data is available.

ISBN 9780525426820
1st Printing

Printed in the United States of America

LSCH

Edited by Julie Strauss-Gabel
Design by Anna Booth
Text set in Joanna Nova Regular

For my people—the young, wry, and chronically ill.
At least we're in excellent company.

Chronically Dolores

Chapter One

Bathroom #62: St. Francis of Assisi Catholic Church. The classic multiseater, one-ply experience. If you enter with expectations of Gregorian chants, candles, and incense, you will leave disappointed. Two and a half stars.

~~~~~~~~~~

Me: Uh, hi, sir. *Father?* Is that right? It sounds weird. I've . . . um, I've never done this before, and I'm going to be honest, I'm not totally sure how this works. Jesus Christ, it's stuffy in here. Oh, I'm sorry, that's like, *your guy.* I probably shouldn't say that to you! Can I say that? What are the rules?

Priest: Why don't you start by taking a deep breath.

Me: Good idea . . . okay.

Priest: Are you a Catholic, daughter?

Me: I think so. My aunt says I'm baptized, but I don't remember it.

Priest: An infant baptism, then?

Me: I guess.

Priest: That's perfectly valid. You're a Catholic.

Me: But I've never been to church. I don't even know if I believe in God or Jesus or anything like that. Mom raised us to be atheist secular humanists.

Priest: Then what brought you here today, might I ask?

Me: My aunt. She's been trying to guilt me into coming with her to a prayer service, saying *You know, us older folks aren't going to be around forever*, and *Wouldn't you like to do something to make your tía happy?* And today I gave in, because I'm having a bit of a crisis, actually, and I guess I thought, *why not?*

Priest: "Why not?" You'd be surprised how many people that question brings in. Almost as many as "Why?"

Me: If I tell you something, you have to keep it a secret, right? That's your whole thing?

Priest: Canon law requires that confessors keep private all things said in the Sacrament of Penance. Not even to save my own life could I divulge one word you tell me.

Me: Well, damn, it's probably not going to come to that.

Priest: All the same, you should know that anything said in here is between you and God. I'm merely a placeholder, a kind of stand-in, to remind you of God's forgiveness. What's troubling you, child?

Me: It's hard to know where to begin. I've got a problem. Well, three separate problems, really, if you break everything down. And normally, that's what you're supposed to do, right? Break things down and tackle the issues one at a time? But I can't really do that—make the three things separate, I mean—because they're all kind of the same.

Priest: Much like the Holy Trinity.

Me: No, it's not like that at all. It's more of a . . . I don't know. Wait, have you ever seen that thing that happens in sewers when a bunch of rats get their tails tangled up? I don't remember what it's called, but after a while of being stuck like that, they eventually become one big, wriggling creature just writhing around in pain, all fused together with blood and grime and feces . . . That's how it is with my problems.

Priest: How vivid.

Me: Thank you. And I've got to talk quickly. My tía thinks I'm in the bathroom, which I was, but I was on my way back when I saw the little door open to this wardrobe—

Priest: Confessional.

Me: Right, well, I saw the door was open, and I thought maybe I could climb inside and get mauled to death by a giant Narnia animal. But that's not going to happen, is it?

Priest: I'm afraid not, no.

Me: I figured. Then I realized that this was one of those rooms with a priest on the other side of the wall, and I thought, maybe it would help if I could just talk to someone, even if I couldn't see them. Especially if I couldn't see them. Does that make sense?

Priest: Of course. Go ahead.

~~~~~~~~~~

"Naranja dulce limón partido dame abrazos que yo te pido."

Tía Vera drummed her fingers on the steering wheel as she sang. Now and then, when the road required more focus, she switched to humming and leaned forward, squinting through her cat-eye glasses. Her rosary swung back and forth from the rearview mirror, almost taking out the plastic St. Christopher suction-cupped to the dashboard.

"Si fueran falsos mis juramentos dame los besos que yo te dí."

My aunt's car didn't have working air-conditioning, because

why would she need some expensive nonsense like that when there were perfectly good windows we could crank down—halfway? Somehow, remarkably, the sixty-five-year-old wasn't even sweating. Her makeup—red lips and thick foundation one shade too light for her brown skin—stayed perfectly still, held there by her monumental willpower. I, on the other hand, was not so lucky. I was sure that, should this drive take too much longer, police officers would find me melted, my flesh permanently fused to the rainbow granny-square seat cover. *The poor kid,* they'd say. *Dead one week into summer vacation. A real tragedy.*

Tía Vera hit a pothole, and I gasped, clutching the door with white knuckles. I wasn't the only one struggling. St. Chris (and by extension the piggybacking Christ Child) took a tumble to the floor of the driver's side, rolling under the pedals. Tía Vera mumbled something in Spanish as she fished around for the figure, taking her attention away from the road.

"Tía, watch out!" I shouted as the car swerved.

"Aha!" she replied, returning the holy action figure to its rightful place and the vehicle to the correct lane. "Cálmate, mija. I've had this car for three decades—that's more than twice as long as you've been alive—and I've never once had an accident."

We drove in silence for a minute before she looked over at me, studying my expression of discomfort as I loosened the seat belt across my lap. "You've still got your affliction?"

I sighed, shifting my hips into the seat and looking out the half-open window. My *affliction.* Crusty rodent number one. "Interstitial cystitis is chronic, Tía. Ongoing. Persistent. Long-lasting. Occurring over an extended period of time. So yes, I still have my affliction."

"Ay, niña, you know I meant nothing by it," she chided softly.

Tía Vera's eyebrows touched in the middle like two fuzzy caterpillars kissing. My brother Mateo had those same eyebrows, and my dad, and I guess I would too if Shae Luden hadn't discovered waxing strips back in sixth grade and insisted we learn to use them. I could picture us in her parents' huge master bath, leaning over the double vanity, goading each other in the mirror to finally rip away the paper. Thinking about Shae made my throat tense, like when you swallow too hard and pull a muscle.

"Vitalis of Assisi," Tía Vera said.

"What?" I asked, realizing I'd filtered out my aunt's chatter.

"I was telling you I looked it up. Vitalis of Assisi, that's the patron saint of"—she lowered her voice to protect my modesty—"pee-pee problems."

I pursed my lips. "Tía, I went to church, like you asked. But going once doesn't mean I believe in any of . . ." I pointed to the poorly painted martyr on the dashboard. "This."

Tía Vera put her hands up, letting go of the wheel. "Claro que sí, of course. I'm grateful for you indulging me. The viejitas are always bragging about their children and grandchildren, and now they know that I have the most beautiful niece." She lowered her hands and glanced at me with the glimmer of a smile. "And you never know. Belief might come later."

It wasn't going to do any good to argue. The car rolled to a stop in the side alley next to Mendoza Printing. "You coming up?" I asked, opening the door and extracting my bare thighs from the drenched seat cover.

Tía Vera tilted her head. "Is your mother home?"

I checked the time on my phone. The lock screen was a picture of Shae and me from a couple summers ago. We were sitting on the swim deck of her parents' boat, grinning at the camera. Shae still had braces back then, and I had a line of way-too-short bangs, which she'd cut the night before. It had seemed like a brilliant idea at the time. I quickly clicked the screen dark. "Friday at six thirty?" I answered, trying to remember Mom's schedule for this week. "Maybe. If not, she will be soon."

"Then no thank you, mija," Tía Vera answered, leaning over the console for the mandatory kiss on the cheek. I ducked back into the car to oblige. "Anyways, I have to get home in time for *Rosa Mi Vida*," she continued. "See you Sunday."

"See you Sunday."

I watched my aunt's red '87 Ford Escort careen down the alley, narrowly avoiding the corner of our big metal dumpster. *St. Christopher sure has his work cut out for him*, I thought, pulling out my keys and turning around to face the MENDOZA PRINTING sign.

My parents rented a two-story walk-up downtown. That was how I always described it to people, because it sounded a lot nicer than the reality. The skinny brick building was wedged between two neighbors: a barbershop and a sketchy ice cream parlor that Mateo and I were sure doubled as a front for some kind of money-laundering scheme. Mom told us that was crazy, but they only offered six flavors, and one of them was black licorice, so how else could they stay in business?

Our rental price included the ground-floor storefront and an upstairs apartment accessible only by a shockingly noisy set of green metal stairs on the outside of the building. Dad said we were lucky the stairs were so loud. It was like having a free alarm system.

"Hey, you," my brother, Mateo, said. He'd opened the door before I had time to reach the top step.

I pushed past him. "Move, have to pee."

"Rude."

~~~~~~

Bathroom #1: Mendoza Apartment. Shared by three adults and one teenager, this noisy commode is in high demand, although its amenities leave much to be desired. The cleaning crew is understaffed, and essentials like toilet paper and hand soap often go unreplaced. The location is redeemed only by its excellent internet reception and a novelty elephant light switch. Expect long wait times, angry door banging, and a disturbing yellow ring on the underside of the toilet seat. One star.

~~~~~~

Feeling moderately better, I made my way back to the living room and flopped face-first over the back of our ancient beige sofa. It groaned in protest, sagging unhappily into its frame.

"Look at all this sweat," I announced, voice muffled by the cushion. "I'm a bog monster." I flicked my sandals onto the floor.

"Love that it's all seeping into the couch," Mateo replied, the recliner squeaking as he sat down across from me.

"Oh, please. This couch is held together by farts and wishes at this point. A little bit of sweat isn't going to make a difference." I rolled over. "Hey, why aren't you downstairs?"

Mateo was almost twenty-one but still lived at home. Mom and Dad made him "manager" of the family business, which meant he stayed here and didn't leave for college like his friends two summers

ago. My brother was clean-shaven, with dark, curly hair and a con-
stellation of zits above his bushy unibrow. Like my dad, he was
barely five foot six, but where Dad was burly and beer-bellied, Mateo
had that lean, sinewy Jesus look. Shae always had the biggest crush
on him.

"I needed to throw in a load of laundry," Mateo answered defensively. "Plus, no one was downstairs, so I figured Johann could handle
things by himself for a few minutes."

"Johhhhhaaaaaann," I sang.

Mateo's cheeks got red. "It's not like that. We're just friends."

Johann Dietrich was a junior at the local arts college. His mother
was an American who went to study abroad in Germany and never
came back. Johann decided, in the spirit of tradition, he wanted to
do the reverse for his college experience. Mom hired him two years
ago to run the design aspects of the print shop, back when the business was making money instead of hemorrhaging it. Mateo had been
madly in love with Johann since his first shift. But my brother was too
chicken to ever say anything.

"You want to lick his pretty German face," I teased.

Mateo sighed. "It's *so* pretty."

I lifted my head, listening as the stairs clanged in that slow, purposeful way that meant my mother was home. When things at the
print shop started going downhill, Mom got a new job as a janitor
at the twenty-four-hour gym on the other side of town. She hated it
there. She never said so, but the sounds her feet made when she came
up the stairs did.

Dutifully, Mateo opened the door for her, and Mom shuffled in,
unceremoniously sliding two pizza boxes onto the kitchen counter.

My heart sank. "Pizza, again?" I asked, trying to keep the disappointment out of my voice.

Mom sat down at the table to take off her orthotic sneakers. "Yes. And?"

I made a face and asked a question I already knew the answer to. "Did you get the kind with white sauce this time? You know I'm not supposed to eat tomatoes."

Mom closed her eyes and turned her face up to the dusty light fixture. I watched the lines on her forehead tense and then relax as she took a long, drawn-out breath before looking back at me. "I'm sorry, Dolores, it completely slipped my mind."

Mateo swooped a piece of pizza out of the box. "You can have my crusts, Dolores. Stick them in the oven under the broiler with some cheese, dip them in a little bit of olive oil and oregano. Make it fancy."

I stood up and shook my head as I began to investigate the kitchen cupboards. "It's fine. I've got some canned pears and saltines around here somewhere."

"Well, can't compete with that," Mateo replied sarcastically.

I flipped him off.

Mom examined my brother with suspicion, then glanced down at her watch. "What are you doing here?" she asked Mateo. "We don't close until seven thirty. People pick up their orders on the way home from work."

Guiltily, Mateo ducked his head. "Johann's got it," he mumbled through his greasy mouthful of pizza.

"You should be taking some of his hours," Mom said. "We have to pay Johann. We don't have to pay you." She paused. "If things keep going like they are now, we'll have to let him go."

Mateo's unibrow shot up to his hairline. "You wouldn't dare," he said, tossing his pizza back in the box as if to punctuate the gravity of the situation. "He's the only good thing about being here."

"Rude," I interjected.

Mateo changed his expression to one of gentle pleading as he approached Mom. "I mean, besides my wonderful family and my beautiful, compassionate mother who would never, ever scrape out the last remnants of my soul by firing the love of my life." Mateo took Mom's hands in his and batted his long black lashes. "And might I add that you look radiant in that navy-blue uniform. It really brings out your eyes."

Mom hid the slightest of smiles. "Send him home for the day," she said. "But you need to stay and make sure those table signs are perfect. One more mistake, and Mr. Kim is going to take his business elsewhere."

"Yes, ma'am," Mateo replied, saluting with his reclaimed pizza before disappearing out the door. His rapid descent down the steps was the only noise in the apartment for a while. Mom sighed and went to her bedroom to change.

Silence. Silence had been my enemy for the last two weeks. In the silence, I couldn't help but remember the terrible thing that stalked me from the shadows. I imagined that it looked like the jaguar statue holding up the glass coffee table at Tía Vera's house—a frozen beast with its back arched low, gemstone eyes locked on its target, eternally waiting for the right moment to pounce.

I'd played the scene over so many times in the last fourteen days that the memory had taken on a rather cinematic flare. Perhaps it was a coping mechanism to deal with the misery of my degradation, perhaps it was a result of the traumatic brain injury, but I pictured the moment as one of those brightly colored, soapy telenovelas my aunt loved so much: *Rosa mi vida, Los ojos del amor, El corazón palpitante.* There was dramatic lighting, extravagant camera angles, and a sweeping score carried by a string quartet . . .

~~~~~~~~

INTERIOR SUSAN B. ANTHONY MIDDLE SCHOOL, LATE AFTERNOON, TWO WEEKS EARLIER

We open on an eighth-grade homeroom set up for end-of-the-year standardized exams. MS. HARPER paces while STUDENTS at metal desks scratch exaggeratedly at their tests. We hear the *click, click, click* of the teacher's heels on the floor. DOLORES chews the end of her pencil, fidgeting, sweating. The camera lingers on the empty water bottle at her desk. Dolores presses her legs together and glances up at the clock, the shot closing in on her terrified eyes. The ticking of the clock adds to the clicking of the teacher's heels, the noises stitched together by the urgent melody of a lone violin.

                    MS. HARPER
          One minute left, class.

Dolores's face is contorted into a mask of pain as she fills in the last bubble on her Scantron. She flips her test and stands up, victorious, practically toppling the desk. But it's too late! A river of humiliation trickles down her legs. We zoom in as her mouth opens, letting out a despairing wail.

                    DOLORES
          Noooo!

Her classmates turn one by one with amplified expressions
punctuated by percussive strings. Horror! Disgust!
Amusement! Devastated, Dolores covers her eyes with her
arm as she attempts to flee the classroom. But it is not
to be! Dolores slips in the puddle and falls down, down,
down, in slow motion. The loud smack of her skull on the
linoleum floor stops the music. Ms. Harper rushes to her
side, her face looming above the camera. Her voice is
muddled.

                    MS. HARPER
          Don't move, Dolores. Don't move. You
          might have broken your neck!

The fluorescent lights drift in and out of focus.
Dolores blinks silently, tears photogenically frozen
on her cheeks. From above, the highlighter-yellow urine
pool inexplicably spreads across the floor, soaking
the girl, the teacher, and the shoes of the disgusted
onlookers. In the background, we hear students'
laughter and mocking, distorted, sharp, echoing over
everything.

                    MS. HARPER
          Someone call 911!

                    STUDENT #1
          We can't! You took our phones away
          for the test!

EXTERIOR SUSAN B. ANTHONY MIDDLE SCHOOL, LATE AFTERNOON

The music returns, gentle and melodramatic. An ambulance
screeches to a stop outside the front of the school. Two
PARAMEDICS rush inside and return only moments later,
carrying the pitiful eighth grader from the scene,
sopping wet and immobilized by a neck brace. At the

windows, the students of the school push their faces against the glass to get a look. Again, we see close-ups of their expressions. Scorn! Pity! Delight! The paramedics load a drenched and dripping Dolores into the back of the ambulance. Over this commotion, the title appears across the screen in curly lettering: A TEENAGE CATASTROPHE . . . starring DOLORES MENDOZA and HER JUDAS BLADDER. Produced by TELEVISIA.

~~~~~~

"Dolores. *Dolores!*"

I jumped, turning to face my mother, who was leaning over the back of the couch. "What?"

"You were just staring into space." She squinted suspiciously. "It's that concussion, isn't it? You know, this is why I never let Mateo join football."

"Mateo didn't want to play on the team; he just wanted to play the field."

Mom's lips pursed into a tight line. "That's not funny."

"It's hilarious. And true."

The couch creaked ominously. My mother straightened up and crossed over to the recliner. "I guess your brain is fine, then. What were you thinking about, anyway?"

"Nothing," I answered.

"Nothing?"

"Mm-hmm." I wasn't going to tell her the truth about the Mexican soap opera playing out in my mind. No way she'd think my brain was fine then.

"*You know,*" Mom began, stretching out the words like taffy as she pointedly changed the subject. "Mrs. Luden hasn't contacted me about the dates for their lake trip this year."

I was overcome by the strange, tilting feeling I got whenever I looked at my lock screen photo.

"Is that just an oversight," Mom pressed, "or is there something you want to talk about?"

The tilting turned to seasickness. It was like being back on the lake, Shae and me lying around in our swimsuits and T-shirts. I could picture Mr. Luden standing at the wheel, looking a lot like the men in Viagra commercials: tall and fit with thick, graying hair and a white-capped smile. Mrs. Luden's face was always completely obscured by her wide-brimmed hat. She wasn't a person: she was a glamorous cover-up, an open paperback novel, a clawed hand holding a vodka soda with lime. And then there was Shae, Pepto-pink from the sun, snorting with laughter at something happening on-shore.

"I'm not sure they're going," I replied, trying to keep my voice casual. "They might be too busy this summer."

"Uh-huh." Mom pursed her lips. "Dolores—"

The sound of footfalls, *bump, bump, bump,* came up the stairs outside. "Dad's home!" I leapt to open the door, desperate to get away from the question I knew my mother would ask next.

My father's face was beaming as he swept me up into his arms and kissed my cheek. "Mija, you'll never guess what I've brought!" he exclaimed in that rough, round voice that scared away childhood monsters and narrated bedtime stories. "C'mon, boys, bring it up, but be *careful!*"

I leaned over the metal railing. Mateo and Johann were carefully lifting a massive television box out of the bed of Dad's old Chevy truck. The two of them struggled to navigate the monstrosity to the thin, steep staircase. "No way."

"It is very big, Mr. Mendoza!" Johann exclaimed in his lilting German accent. His choppy blond bangs poked up over the box. "Oh, hello, Lola!"

Johann always called me Lola. It reminded me of that song. "Her name was Lola . . . She was a showgirl . . ."

Dad and I pushed back into the apartment to make way for the boys. Mom's face darkened as the pair navigated the TV box into the living room.

"Hold on," she said in a hushed, sharp tone, "we can't afford that. You've got to take it back."

"Don't worry," Dad replied, wrapping his arm around my mother's waist. She stiffened. "They gave it to me on a store credit card," he explained. "We only pay a little bit every month, so it's practically free. Plus, I've got a feeling that things are turning around. And it's such a special occasion . . ."

Dad had this ritual when he brought home extravagant gifts, a script that we'd followed since before Mateo and I could even remember. It was a formula he'd probably used on my mother when he first wooed her, a million years ago.

"What special occasion?" I asked.

My father smirked and raised his unibrow, his dimples practically drilling holes into his cheeks as he looked over at me. "Why, isn't today your birthday?"

I shook my head. "No, Dad, it's not." He faked confusion, then turned to my mother. "Well, it must be yours?" he asked, and when she didn't answer, he jostled her gently until her expression softened and she shook her head. "Mateo?"

"Nope," my brother answered.

Dad pointed to Johann—a new addition to the ritual. "What about you? Is it your birthday?"

Johann's green eyes betrayed his confusion. "No, it is not my birthday," he said slowly, glancing at Mateo as if this was some kind of strange American tradition that he didn't understand. "In Germany, we do not have early birthday wishes. It is bad luck."

Dad raised his hands in the air dramatically. "*Mea culpa!*" he cried loudly, beating one arm to his chest. "I must have gotten the dates mixed up. Forgive me."

Mom dug her fingers into her temples. "Diego," she said, just that one word. They don't teach you in school that sometimes a name can be a sentence all on its own. Mateo glanced at my mother with concern, but I knew he wasn't going to say anything when Johann was around.

"Who's manning the store?" my mom asked.

Dad refused to have his mood brought down. "No one, we closed it. I gave the boys the last thirty minutes off." He gestured to the pair. "They're going to help me put this thing on the wall. It's a three-man job!"

Mom pulled away. "I've got a migraine coming on," she mumbled. "I'm going to bed."

Dad seemed surprised. "Abigail—"

The bedroom door shut, and Johann, Mateo, and I were left looking at each other and the TV box and the floor, anywhere except my father.

"It's fine, it's fine," Dad reassured us. "Your mom, huh, always keeping me in line." He paused. "It's good, you know, but so is this brand-new TV. Right?"

The three of us nodded, maybe a little too hard.

"I just love you so much," Dad added earnestly. "I want you to have everything, mijitos."

Mateo swallowed. "We love you too, Dad. Uh, let's get this thing on the wall, I guess."

But they didn't. It turned out that Dad bought the wrong size TV mount. And even if it had been right, he couldn't find any of the tools he needed to get it put up.

"I know I have a stud finder somewhere," he repeated over and over again as he tore through the cupboards. Sweet Johann toughed it out for almost an hour before making an excuse to leave. Once he was gone, Mateo and I went back to our rooms. I doubt that Dad even noticed we weren't there. Late into the night, the first two times I got up to go to the bathroom, I could hear him muttering to himself, rummaging through the house until finally, quietly, he went to bed.

Chapter Two

My bladder woke me up before the sun rose. By the time I got back under the blanket, I knew I wouldn't fall asleep again. I tried anyway, flopping around on my bed like a seal on a pier, desperate to find a comfortable spot before the light from the window changed from blue to pink. It was no use. Despite my best efforts, I was denied the sweet oblivion of unconsciousness. I screamed into my pillow and kicked the duvet off my legs.

As I'd told the priest, there were three problems looming over me—my unholy trinity. It started with problem one, my leaky pee balloon, which led to problem two, accidental public urination during the last week of middle school, which caused problem three, my status as a leper. A leper without a colony. A lonely little leper lepping around.

I picked up my phone and frowned. No notifications. I opened up my texts anyway and scrolled to the bottom of the long string of blue bubbles along the right-hand side of the screen. Desperate, I sent another barrage into the abyss between us.

It's been two weeks Shae why are you ghosting me?

Did your parents take your phone?

Please just say something so I know you're okay

Really you should be asking if I'm okay

I'm not, by the way

I have a funny Mateo story wanna hear it?

Shae please

Mom knocked on my door and cracked it open. "Can I come in?"

I set my phone face down on the bedside table next to my pet project: The Totally Unessential Restroom Digest (the T.U.R.D., for short). After spending an alarming portion of the past year in bathrooms, it seemed only fitting there should be some written record commemorating it. So I started a binder. I had sixty-two glossy, page-protected entries rated between one and five stars. It had started out as a stupid little private joke. But I kept it up long after the humor wore off. I wasn't sure why.

Mom cleared her throat.

"Do I have a choice?" I asked.

"Not really," Mom replied, crossing over to sit at the end of my bed. She was already in her janitor's uniform with her hair pulled up in a ponytail. She set a pamphlet on the duvet between us.

"What's this?" I asked, studying the stock photo on the front. A racially diverse group of teenagers grinned widely at each other as if they couldn't believe how well they were getting along.

Mom pointed to the heading. "It's a workshop, see? Building Communication Skills for Girls Ten to Thirteen. I signed you up."

I blinked at her, not comprehending what was happening. "I'm fourteen."

"You were thirteen not that long ago." Mom leaned back on one hand and picked up the pamphlet with the other. "No one will be at the door checking IDs. Anyway, it's free, and it looks . . ." She opened it. "Insightful," she decided.

"Insightful?"

"As in helping you to 'gain insight into common communication issues,'" she said methodically, her eyes scanning the first flap. "'Growing your confidence in making and navigating friendships, practicing scenarios—'"

"Stop reading the pamphlet to me," I interrupted, pulling the paper out of her hands. "I don't need that. I know how to communicate just fine."

My mother glanced around the room, taking in the messy drawers, the floor covered in dirty clothes, the impressive stack of mugs and spoons on the dresser. "Dolores, I know you're having a hard time right now." She spoke in the same calm, measured voice one might use when encountering a wild animal. "Maybe it has to do with your mishap at school or Shae not inviting you to the lake this year. It's okay that you don't want to talk to me about it. I didn't want to talk to my mom about anything when I was your age. But maybe . . ." She thought for a second. "Maybe you can talk to Mateo about it?"

I rolled my eyes. "Because Mateo has so many friends."

"He's had more than one," Mom countered.

I frowned.

"I only mean that you and Shae were inseparable. Since you were tiny," my mother explained, backpedaling diplomatically. "You haven't needed to make any other friends, and that was *great*."

The way she stressed the word *great* made me know that she thought it was anything but. "What's your point?" I asked, narrowing my eyes.

"My point is that the two of you spent so much time together that you invented your own special way of communicating, like . . ." Mom sucked her teeth as she searched for an analogy. "Like feral twins. The way you interacted made sense to each other, but it was a lot less clear to everyone else."

"This is a whole lot of criticism for seven a.m. Anyway, me and Shae, we're fine. I *told* you. Her family isn't going to the lake this year."

Mom held up her hands. "All I'm saying is that you missed out on learning how to talk to anyone else, how to form new friendships. This workshop seemed like a start in the right direction. Best part, you can walk there. Isn't that great?"

"Only weirdos would go to something like this," I groaned. "Like sixth graders or masochists or aliens in human flesh suits learning how to blend in."

Mom shook her head. "Make fun of it all you want, I understand. But I saw this pamphlet, and I thought of you, and I just . . . had a really good feeling. Like it was something that could really help." She pursed her lips and stared at her hands. "That's all."

I looked at my mother, really looked at her—at the deep furrow running across her forehead, the wrinkles starting to form around her eyes, and her eyes themselves, all red like she'd cried herself to sleep. She had, I bet, after what happened yesterday with Dad and the TV. With the way she worried about money, she probably cried herself to sleep most nights. And then there were my medical bills—God knows how much those were.

Mom looked old. That was the word. As soon as I thought it, my skin got all hot and itchy, and I remembered what Tía Vera said about all the old folks being dead someday.

Oh my God. "Fine!"

"Really?" Her face lit up so much it made me feel bad for putting up a fight.

"Yeah. Whatever," I said, leaving out the fact that it took imagining her mortality to motivate my compliance. Oh, Tía Vera and those Mexican-Catholic guilt trips.

Mom wrapped her arms around me. "Thank you."

"For what?" I mumbled into her uniform.

"For stomping down your independence enough to let me be a parent." My mother released me and stood up. "It's today from two to four. The address is on the pamphlet." Then she disappeared out the door before I could change my mind. "And wear real clothes! No sweats!"

~~~~~~~

Bathroom #2: Mendoza Printing. This immaculate, tile-coated single-seater is everything the upstairs bathroom wishes it could be. The lack of customers ensures that this quaint little haven remains perpetually empty, but the owners keep it fully stocked with expensive toilet paper and air freshener, "just in case." The only downside is the manager's attitude toward noncustomers taking refuge in this sacred oasis. Four and a half stars.

~~~~~~~

"I've told you before, Dolores." Mateo straightened a display of greeting cards. "That bathroom is not for you."

My fingers lingered lightly on the door handle. "That only makes me want it more."

"Customers. Only." He pointed to the sign hanging at my eye

level. "Unless one of us is the only one manning the store, Mendozas hike up to the apartment. Mom's rules."

I had two things to look forward to in my future: holes in my bladder lining and four years of my name being immediately followed by "You know, in eighth grade she slipped in her own pee, hit her head, and was taken away in an ambulance." With that on the horizon, the forbidden bathroom was one of the few precious comforts I had left. I wasn't going to let it go without a fight. "You don't make Johann go upstairs," I argued.

Mateo snorted. "I love Johann. You think I want him to witness our bathroom? You think I want him to see your hair art on the wall of the shower, or Mom's disgusting bite guard, or Dad's collection of not-so-lucky money soaps?" Mateo's mouth formed that same small line that Mom's does when she's upset. "I mean, I don't even know how I'd begin to explain that last one."

"There's probably not a German equivalent." I looked around the store. "Where is Dad? The truck's gone."

Mateo shook his head. "He's doing some work for one of Vera's friends, I think. Which is good, I guess, as long as he remembers to charge her."

Dad had always supplemented the family income with some under-the-table contracting work. It was hard to know exactly how much he made, but he seemed to spend it pretty freely. I thought back to earlier that morning, when I'd gotten myself a bowl of Crispy Rice Squares and noticed the TV, back in its box, still wedged awkwardly into the living room. The scattered pieces of the wrong-sized mount were strewn across the carpet. I doubted if the washers or screws would ever be found. "Did we really have enough money for that TV?" I asked, dreading the answer.

Mateo stared at me sternly. "Listen to me, Dolores. It's not *we*, it's *they*. Their finances. Their decisions. Their messes. It's between *them*." He rubbed his eyes. "None of it is on you, got it?"

"But the ambulance bill was mine," I groaned.

"No," he said firmly. "You are their *child*. A dependent. It's your parents' job to take care of you."

I nodded, taken aback by his tone.

"Anyway," he said, shaking off the seriousness, "Mom said you were going to that sad kids' meeting at that event space a few streets over, and I was wondering if you'd put up some flyers on the way."

"For what?"

Mateo went behind the counter and retrieved a box with papers, thumbtacks, and packing tape. "A special promotional offer for the shop." He gazed mournfully out the large window at the front of the store. "I *have* to keep Johann working here. My fifteen-year plan depends on it. It starts with workplace romance and ends with us owning a bed-and-breakfast in some little German village with cobblestone streets and a castle in the distance." He pushed the box into my arms. "Don't screw this up for me."

I forced a smile. "Wouldn't dream of it."

<hr>

I knew it was going to be a bad bladder day by the time I'd reached the ice cream parlor. One Fell Scoop had moved in two years ago, replacing a sleepy beige temp agency. Since then, it had been my tradition to duck under the big front window as I walked by. As soon as I was nearly past, I would sneak a quick peek inside to see if I could catch the two men who worked there in the middle of some nefarious deed. I had nicknames for them based on their face tattoos: Spider and Teardrop. Today the pair stood behind the pink-and-teal counter cleaning the waffle cone maker. A couple of kids were working on massive ice cream cones at a booth in the corner, and an older woman was at one of the small round tables, flipping through a magazine and drinking a milkshake.

As soon as I stood back up from crouching, I felt it. Sometimes the pain came on fast and sharp first thing in the morning, pinning me to my bed like a butterfly in a display case. Other times it changed throughout the day, starting uncomfortable and growing sharper, meaner, gnashing its teeth into my pelvis. But always, always it was there. That was what I couldn't explain to my family or Shae, what no one I talked to could understand.

It was probably the jeans. Balancing the box of flyers against my hip, I tried to adjust the waist a little higher. Ever since my diagnosis, I'd prioritized comfort, living exclusively in my brother's old joggers and cut-off sweats. They were from his eleventh-grade sporty crop-top phase—a period of his life we were not allowed to mention. Lucky for me, Mateo never got rid of anything.

I stopped at a spot of wall covered in posters that said things like "Cheap Piano Lessons All Ages" and "Purebred Puppies for Sale" and "I know where I'm going after I die, do you? GET SAVED today before it's too late!" I pulled out one of Mateo's flyers. In large capital letters, it read "MADE YOU LOOK!" and then, under that, "Design your own eye-catching paper goods at Mendoza Printing. 25% off your first order!" In rich, saturated color, my brother had edited together an image of a cat in a top hat riding a pterodactyl through space while both of them shot laser guns. Clearly, Johann had played no part in this design.

I hung up four or five flyers on the way to the workshop, which was at a rentable event space at the edge of downtown. I'd never been inside, although we'd printed the address before on invitations: wedding receptions, birthday parties, lock-ins. That's when I realized how my mother had heard about it. I pulled the brochure out of my pocket and checked the bottom left-hand corner. Sure enough, there was our logo, an artsy-looking MP that Johann had designed when he first started working for us. We hadn't run off all our business then.

"Are you here for the workshop?"

I looked up. A woman, probably not much older than Mateo, was holding the door open for me. She was wearing an ill-fitting salmon blazer over a casual dress that fell at her midthigh. I glanced down at her heels, which were probably a bit too high and sparkly to have been purchased as professional wear.

"Um . . ." Surely someone hadn't left this baby adult in charge.

It's too late to turn back; you have to pee, my bladder reminded me.

Rot in a ditch, I responded. But it was right.

The woman made an exaggerated show of waving me in. "Don't be shy, come on, everyone is just getting seated, mingling. There's lemonade and chocolate cookies on the table. You can set that box right in here if you want."

"Can you please tell me where the bathroom is?" I asked politely.

"Of course. It's just right back here to your left. You can't miss it."

Chapter Three

Bathroom #63: Events on Green. For a space designed to be customizable, the bathroom is rather distinctly decorated. The theme appears to be "beach getaway," which might be fun if we weren't several hundred miles from the ocean. Aside from the decor, it is clean, well-stocked, and the fan turns on automatically. Also of note is a particularly nipply mermaid wrapped around the soap dispenser. Quite saucy. Four stars.

~~~~~~~~

Walking back around the corner and into the main space, I realized at once that I'd made a terrible mistake agreeing to come. Thirty or so Girl Scouts—all sashed and khaki'd and entirely prepubescent—stood crowding the lemonade table. My stomach sank as I searched helplessly for someone, anyone, who wasn't still in elementary school.

As I spun around, ready to make my escape, I barreled into the woman from the door, nearly toppling her over.

"I need to give you your questionnaire," she said, righting herself on her party heels and forcing a clipboard and pencil into my hands.

"But—" I protested.

"Don't worry, it's just for my professor. I don't get credit for this project otherwise."

I made my way to the back row of metal folding chairs and skimmed through the half sheet on the clipboard.

Rate each statement strongly agree, agree, somewhat
agree, unsure, somewhat disagree, disagree, or strongly
disagree.

1. *I consider myself an effective communicator.*
2. *I feel comfortable introducing myself to strangers.*
3. *I can advocate for my needs when necessary.*
4. *I know how to communicate healthy boundaries.*
5. *I can work through a disagreement with a friend.*

I shoved the paper in my pocket, and set the clipboard and pencil
on the empty chair beside me. No way was I going to do that stupid
survey. Damn door lady's school credit. And damn these jeans! I dug
the waistband out of my gut as the Girl Scouts shuffled, giggling, to
their seats, leaving me the entire back row.

The woman walked to the front of the room and clapped her
hands. "Hello, everyone! My name is Nora Evans, I'm a psychology
major in college, and I am so excited to be here with you guys today
to talk a little bit about communication—"

"A little bit?" interrupted a voice from the front row. I couldn't see
who it belonged to. "This was meant to be a two-hour workshop. My
mom isn't going to pick me up until four."

The girls in front of me snorted and whispered to each other.

Nora seemed slightly flustered. "I mean, yes, that's right. We are
going to be here until four."

"Well, that's quite a lot of talking, isn't it?" the voice pressed.

Real laughter from the crowd, less stifled now.

"I mean, isn't it?"

The sass! Tía Vera would have smacked my mouth if she heard

me talk to an adult that way, even an adult-in-training like Nora. I almost felt bad for the psych student, blushing the color of her blazer, at the front. Lifting a little off the seat, I finally laid eyes on the culprit.

She wasn't a Girl Scout, that was for sure. She was my age at least and dressed in a white sleeveless blouse. Her hair was silver-blond and neatly fishtail-braided down her back. For the briefest moment, she turned around and our eyes met. Hers were hazel, enlarged by gold eyeliner and a pair of round, wire-rimmed glasses. I ducked down into my seat. *God, Dolores, way to be subtle.*

"Yes, um," Nora stammered, setting up her slideshow on the projector. "Well, why don't we just go ahead and start! I've made this, uh, presentation, so maybe we can hold our comments until the discussion. Is that good with everyone?"

The presentation was long. Too long. The Girl Scouts in front of me were rapidly losing focus, staring at the ceiling or whispering or twisting and untwisting their sashes. I gnawed unhappily on the yellow pencil as the pain in my pelvis crept into my lower back and down my thighs. I returned to the bathroom.

<hr />

INTERIOR LOWER EAST UROLOGY CLINIC, MORNING, ONE YEAR PRIOR

Inside an exam room, DR. THATUS, a bald, spindly man, wheels over to DOLORES on a swivel stool. His villainous mustache and the musical accompaniment full of minor chords indicate immediately that this man is an unsavory character, not to be trusted. He hands Dolores a glossy sheet of photo paper with pictures of her bladder.

                    DR. THATUS
          The condition has no cure.

Dolores examines the photos with brave stoicism. The
pictures are cropped into circles, with the pink veins
and red splotches giving them the look of a barren and
unfamiliar planet suspended in darkness. The camera
zooms in on MOM MENDOZA's trembling hand as she clasps
it to her chest in fear.

                    MOM MENDOZA
          But there is a treatment?

The doctor is silent. He rolls himself to an overflowing
bookshelf as he lets the suspense build. Licking his
finger, he shuffles through a stack of papers until he
finds one. We pause here long enough to read the title:
IC FOOD LIST.

                    DR. THATUS
              There's a low-acid diet that many
              people find quite helpful. No
              chocolate, coffee, spices, citrus,
              tomatoes, alcohol, things like that.

                    MOM MENDOZA
          Is it just the diet?

                    DR. THATUS
              There are medications and therapies,
              but I don't want to start her on
              them when she's so young.

We pan back to the patient. Dolores, while indeed young,
is clearly quite mature and intelligent for her age. Not
only that, her long dark hair is rustled by a magical
breeze wherever she goes. Even indoors.

                    MOM MENDOZA
         Of course. When her pediatrician
         kept finding blood in her urine, we,
         my husband and I, we were so worried
         it was something serious.

                    DR. THATUS
         No, nothing like that. Nothing . . .
         life-threatening.

The camera closes in on Dolores's suspicious eyes. The
minor chords of the score increase in speed and urgency.
Dolores glances at her mother and sees that the woman
is taken in by the man's lies, entirely hypnotized. The
doctor swivels to face his patient.

                    DR. THATUS (cont.)
         It'll go through cycles, most
         likely. Sometimes better, sometimes
         not. There are things that are
         almost sure to make it worse:
         stress for one, bike riding, and it
         might cause you more trouble around
         your . . .

We zoom in on the doctor's mouth as he lowers his voice.
His mustache hairs bristle with his breath.

                    DR. THATUS (cont.)
         . . . lady's days . . .

Dolores straightens up in righteous indignation.

                    DR. THATUS (cont.)
         . . . which is normal. Get yourself
         a heating pad and an ice pack.
         You'll learn how to manage it. We

won't be needing to schedule a
follow-up.

The deceptive doctor wheels himself to the door and then
backward out of the room. Dolores stands and tries to
stop him.

>   DOLORES
>   Come back! Period! It's called a
>   period! Why can't you say it? You
>   stuck a camera up my urethra! Say
>   it, dammit! Say it!

The doctor is too fast, rolling himself down the hallway,
zigzagging in reverse like a scuttling crab, a wicked
smile on his lips. The music crescendos as Dolores,
standing in the doorway, watches the cackling urologist
disappear into a puff of smoke. As soon as he's gone,
Mom Mendoza blinks as if waking up from a trance.

>   MOM MENDOZA
>   What a sweet man! Aren't you
>   relieved it's no big deal?

Dolores looks back at her mother. She gives a rueful
smile at the woman's naïvety.

>   DOLORES
>   Yes. So relieved.

~~~~~~~~~

Dr. Thatus had been wrong, of course. The condition *was* life-
threatening. Between humiliating me, driving away my best friend,
and landing me in the hospital, interstitial cystitis was threatening to
ruin my entire life.

While I washed my hands, I noticed the naked mermaid again, not that she was hard to miss. She was beautiful and happy and, well, cold by the looks of it. I coveted her. How much better to be something, anything, else from the waist down.

As I went back to the room, Nora finally turned on the lights. "Okay, everyone, I know that was a lot of information, and I'm sure you're tired of sitting. So now we're going to play a game!" She picked up her KEEP CALM AND TRUST CARL ROGERS tote bag and retrieved a bell. "I want you to move your chairs into pairs, facing each other, all around the room."

There was a terrible scraping sound as the attendees followed Nora's instructions. The Girl Scout in the row in front of me turned her chair around to face mine. She smiled shyly, showing off her braces, then turned in her seat to see the instructor.

"Now, I'm going to give you all a topic, and you need to introduce yourselves and have a conversation for one minute." She held up a finger on one hand and the bell in the other. "When I ring this, that means you need to run and find a chair with someone you haven't sat with before. Every round will have a new topic. Are we ready?" She grinned. "Your first topic is food! Go!"

The big empty space suddenly echoed with conversation. My partner looked back at me.

"I just got my braces on yesterday, so it really hurts to eat anything. Especially sour stuff." She leaned forward and turned her upper lip inside out. "I've got lots of cuts in my mouth, see?"

"Uh-huh."

She flipped her lip back down and gazed forlornly at the refreshments table. "I drank the lemonade when we first got here," she said, getting a little teary-eyed. "It was a mistake."

"You know, they sell wax that you can put over your braces. That helps sometimes."

The girl shook her head. "I tried that, but it tastes bad. What's your favorite food?"

"Um." I thought for a second. "I don't know." It was true. At one point the answer would have been carne guisada, or Abuelita brand hot chocolate with coffee, or chorizo with eggs and potatoes, but those things fell solidly into the "Avoid" category of the IC diet. Many of the foods I loved had been taken away or made bland beyond the point of recognition. "Vanilla ice cream, I guess."

The bell rang, and we both stood up. "Nice to meet you," Braces Girl said, and went to find a new partner.

I sat in one of the chairs nearest me as a girl with red hair bounced into the seat opposite.

"School!" Nora announced.

The girl in front of me took a deep breath. "My name is Emory, and last year in fourth grade, my homeroom was with Mrs. Taing, and we read Where the Red Fern Grows, and all the boys in my class cried, but I didn't cry because one time I saw a dog get run over by a truck, but my mom said it was just a stuffed animal, but stuffed animals don't have red in them, so I bet she was lying to me like she did about the tooth fairy." She paused. "Do you ever wonder where all your baby teeth are now, like, what your mom did with them, if they're in a garbage dump somewhere or a bag or a drawer?"

"No," I answered. Mateo and I hadn't grown up with the tooth fairy, or Santa Claus, or God. Mom was adamantly against lying to children.

The bell rang.

The roulette of awkward, forced small talk continued for ten or so rounds. Animals, sports, vacations, movies, art, siblings. The more we went on, the more aggressive the younger kids got trying to beat each other to the chairs, weaponizing their pointy little elbows and knees.

"This is the last round," Nora called out. "So you can pick what you want to talk about this time."

I sighed and put my head in my hands, running my fingers through my hair. The action left a greasy film on my palms. When was the last time I showered? *Do better, Dolores.*

The chair in front of me squeaked. I looked up.

It was her. The girl from the front row in the white blouse. She sat down and crossed one ankle over the other. Somehow, she managed to look even more out of place than I did. I could see the rest of her outfit now, gray pinstripe slacks and low heels. It was closer to what I'd expect our instructor to wear, like she was going to a job interview. Or conducting one, even.

The girl leaned forward, studying my face like it was a difficult question on an exam.

"I've been watching you," she said finally, pushing her glasses up her nose.

"What?" I asked, looking around nervously.

She nodded. "You have a problem."

Chapter Four

Me: Hi, sir, it's me. Wait. You can't see me, can you? Uh, I'm the, well . . . I was here two days ago. You *are* the same person I talked to, aren't you? Because this would be really awkward if—

Priest: Yes, child, I remember you. And I'm the only priest at St. Francis, so if you come back in the future, it will also be me.

Me: That's a relief.

Priest: So, what brought you here today? Did your aunt threaten to die again?

Me: No. I came by myself. And I don't know why, totally. Mostly I just needed to process something that happened, and you're the only one who knows everything that's going on. I mean, you were. That's kind of the whole issue, actually.

Priest: How so?

~~~~~~~~~

"You have a problem," the girl had said.

My hands went cold. "What?"

She rested her chin on her clasped hands. "You've gone to the bathroom three times in the last ninety minutes." She tilted her head. "Is it some kind of intestinal disturbance? Crohn's, irritable bowel, ulcerative colitis—"

"I wasn't . . ." I stammered. "I mean, I don't . . ."

"No, not that." Her stare was like flypaper, her yellow-amber eyes leaving me mostly immobilized, squirming hopelessly in mortal terror. "Something reproductive," the girl continued, "or a urinary tract infection, perhaps? Do you take baths? You shouldn't."

I braced myself to stand. "I've got to go—"

"You have to tell me," she objected. "The time isn't up yet."

I shook my head in disbelief. "I don't even know you!"

"Terpsichore Berkenbosch-Jones," the girl announced. Then she rolled her eyes and added in a quick, rehearsed tone, "Tirp like chirp, sick like ill, ore like the metal, ee like the letter. Tirp-sick-ore-ee."

I didn't say anything.

The girl fidgeted with a gold spinner ring on her thumb. "You're Dolores Mendoza. I saw your name on Ms. Nora's sheet. You're the only one here my age." She looked around the room and ran her teeth over her bottom lip. "And unaffiliated with a sororal organization."

Nora rang the bell. The sound seemed to rub Terpsichore the wrong way. She made a face and put her thumb against her ear.

"Great job, everyone," Nora sang. "I heard some excellent conversations! Now, you're going to stay with that partner for the rest of the workshop, so go ahead and put your chairs together facing the front."

Terpsichore stood and lifted her chair, swinging it around so it was touching mine.

The rest of the workshop? I glanced over at the girl as she sat down. *No way.*

Nora clapped her hands to quiet the room. "We're going to do a role-playing activity. In your pairs, you're going to come up and improvise a conversation with the prompt that I give you. These prompts are going to be a little harder than the last ones, because I really want to help you practice communication in more difficult, real-life scenarios."

My phone buzzed in my back pocket.

"Can we make up characters?" a girl asked.

"If you'd like to, you can," Nora answered. "If not, you can just be yourselves, acting how you think you'd act in that scenario. I'll show you an example, um . . . Marisol, why don't you come up and demonstrate with me?"

My phone buzzed again. Inside my rib cage, my heart started to flip-flop. *It's probably Mom. Or Mateo. Do not get your hopes up. Do not check it.*

One of the taller Girl Scouts stood shyly from her seat and met Nora at the front of the room. She fiddled nervously with the edge of her sash.

"Okay, Marisol," Nora began. "In this scenario, you will play a shop owner. And I'm going to play a customer returning a product that I've purchased."

"Why are you returning it?" someone asked.

"That doesn't really matter," Nora answered. "The most important part of this exercise is practicing self-advocacy in an everyday situation." She turned to Marisol. "Hello, there."

"Hello."

Nora pantomimed that she was holding a large object. "I was hoping you could help me with something."

Marisol was silent.

Nora's smile remained fixed on her face. *I bet her cheeks hurt.* "I need to return this item to your shop," she continued.

"Why are you returning it?" Marisol asked.

Some of the girls started to giggle. I snuck a glance at Terpsichore, who was twisting that ring on her thumb as she focused on the swiftly devolving presentation happening at the front of the room.

"Can you stop chewing that?" she asked, catching me staring. "It's very distracting."

I hadn't realized that I'd been carrying the pencil around. It was a mess of slobbery splinters at this point. Embarrassed at being called out, I balled it up in my fist against my bouncing leg. My phone buzzed a third time. *It's not her. You know it's not her. It's been two weeks.* I licked the graphite from my teeth.

A fourth buzz. Then a fifth. I couldn't ignore my phone any longer and quietly pulled it out of my pocket. I felt shaky all the way down to my ankles when I read Shae's name on my notifications. God, the relief! I opened the messages and read them one by one as Nora and Marisol continued their verbal joust at the front of the room.

Hey sorry I didn't text back

"Well, uh, as I said in the introduction, why I'm returning it is less important."

"It might be important to me. As a shop owner."

Things have gotten really busy

"I guess I decided the product wasn't what I wanted after all."

"I'm sorry, but we only give refunds on items that don't work. It's store policy. The sign is right there."

I think I need some space from you for a little while.

"I just remembered. It doesn't work."

"Yes, it does. See?"

Just give it until everyone forgets about your accident. Then we can be best friends again. Promise.

"I guess you're right. You know what, I've decided to keep the product after all."

Love you.

"And scene!" Nora's voice came out as a strained squeak. "Thank you so much, Marisol, can you go back to your seat? Why don't we have another group come up, maybe some older girls this time . . . Dolores, why don't you and your partner go next . . . Dolores . . . *Dolores.*"

I stood up, putting my phone back in my pocket. The movement was mechanical, reflexive, empty. All the while those two words pierced my brain like red-hot pokers, sizzling and spitting and burning. *Love you. Love you. Love you. Love you. Love you. Love you. Love you.*

"Remind me of your name," Nora requested.

"Terpsichore," Terpsichore said.

"Yes, that's right. It's such a pretty name. Did your parents make it up?"

"No. The Greeks did. Two thousand years ago. Terpsichore is the muse of dance and choral song."

Nora pulled a stack of handwritten notecards out of her bag. "That's fun." She undid the rubber band and flipped the first card over. "I think we're all ready to get started with our next scene." She looked at the girl in front of me and stammered. "Uh, Twer—"

"Terpsichore," the girl interrupted.

"Yes," Nora continued, "has, uh, noticed that Dolores is anxious about a problem."

"What kind of problem?" The question came from a kid on the floor with her feet up on the seat of a chair. Her skirt had hiked up to her waist, showing off a pair of bright purple bike shorts.

"They can pick," Nora snapped. "It's their scene!" She took a steadying breath. "Okay, girls, go ahead."

Terpsichore glanced around quickly before she spoke. "I have noticed you are anxious about a problem," she said robotically.

I think I need some space from you . . .

I coughed and cleared my throat. "I am anxious about a problem, Tirp-sick-ore-ee. Thank you for noticing." I turned to sit back down.

"Wait, it needs to go a little longer than that," Nora insisted, stepping into my path. "Terpsichore, why don't you ask Dolores about what's bothering her?"

Terpsichore rolled her left ankle so she was balancing on the outer edge of her foot. "What's bothering you, Dolores?"

I stared at my shoes, every cell in my body willing this moment to be over.

"Is it because your best friend doesn't want to be your friend anymore?" Terpsichore asked, switching feet.

My stomach dropped. I looked up to read the girl's expression, but she was focused on her ring again, twirling and twirling it, as if she hadn't spoken to me at all. I might even have believed it was all in my head if Nora hadn't commented.

"Wow." The woman leaned backward. "That is . . . creative. Dolores, it's your turn to respond."

The blood rushed to my face, flushing my cheeks and leaving my fingers and toes icy cold. "I don't know what you're talking about," I lied.

"The texts on your phone," Terpsichore said without looking up. "A girl named Shae said she didn't want to be your friend until everyone forgot about something that happened. She said she needed space."

I was going to cry. I could feel the pressure in the corner of my eyes, that tickle in the back of my nose. It was like a countdown to a bomb going off. "You saw that? You read my texts?"

Terpsichore nodded, unremorseful. "It wasn't a very kind thing for a best friend to say."

Nora clapped. "That's, uh, that's great, you guys. Why don't we just end that there, you two can go sit down, and maybe we can all try a different activity—"

My hands hit the front door, throwing it open just as the bomb made it to zero. If I ran fast enough down the street, maybe no one would notice that I had shattered. The tears and ragged breathing could be explained away by a breathless, sweaty sprint. My feet pounded the sidewalk, bringing me closer and closer to the print shop. I was almost home. Almost safe. Just a little farther.

You have to pee, my bladder lied, stabbing a knife into my pelvis. I stopped and leaned against the building beside the ice cream parlor, pressing my forehead hard into the brick.

"Dolores! Dolores, wait! You forgot your box!"

I recognized the voice. I spun around as Terpsichore, hardly winded, caught up to me. Her braid had started to come undone, and stray white hairs fell softly around her too-sharp cheekbones.

"How . . . could you?" I asked, between sobs.

"I thought you might need it." She offered me the box.

I pushed it out of her hands onto the sidewalk, sending Mateo's flyers into the road. They flapped under the tires of passing cars like suicidal pigeons. "How could you just humiliate me like that, someone you don't even know!" I wiped my nose on the inside of my shirt. "What did I do to you?"

You have to pee, my bladder persisted, twisting the knife. I leaned back against the wall.

Terpsichore studied me, an expression of deep confusion passing across her face. "You didn't do anything to me," she said, wrinkling her forehead in concern. "You lost a best friend. It's serendipitous. I'm looking for a best friend, actually. Quite urgently."

"What the hell is wrong with you?" I shouted.

Terpsichore stepped back. "Nothing's wrong with me," she said, looking at the ground. "My brain just works differently than yours. It's not bad. It might even be helpful."

Round and round went the knife, digging up my insides. I had no more patience for this girl and her riddles. "What are you even talking about?" I dug my palms into my forehead. "You don't make any sense!"

"I'm autistic," she explained, staring at a stray flyer on the concrete. And then softer, as if just to herself, she said, "Not wrong, just different."

That terrible knife became a sword and pierced me through, impaling me. I cried out and sank down onto the sidewalk. I hugged my knees to my chest, perched, as the tears and slobber and snot melted into my shadow on the concrete.

Terpsichore lingered a moment. I watched her black heels as she swayed from side to side, debating her next move. She picked the flyer off the ground.

Whatever. I didn't care what she did. I closed my eyes and waited until my breath was no longer coming in ragged gasps. By the time I'd wiped my face and stood up, Terpsichore was long gone. I turned around. Spider and Teardrop stared at me through the window of the ice cream parlor, rags and Windex in hand. When I made eye contact, they quickly turned their attention to the smudged handprints on the glass.

You've really made a spectacle of yourself, Dolores, I thought.

And you still have to pee, my bladder added.

I opened the door of the print shop and made a beeline for the good bathroom. Mateo came and pounded on the door, but I ignored him.

"Dolores!" he yelled. "Dolores, I've told you a thousand times!" And then, "Are those my flyers on the street?"

~~~~~~~~

Priest: Quite the story.

Me: It was the second-most embarrassing moment of my life.

Priest: Have you told anyone about the texts from your friend?

Me: No. And I'm not going to either.

Priest: That must be a heavy secret. May I ask you a question?

Me: Sure.

Priest: Was there any part of you that felt relieved when the girl saw those messages?

Me: That's a stupid question.

Priest: Forgive me, I don't mean it like that. I'm only wondering if it helped at all to share your pain with someone? We're not meant to shoulder life's burdens alone. Even Christ needed someone else to carry his cross.

Me: I'm not alone. I've got you.

Priest: And I'm grateful, if perplexed, by your trust. But I'm worried you're trying to handle this significant loss on your own. Wouldn't you rather have support? Your brother? Your parents? Your aunt? This girl, even, or someone like her?

Me: I'm fine. Really.

Priest: Well, child, what will you do now?

Me: That's a better question.

Chapter Five

"I don't want to *go*."

Mom pulled the covers from over my head. "It's not up for discussion. I have to be there, you have to be there." It was Sunday evening, five o'clock. Mom was already dressed in a skirt and blouse with her makeup done. "Besides," she continued, "experience has taught me that the more buffer-people there are between me and your aunt, the better it is for everyone."

I rolled onto my stomach and groaned into the mattress. "I'm in a flare. My bladder—"

My mom sighed. "Dolores—"

"I'm not making excuses!" I interrupted, lifting my head. "Do you know what they call IC in other places?"

Mom put her earrings in, the little dangly silver birds that Mateo got her for Mother's Day. "What do they call IC in other places?"

"Painful bladder syndrome. Does that sound like an excuse to you?"

My mom turned around, making her way out of my room. "Just remember what Dr. Thatus said—you can manage it. Just like I manage your aunt. Talk about chronic pain. We're going." Mom put her hand on the doorframe. "I really hoped the workshop was going to help your attitude."

I shoved the T.U.R.D. binder off my nightstand. "Sorry I'm such a disappointment!"

"Car," she warned. "Now."

My mother marched our family through the apartment. Out we went, down the hall, past the pile of unfolded laundry, past the empty pizza boxes in the kitchen with their snowflake-shaped grease stains, past the recliner and the sofa and the TV still in the cardboard box. The metal stairs shook as the four of us made our way down the side of the building. It sounded like thunder.

Johann was locking up the print shop, but stopped to wave cheerfully as we passed. "Hallo, Mendozas! Where are you going?"

"To our aunt's house," Mateo answered, brushing his hair back. "For dinner."

Mom looked around, the little birds twirling under her earlobes as she calculated. Then she smiled. "How would you like to come with us, Johann?"

"Really?" Dad asked, staring at my mother in surprise.

She shrugged innocently. "You know Vera would want us to invite him, and there's always plenty of food."

Dad nodded, rubbing his hand across his chin before turning to Johann and asking, "Well, what do you say?"

Johann seemed pleasantly surprised by the offer. "Why not?"

"Why not?" Mom repeated brightly. "It will be lovely to have you join us."

I glanced at my brother. Mateo's expression strobed back and forth between sheer elation and abject terror as he, Johann, and I got into the back of the family car—Mom's Toyota Corolla. Johann was the skinniest, so he took the middle seat, folding his knees to one side.

Dad checked the rearview mirror as we found our seat belts. "If you could just keep your head ducked a little, Johann, so I can see out the back window," Dad called. "You're very tall."

Johann leaned over until his ear was almost against Mateo's clavicle. "Good?" he asked.

Dad took the car out of park. "Perfect."

Johann glanced over at Mateo apologetically, as if acknowledging the deep invasion of personal space. I rolled my eyes and looked out the window, dreading the next ten minutes of my useless brother's silent, lovestruck panic.

But that's when Mateo surprised me. "Hallo, Johann," he said carefully, staring at the crumbs on the floor of the car. "Wie geht es dir?"

Johann looked surprised. "Nicht schlecht," he replied, eyes sparkling. "Gut gemacht, Mateo. Lernst du Deutsch?"

"Ja." Mateo smiled so hard I was sure his mouth would end up slack—loose like the elastic on an old pair of underwear. "I mean, I got an app on my phone."

I nudged Johann. "Maybe you and Mateo could go out for lunch sometime," I teased. "You could help him practice."

"Of course!" Johann answered earnestly. "That would be excellent."

For the rest of the ride Johann quizzed Mateo to find out what words and phrases he knew, offering pronunciation corrections and excited praise. It turned out my parents were the silent ones, not speaking to us or to each other until we pulled up the steep hill of Vera's driveway.

My aunt was out the door to greet us before Dad had turned off the car. She had on a housedress and her yellow cobbler apron with the pockets that looked like chickens. "¡Mis amores!" she exclaimed, pulling me into her arms. She smelled like onions in cooking oil and coffee and cumin. She kissed my cheek and released me, looking around for the rest of the family. Her eyes paused on the tall, slender German.

"Johann," I whispered into her ear. "He works at the print shop. I'm sure you've met him loads of times. He and Mateo are friends."

Tía Vera nodded in an understanding way and then winked at me. "Claro que sí, 'friends.'"

I shook my head, "No, not like—"

But she'd already kissed the German on the cheek, causing him to blush beet red. "Oh, and Johann! How wonderful!" Tía Vera hugged my brother, brushing one of his long curls behind his ear. "And, Mateo, you get more handsome every day," she told him. Then she embraced my father.

Vera was thirteen years older than Dad. In other families that kind of age gap might have hindered a close relationship between the pair, but fate had other plans. My grandma got an infection and died shortly after Dad was born. Tía Vera dropped out of school to take care of him and all the other siblings while my grief-stricken grandpa worked long hours, disappearing until he was just a hollow shell of himself moving silently through the world. He was a living ghost, that is, until seven years later, when he decided he just couldn't go on living anymore. Vera single-handedly raised and provided for her siblings, who eventually went away to college and built families and successful careers in other states. Only my dad stayed close by, devoted to the woman who had carried him on her hip when she was my age. Vera is the only mother that my father's ever known, and she loves him just as fiercely as if he were her son.

Which made Mom less like Vera's sister-in-law and more like a daughter-in-law. And it showed.

Tía Vera crossed over to my mother, kissed her, then pulled back, squeezing her hand tenderly. "Abigail," she said, searching Mom's face. "You look . . . tired."

Mom forced a pleasant expression. "Hello, Vera."

"You know I worry about you," my aunt insisted, shaking her head, "about your health. I've been praying for you."

"That's not necessary," my mom replied.

Tía Vera shrugged. "I disagree. Come in, come in, everyone!"

The path up to Vera's front porch was lined with summer annuals: marigolds, geraniums, cosmos, zinnias, poppies. One of my first memories of my aunt was her hands around mine as she showed me how to loosen and untangle the roots of an African violet after we freed it from its plastic nursery container. "Now, you make sure you talk nice to it, mijita," she'd told me, as we filled soil into the violet's new Talavera pot. "Plants are like people. They grow better when you tell them how strong and beautiful they are. You be good to them, you understand?"

When Mom caught me talking to the dandelions growing in the concrete, she was furious at my aunt for putting all kinds of silly ideas in my head, confusing me about what was real and what was fantasy. She about blew a gasket when I told her that I had to eat my vegetables or El Cucuy would come and get me.

Mateo pointed between two of the flowers. "What did Anthony do this time?" There in the bed, partially buried in the dirt, was an upside-down statue of a saint. His sandaled feet and brown robe pointed to the sky.

"My reading glasses," Tía Vera answered. "I've told him he can come back inside once I've found them, but until then, he stays right where he is."

Mom's mouth shrank into a pucker, but she said nothing as we climbed the steps to Vera's porch and followed my aunt inside.

"Can I help you with anything, Ms. Mendoza?" Johann asked politely, making an exaggerated show of wiping his boots on the welcome mat. He still felt guilty about wearing shoes inside other people's homes. "It feels disrespectful," he'd explained once. "We take our shoes off in Germany."

Vera smiled and led him to the tiny kitchen at the back of the house. "Sí, yes, right through here. You can help me roll tortillas."

Dad went to sit down on the green, doily-covered sofa across from the jaguar coffee table while Mom excused herself to use the bathroom. Mateo stared nervously into Tía Vera's china cabinet like he was suddenly very invested in counting the tiny porcelain women with parasols.

"Hallo, Johann," I teased, leaning over to him.

"Shut up," he warned.

"Your legs were touching."

"I swear to God, Dolores."

"I get the downstairs bathroom," I said. "No restrictions. As your wingman, I think I've earned it."

He spun around flustered, picking at a thread on his T-shirt. "Fine, whatever, just stop, I don't know, looking at me."

From the kitchen, the tortilla lesson had quickly taken a turn. "You know"—Vera spoke over the sound of the wooden rolling pin on the cutting board—"I could always tell that Mateo would be a homosexual. From the time he was in the womb—"

The blood drained out of my brother's face. "Nope." He raced to interrupt the conversation. "Tía, Johann doesn't want to hear that story!"

~~~~~~~

No one set out a spread like Vera. Fresh flour tortillas in their straw warmer, beans refried in bacon fat, salsa, red rice, guacamole, carne guisada. She laid out the food on her immaculate kitchen counters. My eyes watered with envy as my brother piled the braised roast, potatoes, and onions onto his plate, drizzling Valentina over the entirety of his meal. It wasn't fair. Once we'd made our plates, we wedged ourselves around the tiny circular table—Mom, Dad, Vera, me, Johann, Mateo—elbows folded in against our bodies so we didn't hit the person next to us.

Tía Vera cleared her throat. "Diego," she said expectantly, holding her hand out to my father.

Dad cast an uncomfortable glance at Mom before taking his sister's hand. I followed suit and then reached out to Johann.

"It's for a prayer, is that okay?" I asked.

"Of course," he answered, taking my hand and then Mateo's. My brother stared in wonder at their fingers before shaking himself out of it and looking over at my mother. Mom had her hands folded in her lap. This ideological standoff had been going on for as long as I could remember. It would probably continue until one of them died and the survivor claimed victory.

Dad bowed his head. "Bendícenos, Señor, y bendice éstos alimentos que nos vamos a servir, y que Tú nos das por Tú infinita bondad. Te lo pedimos por Cristo, Nuestro Señor. Amen."

"Amen," Vera repeated. "Now, let's eat."

As always, the first few minutes were devoid of all conversation. Just the sounds of chewing and glass bottles of Jarritos lifted and set down on the vinyl gingham tablecloth. My aunt's food was a fully immersive experience and deserved the moment of silent, contemplative appreciation it elicited. Not even my mother could find fault in Vera's cooking.

"It's delicious," Mom said, breaking the spell. "I don't know how you do it. And never with a recipe."

Tía Vera shrugged modestly, ripping her tortilla. "It's not so hard. Just takes some common sense." My aunt glanced over at me and wrinkled her forehead. "Mija, that's all you want?" She studied my plate of plain tortillas and beans. "You aren't chubby, if that's what you're worried about. Big-boned, yes. Sturdy. But not chubby."

I tried not to feel conspicuous as the rest of the family glanced up from their food. Johann tilted his head in curiosity.

"I'm not supposed to have the other stuff," I reminded her quietly. "Because of my bladder."

"Yes, yes, I know that," Tía Vera said, piling three more tortillas on my plate. There was a slight outline of a handprint in the center of each where she'd smacked it down on the cast iron comal to cook. "But you have to eat more of the rest to make up for it. You know, I made the beans for you, special—half the salt!"

I shook my head. "Salt isn't . . ." Looking at her expectant face, though, I decided not to correct her when she was making such an effort. "I mean, thank you. It's great."

"And you know I'm happy to cook this for you anytime," my aunt reassured me. "But we've got to get you cured."

I sighed. "There isn't a cure, Tía."

"I have this friend," my aunt said. "She's got a special gift for healing. I want to take you to see her."

"You are not taking my child to a witch doctor, Vera." My mom's voice had a false levity to it, but the little birds on her ears started quaking, as if they sensed the coming storm and wanted to take flight. I couldn't blame them.

"Your daughter has been struck down with an affliction," Tía Vera answered.

I could tell from Dad's face that Mom had kicked him under the table. He'd been tapped into the ring, and there was nothing he could do to get out of it. "It's not an affliction," he began, breaking up the reply with a sip of his drink. "It's a common medical condition with plenty of treatment options."

Johann had stopped eating and was sinking slightly into his seat. "This food is wonderful, Ms. Mendoza," he said, glancing around nervously as the tension rose.

"Thank you, Johann." Tía Vera smiled at her guest before turning back to my mother. "And what are you doing to treat this condition?"

"She's got the diet," Mom shot back. "But we're not going to try anything more invasive until she's older."

Mateo covered his eyes with his hands while Johann searched for something else to compliment. "And the plates on your wall. Wow. Very cool. The flowers."

"She needs help now," Vera insisted.

Mom pushed her hair behind her ear. "Even if that was true, no superstitious, primitive magic trick is going to fix it."

Both my father and Mateo winced at the word primitive. Vera, however, remained unreadable.

I turned to my mom. "Even if that was true?" I repeated in disbelief. "What, you don't believe that I'm in pain? That I'm miserable? You know what happened at school!"

Johann was talking to himself by this point. "And these place mats. I like these very much. Yes."

Mom sighed. "Dolores, that is not the point. The point is your aunt is inserting herself into personal family matters and making everything about her." She wrung her paper napkin. "This is just like the baptisms."

"Here we go," Mateo mumbled under his breath. He looked over at Johann and whispered, "I'm sorry."

"They were at death's door; what was I supposed to do?" my aunt asked.

"They were not! They were getting better, actually." Mom's voice was strained. "But that shouldn't matter, not when you knew how I felt about it."

"You don't believe, so what harm does it do to you?"

Mateo leaned over to Johann and lowered his voice. "Me and Dolores had a really bad case of the flu when we were little," my brother explained sheepishly. "I only sort of remember it, and Dolores was a baby, but apparently Tía Vera decided we were in mortal peril. Normally only priests can baptize someone, but in situations where there's a threat of dying, any baptized person can step in and use whatever's at hand." Mateo swallowed. "Which is what Tía Vera did with an Evian water bottle. When Mom wasn't looking."

"The bottle is on a bookshelf around the corner if you want to see it," I said, still reeling. "Next to a family photo and some phallic pottery Mateo made in first grade."

My brother glared. It was my turn to be kicked in the shin.

Mom shook her head at Vera. "It wasn't your call to make."

My aunt stood abruptly from the table, knocking me into my brother. She picked up the empty plates and placed them in the sink.

Then she loitered there silently with her hands on the counter, her back to us. "Well, we clearly remember it differently." She turned the faucet on.

That was the cue. Everyone but Johann knew what came next. Instinctively, we all began to set the stage. My father pushed his chair closer to the table, giving my mother just enough space to wiggle out behind him.

Mom stood up. "Dinner was lovely, Vera . . ."

Mateo and I silently mouthed my mother's next five words to each other. I hate to do this . . .

"I hate to do this," Mom continued. "But I've got to run a few errands before we get the week started. Could you—"

My aunt spun around with a magnanimous expression. "Of course, Abigail! Don't you worry about it for one second."

"Thank you. Really."

Mateo and I tilted our chins up so Mom could kiss our foreheads. She gave the back of Johann's chair an acknowledging squeeze.

The German looked around inquisitively, possibly trying to navigate the sudden, dramatic shift in tone. Or perhaps wondering how he was going to get back to his car at the print shop. "Uh, are you leaving, Mrs. Mendoza?" he asked. No one answered him.

"See you at home, Mom," Mateo murmured. Dad stared at the tablecloth, holding his breath until my mother closed the front door behind her. Then he laughed nervously and stood up to help with the dishes.

"It's fine," Mateo explained to Johann. "Vera will drive us back. We've been doing these twice-monthly Sunday dinners since I was born. In twenty years, Mom's never once stayed for dessert."

"It's a shame," I added dryly. "Tía Vera makes a mean flan."

Chapter Six

Bathroom #3: Tía Vera's House. Like everything else on the premises, this bathroom is well-kept, clean, and crowded with mementos. The patterned Mexican tile and large tin-framed mirror create the illusion of more space than is actually there. The owner's love of plants continues into this room, with two hanging pothos creeping from their pots, obscuring the light from the frosted window. Lining a small wooden shelf is a row of tall votive candles with colorful illustrations of saints on the glass. Since the shelf sits across from the toilet, one always gets the feeling of having an audience. St. Jude's stare is particularly plaintive. Four stars.

~~~~~~~~

As the sun started to set, Mateo, Johann, and I watched the fireflies from Tía Vera's front porch. The bugs' flickering yellow lights meandered lazily through the garden, dipping between the flowers and St. Anthony's skyward feet, in no particular hurry to get anywhere.

"What are they doing, anyway?" I asked my brother. "The fireflies."

Mateo made a face. "What do you mean? They're doing *that*. Phosphorescence isn't enough for you?"

I hugged my knees to my chest. "No, like, are they hunting? Pollinating? They're flying around using up energy, so they have to have some motivation."

"They don't need a motivation," Mateo scoffed, leaning forward to pick at a water-damaged deck board. "They don't have to prop up a capitalist hellscape. They can do something just because they feel like doing it. *Dolores.*"

"Okay, geez." I grabbed the railing and pulled myself up. "Sorry I asked."

Behind me, I heard the door creak open. "It's a nice night," my dad announced, swinging a six-pack of beer by the cardboard handle.

Johann, who'd been silently sweating through his clothes in the muggy evening air, glanced around, waiting for me or Mateo to acknowledge our father. When we didn't, he took the task upon himself. "Yes," he agreed, wiping his drenched bangs from his forehead. "Very pleasant, Mr. Mendoza."

Dad nodded, satisfied. Groaning, he sank into one of the colorful rocking chairs that scraped up against the siding of the house. Mom had always warned Mateo and me about sitting in them. Those things were older than Vera and slathered with layers of peeling paint that probably (definitely) contained lead. Poisonous or not, I guess Dad had spent his whole life around them, so it couldn't make much of a difference now either way.

"It's too bad your mom had those errands to run," Dad mused. He lifted a drink from the caddy and used a bottle opener to pop off the lid. Then he held it out. "Johann, beer?"

"Yes, thank you," Johann replied gratefully, immediately placing the chilled glass bottle against his cheek.

My brother looked at his twenty-two-year-old crush, then back at our father. "Can I have a beer?" he asked with a tone of forced casualness.

"Oh, shut up, Mateo," I told him. "You're not old enough."

"I will be in October." He flipped me off behind his back, but kept his tone light as he reasoned with Dad. "Plus, you know, the legal age for buying alcohol in most other parts of the world is eighteen. Including Mexico." He paused and, with one hooked finger, pulled the cardboard caddy slowly toward his legs. "So really this beer is my birthright."

Johann placed the bottle against his other cheek. "In Germany you are permitted to order beer or wine at a bar when you are fourteen years old," he explained. "As long as you are with an adult."

"Fourteen?" I repeated in shock. "You've been drinking since you were fourteen?"

"Alcohol is not so much a big thing in Europe as it is here," he explained, bringing the bottle to his forehead.

Still staring up at my father, Mateo cautiously lifted a brown bottle and rolled it between his hands, the condensation turning his palms slick. "I mean, it's up to you, Dad," he said with forced disinterest. "You know, I'm not bothered either way."

"Geez," Dad grumbled, shaking his head. "Don't tell your mother."

Mateo grinned, and with one smooth, practiced motion, he used the edge of the step to open his drink. Back in high school, my brother had taken drama for his elective, and those kids were wild. Junior and senior year, he'd come home from loads of parties smelling like Fireball whiskey and weed, wearing a letterman jacket that for sure wasn't his. He'd sneak back into the apartment at two in the morning, taking his shoes off and climbing the staircase in his socks. There was a rumor back then that Mateo had a stick-and-poke tattoo somewhere on his body. It was probably just a rumor, though. I'd never seen it.

No way this was my brother's first beer, but there was a good chance it was his first since graduation—when all his friends left for college and started their own lives. Mateo took a long gulp from the bottle, leaned back, and closed his eyes. Maybe he was remembering his carefree firefly days.

I glanced over at the three remaining bottles. Alcohol was on the list of worst interstitial cystitis triggers. So was sex. I knew that those restrictions didn't matter right at this exact moment, but the implications for later on made me more than a little nervous. And it wasn't like I could talk to anyone about it. How was I supposed to bring up something like that? *Hi, (insert name here), someday, not now, I figure I'm going to want to be like every other teenager and drink and have sex. But what if I can't? What if the things other high schoolers get to experience just don't apply to me? What if there's a part of me that's fundamentally broken?*

The noise of the door swinging closed startled me out of my gloomy thoughts. Dad had taken the rest of the beers and gone back inside. In his absence, Mateo and Johann had shifted closer together on the porch. Not so close as they had been in the car, but not as far away as they would have been working behind the front counter at the print shop.

"I'm sorry about all the weirdness over dinner," my brother said, digging his shoes into the concrete. "This literally happens every time. I should have told you not to come. I don't know why I didn't." He set his beer on the step.

Johann looked at my brother with a hurt expression. "Do you not want me here?"

Stupid Mateo didn't say anything. He was still looking down at his feet, scrape, scrape, scraping the soles across the concrete. The scratching sound coupled with the back-and-forth of his legs evoked the image of a cat using a litter box. Two years without friends had left my once-confident brother socially inept. I followed Dad inside. Feeling sorry for Mateo made me uncomfortable. Mateo was there to goad and laugh at, not to pity.

When I made it to the kitchen, Tía Vera was alone with her back to me as she leaned forward against the sink. The radio played softly in the corner, turned to the only Spanish station in town. It was impossible to follow the tune over the slush of my aunt's aggressive scrubbing.

"Tía?"

Vera didn't look up, just held a gloved hand in the air. "One moment, mija. I'm almost finished." She pushed her glasses up her nose with her wrist.

I sat down and picked at the edge of the vinyl tablecloth, that place where the cold, smooth surface gave way to flannel backing. What had I come in here to say exactly? Something about the horrible messages Shae had sent? About that girl Terpsichore and my total humiliation at the workshop? About my *affliction*? My troubles as a just-turned-fourteen-year-old didn't begin to compare to the ones my aunt had faced with a dead mom and a gaggle of younger siblings to raise. How dare I sit here feeling sorry for myself? *Way to self-indulge in your own misery, Dolores.*

Tía Vera turned around and pulled off her gloves, sending a spray of tiny bubbles into the air. "What is it?" She walked purposefully to sit in the chair across from me, giving me her full attention.

I rested my cheek on the crook of my elbow, turning the world on its side. The kitchen, my aunt, my reflection on the vinyl—all skewed at an angle like a work by M. C. Escher. Through the wall, I could hear

Mateo and Johann talking in low voices. I tried to figure out what emotion was suddenly making my teeth grind against each other and realized, with surprise, that it was jealousy.

"I'm getting tired," I said finally. "Do you think you could drive us home soon?"

My aunt nodded. "Of course. Anything wrong?"

"Nothing's wrong," I replied, taking a page from my mom's book. "Just a headache."

~~~~~~~~~~

Mateo and I had long speculated about where exactly my mother went on her Sunday evening "errands." She didn't take anything with her, and she didn't bring anything home. Adding to the mystery, practically everything in town was closed on a Sunday night, but the Corolla was always missing when Tía Vera dropped us off at the apartment. My brother and I had scoured the middle console and seats and floor, but we never found a scrap of evidence in that car of where she'd been. The only clue we had was the odometer—wherever it was my mother went after leaving Tía Vera's, getting there and home bumped the number up by eight miles. That was all we knew.

After climbing the stairs, the three of us went our separate ways. Dad went into the bathroom to start the shower heating—a task that could take anywhere from thirty seconds to twenty minutes, depending on the fickle whims of the pipe gods. I raided the pantry and pulled out a box of humidity-softened Nilla Wafers. Mateo put the leftovers in the fridge: rice, meat, and beans stored in old margarine containers and a stack of tortillas wrapped in aluminum foil. When we were getting out of her red Escort, Vera had passed an identical to-go bag of food to Johann. "You must come back soon. You're too skinny," she'd told him. And then, "Your mother is so far away. She'd want to know you were eating enough, don't you think?" Johann had blinked quickly at that before ducking in gratitude and hurrying back to his own car.

Mateo leaned his head on the arm holding the fridge door open. His eyes were locked on something inside. The fridge began to beep.

"What are you staring at?" I chewed on a cookie and stood on my tiptoes. The fridge looked the same as it had this morning, full of liquifying produce and dry pizza.

"What?" Mateo glanced back at me. "Oh, yeah, the milk is going off. Don't drink it." He paused, shut the fridge with one socked foot, and spun around on the other. "Or do, I'm not the law."

"You okay?" I asked, backing out of my brother's personal twirling space. "You and Johann didn't talk at all on the drive home."

Mateo did a jazz square, raising and lowering his shoulders in time to some unheard music in his head. "I'm fantabulous."

"You're deflecting."

"What ho," Mateo said, adopting a stick-straight posture and formal English accent. "Who is this grubby little street urchin that dares speak to me thus! Begone or else I'll be forced to box your ears. Away with you!"

"What are you—"

Still in character, he picked a dirty spatula off the counter and held it out in front of him. "Away!" he sang, flicking the sides of my head.

I ducked. "Ew, gross, Mateo, it's all greasy!"

Mateo dropped back into his normal voice. "No need to be so judgmental, Dolores. So are you."

I put my hands up in surrender. "Fine," I spat. "I was just trying to be nice. Good night, dorkface."

My brother waved his fingers at me, shooing me off. "Toodle-oo."

And just like that, I didn't feel sorry for Mateo anymore.

Shae didn't have any siblings. I was so jealous of that growing up, of the undivided love and attention that her parents showered on her. She had no older brother to steal her limelight or tranquility or hair-care products. But it wasn't just her only-child status that made Shae's life magical. As a kid, I believed that the perfection and affluence of her world was a direct result of the Ludens being the kind of people who deserved good things. Comfortable things. Easy things. My family couldn't be allowed a home or a car or a life like theirs. We weren't *those* kinds of people. We didn't deserve it. Somehow, I was sure we would mess it all up.

~~~~~~

INTERIOR MENDOZA APARTMENT ABOVE THE PRINT SHOP, NIGHTTIME, SIX YEARS PRIOR

We open on a shot from above. DOLORES and SHAE both shiver next to each other on a cramped iron twin bed. Although the girls are meant to be eight, they are portrayed by their fourteen-year-old selves with wigs and pitched-up voices. The girls are dressed in opposite styles to reflect their opposing economic statuses. Dolores's grubby pajamas are on the verge of falling to rags while Shae's full-length silk nightgown catches the glow from the flickering streetlight. The only sounds are the icy wind and ominous creaking of the building's walls.

                    SHAE
        I've never been in a house like
        this.

                    DOLORES
        It's not a house. It's an apartment.

Outside there is a commotion on the street. The girls
sit up to look out the grimy window. The camera follows,
catching the view from behind their shoulders. Two
BANDITS appear in white masks, one illustrated with a
spider and the other with a teardrop. The pair perform a
cinematically choreographed mugging of some poor unseen
victim, shoving him into a snowdrift. The ruffians hop
onto waiting motorcycles, rev their engines, and ride
off into the night.

                    SHAE
        This doesn't seem like a very safe
        neighborhood.

                    DOLORES
        It could be worse.

Shae, full of concern for her poverty-stricken best
friend, reaches out and takes Dolores's hands, gripping
them with a sense of urgency. Tender piano music stirs
over the sound of police sirens and horny alley cats.

                    SHAE
        Maybe we're secretly sisters. Maybe
        my mom really had twins, but some
        evil doctor gave you to your parents
        by mistake.

                    DOLORES
        That doesn't make sense.

                         SHAE
          Why not? I'll bet it happens all
          the time. If it were true, then you
          could come live with me. We could
          be together every day, and you
          could share my clothes and food and
          everything.

                       DOLORES
          We don't look anything like each
          other!

                         SHAE
          Lily and Saanvi in Mrs. Edison's
          class don't look like each other,
          and they're sisters.

                       DOLORES
          That's because Saanvi's adopted.

                         SHAE
          Well, I can tell my parents to adopt
          you. I know they would if I said so.
          They give me everything I ask for
          all the time without any exceptions
          ever.

Dolores looks forlornly at a cracked picture frame on
her cobweb-covered bedside table. The camera closes in
on the static faces of her father, mother, and teenage
brother, cropping Dolores out of the photo entirely.

                    SHAE (cont. in the background)
          You could be my sister. Forever. For
          life.

Dolores shakes her head. Our protagonist knows she could

never desert her family, not when they rely so deeply
on her. She is, after all, the very glue that holds them
together. In the background, an oboe wails a plaintive
tune as Shae extends her pinkie out to Dolores.

                    SHAE
        Then swear to me that you'll be my
        secret sister. Swear it! Swear!

                    DOLORES
        I swear.

The two lock pinkies, sparking a burst of magenta light
and the sound of ethereal chimes. The pact must never,
ever be broken. Shae's ruddy face is illuminated by the
glow.

                    SHAE
        And you'll love me forever? For
        life?

                    DOLORES
        Forever for life.

~~~~~~~~~

I sat in bed and plugged my phone in to charge. Absently, I pulled up
Instagram and scrolled through my feed of home remodelings and zit
poppings and unlikely animal friendships. I skimmed over the tar-
geted ads of clothes I couldn't afford on models who looked nothing
like me. I skipped to the end of a video where a construction worker
saved a litter of kittens. And then I saw a post that stopped me dead
in my virtual tracks.

I recognized the picture immediately. Two girls sitting on the swim platform of a boat, grinning at the camera. Both were wearing big T-shirts over their swimsuits and sunglasses on their heads. It was the picture I had as my lock screen, Shae and me two summers ago at the lake on her parents' boat. Except something was wrong.

Because it wasn't me and Shae as awkward preteens in the picture, no micro bangs and braces. It was fourteen-year-old Shae and someone else. Another girl, one from our grade—Emelia Ackerson. And there she was on the boat. Our boat. On our lake trip. Reliving our memory.

In the caption, Emelia had typed: *Perfect evening for a dip in the lake!* *#newexperiences #newadventures #newfriends*

It felt like a porcupine had crawled down my throat to chew on my heart. The photo hurt worse than anything Shae had said in those texts. She needed space, okay, sure. Recent events had left me a contagious loser. I couldn't deny that. Made sense she would need to keep our friendship on the down-low. Made sense she wouldn't want to be seen with me. But there was a big difference between passively ignoring my existence and re-creating our happiest memories with some random classmate.

But apparently that didn't matter to Shae. Apparently, the only thing that mattered was the fact that Emelia Ackerson had never wet herself publicly. Emelia Ackerson had never slipped in a puddle of her own urine and cracked her skull. Emelia Ackerson was tall and pretty and came from a functional family that had fresh produce in the fridge and more than one bathroom.

I was too angry to cry. Instead I just sat and stewed in seething rage, staring at the ceiling. Outside, the Corolla pulled up the alley and the engine stopped. My mother's footsteps on the staircase were barely distinguishable over the low, familiar rumblings of the street at night. She must have carried her shoes in her hands and come up in her socks. The front door opened, then closed. Mom slid the deadbolt into place. I heard her trip over the TV box in the living room and suppress a string of low curses. She made her way through the kitchen, shutting cabinets and turning off lights. I heard her put the box of Nilla Wafers back in the pantry. Then she shuffled stealthily down the hallway, stopping directly in front of my door.

For a moment, I thought she might come check on me. I braced for it, picturing the scene unfolding. She'd see right away that I was distraught, sit on the end of my bed, and demand I explain what was going on. She'd give me no choice. I'd have to tell her that I'd become a human-shaped lump of hazardous waste and Shae couldn't risk radiation poisoning. That I was terrified of the future that my bladder would dictate for me. That I had never felt so, excruciatingly, crushingly alone.

But she didn't come in. She simply turned off the hallway light and went to bed.

Chapter Seven

"Dolores." Mateo's voice was annoyed as he pounded on my bedroom door. I sat up. It was almost noon. I couldn't remember falling asleep, and judging by how exhausted I felt, it probably hadn't happened more than ten minutes earlier. I squinted against the bright light streaming through my window. In the first few moments of consciousness, I couldn't recall the specifics of last night's devastation. But I sensed a general aura of doom.

"Dolores!" Mateo kept banging on the wood. "Dolores, wake up! There's someone waiting to see you downstairs. Answer your phone!" I heard my brother leave the apartment and descend to the print shop, mumbling to himself the whole way.

Shae. All at once, I remembered everything. I scrambled out of bed, pulling on a pair of joggers and a tank top. I flopped my hair up into a bun and scrambled to find my deodorant amid the ocean of dirty clothes on my floor. Shae had seen Emelia Ackerson's Instagram post! She had come to console me, to tell me that she hadn't replaced me after all. That the boat photo had been taken in jest and posted online against her will. Where was the deodorant? Screw it, the can of Febreze on the dresser would have to do. Or better yet, maybe Shae was here to say she'd changed her mind about the whole thing. That she didn't need a break from me, that she realized how much she missed me and that she was an idiot to put our friendship in jeopardy. My flip-flops, where were they? Aha! There by the recliner! I flew out of my bedroom, through the front door, and barreled toward the stairs.

This was a mistake. Misjudging my ability to slow down in slick-soled shoes, I catapulted myself right over the railing and tumbled through the sky. The fall seemed to happen in slow motion, my arms and legs moving sluggishly against the resistance, like treading water. It sounded a lot like being underwater too, in a hot tub with the whoosh-ing drone of the jets. A spot of dried, mauve gum grew larger and larger in front of me as the concrete sidewalk eclipsed my vision. I squeezed my eyes closed, bracing for impact, realizing at the last possible moment that once again my skull was oriented directly toward the ground.

Smack.

It hurt. But not nearly as much as it was supposed to. The concrete I hit had give and smelled like sandalwood cologne. And was wearing a cotton button-down shirt. My eyes popped open.

"I have you!" Johann gasped. "It is okay, Lola, I have you." He was holding me against his chest, breathing hard. His voice was equal parts terror and relief.

"*Whoa,*" I whispered.

"Jesus Christ, Dolores!" Mateo shouted, running up to us.

I looked back down at the crusty gum fossil that was almost my final earthly image. It was so small. So sad. So crusty.

Mateo was still shouting. "What are you, a toddler? Do we need to get a baby gate to keep you from killing yourself? If Johann hadn't been standing right there—"

I couldn't breathe. I gawked at Johann, who was still holding me like I was a twenty-pound lapdog he'd ripped from the jaws of con-crete death. My whole body was shivering.

"You're really strong," I squeaked at Johann. I swiveled my head to look at Mateo. "Did you know he was that strong? I didn't."

Mateo's face was bright red. "I'm going to use the giant paper cutter to chop your stupid legs off! Maybe then you won't be able to break your neck being an idiot!"

Johann laughed in a breathless, shaky kind of way. "That sounds like it could be a Bavarian fairy tale." Slowly he lowered me to the ground, supporting me until I could make my knees work. "Do not take it too hard, Lola," he said. "You made your dear brother very scared."

"Not scared anymore!" Mateo shrieked. "Angry! *Murderous!*"

I looked at my brother. "I can see the veins in your forehead," I told him. "All of them. They're, like, pulsing."

Mateo squatted against the building and took a deep breath.

Johann stepped between us. "I will keep him far away from the giant paper cutter, Lola," he reassured me. "Let us go sit down, Mateo. Dolores can watch the store for a few minutes."

Mateo nodded and stuck his head between his knees. He seemed to have lost all ability to speak.

"Thank you, Johann," I said, feeling more than a little embarrassed. "For saving my life probably. I definitely shouldn't do that again."

"No, please. One time is plenty." Johann took my brother's wrists and pulled him to a standing position. Mateo's face was turned away from me. Probably so I couldn't see his strobing disco veins.

I winced. "Sorry for scaring you, Mateo."

My brother grunted in acknowledgment. Johann glanced back at me, his eyebrows lifting suddenly. "Oh, Lola, your little friend is waiting for you inside."

Somewhere on my descent, probably between ten and three feet from the ground, I'd forgotten the reason I was sprinting in the first place. *Shae was here.* She'd come to talk in person, to explain the texts and the post and the weeks of radio silence. I pulled the front door of the print shop open, the bell above me announcing my arrival. There she was, hidden behind a display of vinyl sign options. Riding high on the adrenaline of my near-death experience, I raised my voice boldly, keeping my tone just cold enough. "So, you've come to apologize, haven't—"

I stopped as the girl stepped into unobstructed view. She was wearing a yellow blouse with a big collar and a pair of dark green slacks. Her white-blond hair was tied up in a scarf.

It wasn't Shae.

"Yes, I have," Terpsichore said, her voice betraying her surprise. "That is very perceptive of you."

"Wait, you're—"

"Terpsichore Berkenbosch-Jones," the girl interrupted in that rehearsed, robotic tone. She paused for a second and fidgeted with her ring. "We have met."

I shook my head. "You're not who I was expecting."

Terpsichore rolled her left ankle. Then her right. "I don't know what to say to that."

It was a fair answer. I didn't know what I'd expected her to say. "What are you doing here?" I asked, walking behind the checkout counter, putting the bulky cash register between us.

Terpsichore approached the other side of the barrier. "You just said it. I'm here to make amends." For the first time since I walked in, she made eye contact, that same sticky eye contact from the workshop.

"I've thought through the encounter over and over again, and I can see that the way I acted was not sensitive to any personal feelings of loss you might have been experiencing in the moment." She blinked. I noticed her mascara was dark green. "My behavior added to your hurt feelings," she said finally. "That was not my intention. You have my sincere apology."

Her voice was earnest, even if her eyes did make me uncomfortable. I straightened a stack of notecards on the counter. "Okay."

"I only came to say that," she said, pulling a thin fabric wallet out of her pocket. "And also to buy stamps."

"We're out of stamps," I answered. I didn't know why I said it. I didn't know whether or not it was true. I didn't even know if we carried stamps.

Terpsichore tilted her head. "I guess that's all, then. Goodbye, Dolores." The girl turned to leave.

"Wait." I didn't know why I said that either.

Terpsichore looked back with interest. "Did you find stamps?"

"No," I answered.

Her face fell in disappointment. But she didn't leave. Instead, she opened her wallet and methodically flicked through a pocket of bills. "I have ten dollars and no stamps to buy," she announced. She came back to the counter. "Do you have any money?"

"None," I admitted, not sure why she was asking such a strange question. She wasn't about to rob me, was she? The way things had gone recently, I wouldn't even have been shocked by such a turn of events. "There's none in the cash register, either."

Terpsichore shifted her intense stare back down to her wallet as she counted the money a second time. "Would you like an ice cream?" she asked the wallet.

Somehow that question surprised me more than a stickup. But not as much as my answer.

"Okay."

Chapter Eight

I couldn't actually desert the print shop without finding someone to take over for me. Or at least without getting permission to flip the BE BACK SOON sign and lock the door. Since we weren't supposed to leave any customer in the shop unattended, I told Terpsichore to wait for me in front of the ice cream parlor. I was still a little wobbly with adrenaline, but glad no one else had seen my near-faceplant off the balcony.

I popped my head out the side door and glanced around, hoping that Johann and Mateo hadn't wandered too far. They hadn't wandered at all. In fact, the two of them were standing right there in the alley. At the sound of the creaking hinges, the boys jumped back from each other and stared in opposite directions. Under normal circumstances, I might have thought they were up to something.

"What, Dolores?" Mateo ran his hands down his face, rolling his eyes up at the sky and pulling on his cheeks. *"What do you want?"*

"Nothing," I answered, resting my head on the doorjamb. "I'm going out. Just thought you should know."

Johann dropped to the ground to fiddle intensely with his shoelaces. His face, or what I could see of it at least, was totally pink, like when Tía Vera had given him that big lipsticky kiss on the cheek.

"Well . . ." I prodded.

Mateo's mouth was drawn small, fists balled up tight in exasperation. I figured he was still angry with me for the impromptu skydiving incident. "You can't sit behind the desk for ten . . . twenty minutes?"

"I told you, I'm going out." I narrowed my eyes. "What were you guys up to back here, anyways?"

"Johann was . . ." Mateo stretched out his words. "He was looking at the birthmark on my neck. To predict my future. It's a German thing, right, Johann?"

Johann stood up, nodding like a bobblehead. "Yes, uh . . ." He leaned forward slightly to study the weird mole just under my brother's ear. "You will not grow any taller than you are today," he told Mateo in a serious voice. "But also, not any shorter."

I rolled my eyes. "Wow, so much to look forward to. Are either of you going to take over for me?"

Mateo swallowed. "Um . . . no, not right this second, no."

I shifted my weight impatiently, rattling the door handle. "So, I can lock up?"

"Go, get out of here!" My brother shoved me backward into the print shop and started closing the door between us. Then he paused and lowered his voice. "Don't tell Mom."

"I don't tell her *anything*." I reached my hand through the shrinking crack in the doorway to wave. "Bye, Johann."

Johann stood up on tiptoes to give a little wave back. "Bye, Lol—"

"Okay, bye!" Mateo interrupted, pushing my hand back inside and slamming the door between us.

I locked the front door of the print shop with my employee key.

Terpsichore stood stick straight while she waited for me, staring out into the street. I didn't really know what to say, so I yanked on the door a few times to check that it was secure.

I turned to face her. "So, I guess we—"

Without directly acknowledging me, Terpsichore spun on her heels and pulled open the glass door of the ice cream parlor. She let it swing shut behind her.

"Can go in now," I finished. "Well, okay, then."

The blast of air-conditioning that greeted me wasn't as cold as most of the other shops on Main Street. It made sense; after all, wasn't it in Spider and Teardrop's best interests to keep their business a comfortable temperature for ice cream consumption? The strategy worked. Despite their limited flavor selection, the store was busy, but not crowded, with people sitting along the counter on pink metal stools and tucked into the row of booths that lined the side wall opposite. Terpsichore was standing back from the counter, studying the chalkboard menu suspended from the ceiling. I walked over to her, passing a young woman quickly scraping milkshake out of a glass and into her mouth. She had one leg out of her booth, rolling a bulky stroller forward and back with the toe of her sandal.

"You can't order anything that costs more than four dollars and fifty cents." Terpsichore glanced down at me—she was quite a bit taller—then back to the board. "Sales tax."

"Uh, yeah. Sounds good." I scrunched my mouth to one side. "I'll do a cone, then. Vanilla."

"Single scoop," Terpsichore clarified. "And your topping?"

"Just plain is fine."

From inside the stroller, the baby started to gurgle in an uneasy way. Responding to the infant, the woman started to eat faster and scoot the stroller with heightened intensity.

"You should get a bowl instead," Terpsichore informed me, pushing her glasses up her nose. "Cones are messy."

"A cone is fine, thanks." By this point, the baby had started to cry.

Terpsichore walked up to the cash register to order. Spider went over to greet her, drying a cylindrical ice cream scoop with the edge of his striped apron. I watched the girl lean forward and point at the glass, indicating the flavors she wanted. I decided to take the opportunity to relieve myself.

~~~~~~

Bathroom #64: One Fell Scoop Old-Fashioned Ice Cream Parlor: Nestled in the farthest back corner of the establishment, one has to pass by every other customer to reach these facilities. Upon completing this embarrassing trek, the weary traveler is greeted by two single-seaters, each no bigger than a broom closet. The tiny restrooms are clean, however, and the bright pink-and-teal subway tiles continue from the front of the shop into the bathrooms and halfway up the wall for an undeniably pleasing effect. Staying on brand, the foaming hand soap is cocoa-butter-scented. However, the hand dryer is much too hot. Three and a half stars.

~~~~~~

In my absence, Terpsichore had picked a booth in a quiet corner near the back. I scooted over the squishy pink vinyl across from her. She held out my cone, which she'd completely mummified in napkins.

"I didn't want it to drip," she explained.

"Right. So, what did you get?" I asked, excavating my treat.

She looked down at her scoop of ice cream shaped like an aluminum can. "Fudge brownie with gummy bears."

Ew, I thought. "Why gummy bears?"

"I don't like crunchy desserts." She scraped her spoon methodically down the edge of her cylinder. "I've never seen ice cream served in this shape before."

"Yeah, it's some retro gimmicky thing." I took my first bite and was surprised to find that it was actually very good.

Terpsichore looked over her shoulder to the front of the store. "Your parents' business is right next door. I saw it on the flyer."

"Yup," I confirmed, still not totally sure how I felt about Terpsichore knowing where I lived.

"Do you get ice cream here frequently?"

"No, not really," I admitted, adjusting my back against the hard booth. My bladder was mad I hadn't found a bathroom earlier. "We don't have a lot of money for 'extras'—that's what my mom calls stuff like this." I lowered my voice. "Plus, the owners seem kind of sketchy."

"Do they?" Terpsichore asked at a louder than normal volume. "How are the owners sketchy?"

"*Oh my God! Lower your voice,*" I hissed, hiding my face behind my cone. "*They'll hear you.*"

She indulged my request, but maintained a confused expression. "How are the owners sketchy?"

"I don't know," I stammered, never having been challenged on this particular assumption. "They just seem kind of . . . rough. With the piercings and the face tattoos."

Terpsichore chewed thoughtfully on a gummy bear. "I plan on having lots of tattoos someday," she mused.

I don't know why this shocked me. After all, I didn't know her well. And she hadn't given any indication she didn't want tattoos. But Terpsichore just didn't seem the type. Not with her perfect makeup, perfect clothes, perfect hair. Even the few messy strands that escaped from her scarf were perfect, like she'd just run in breathless from a meadow or something. "That's a big commitment," I said, hiding my surprise between slurps of ice cream. "I mean, what if you're doing something and you don't want them to show?"

"I know how to cover them up with makeup," she explained. "It's simple color theory."

I licked around the edge of my cone. "Maybe that's what my brother does." I said. "I heard a rumor at school that he got a tattoo when he was a sophomore. But I don't think it's true."

Terpsichore's eyes widened in disbelief. "No reputable tattoo parlor would service a minor."

"Oh, he didn't get it done reputably." I watched as the tired mom set her empty glass and spoon triumphantly on one of the carts beside the garbage can before wheeling the stroller to the door. Teardrop quickly hopped over the lowest point of the counter and raced to hold the door open for her. The mother laughed gratefully and waved back at him through the glass. "Do you have any siblings?" I asked.

"No."

I bit into my cone. "You're lucky."

"Maybe," she said, running her spoon down the edge of her ice cream. "I might have had some, only my father left my mother after I was diagnosed. He didn't want to have any more children with her in case they also turned out autistic like me."

I choked a little and looked up, trying to read her expression. Had

I hurt her feelings? Was she trying to make me feel bad for saying something so stupid? "I'm sorry," I mumbled.

She flicked her gaze up to hold mine. "Why? Apologies are for when you've done something wrong. You didn't do anything wrong."

I didn't answer, just shifted again in my seat, trying to find a comfortable spot.

"I have a cousin, though," she continued matter-of-factly. "Casimir. He's six. My aunt is deployed overseas so he's staying at our house until she comes back sometime around New Year's." She took a bite. "My mother wasn't prepared for how . . . spirited Casimir can be."

As if materializing from thin air, a Little League team in orange jerseys swarmed the shop, sweaty and shouting.

Terpsichore tensed a little, folding her shoulders together as if to make a hiding place for her chin. Then she closed her eyes and slowly relaxed, taking a long inhale.

The ball players shoved each other around trying to reach the counter, stomping their cleats on each other's feet. Accompanying the noisy horde was that wet goat smell that little boys get after baking in the sun for a few hours.

"You dripped."

I swallowed the last of my cone. "What?"

Terpsichore stood and leaned over the table to stare at my crotch. "You dripped ice cream on your pants. Like I warned you about." She looked pointedly at the pile of napkins that had once swaddled my cone.

"Oh, right." I grabbed some napkins and shrank my pelvis under the table, out of her line of sight. "It's fine. Don't worry about it."

Terpsichore ignored me and started digging through her pockets, lining up the contents across the table. *Phone. ChapStick. Earbuds. Sunblock. Microfiber cloth. Bobby pins. Hair ties.*

"Seriously, it's okay," I assured her, my face flushing in embarrassment. I looked around to see if anyone was watching us, but the plastic-spoon sword fight between a few of the sweaty hellions seemed to take the main focus. "How do you have so much room in your pockets?"

Keys. Tape measure. Safety pins. Needle case. Thread. "You should take care of your clothes," Terpsichore scolded. *Mints. Stress ball. Pocket knife.* "Someone put a lot of thought into them."

I glanced at the blade in panic. "Uh, not these ones, I promise."

"Yes, those ones." *Tiny spray bottle. Tide pen.*

She picked up the last two items and came around to my side of the booth, trapping me. "It's okay, though, Dolores, I'll help you." She held the pen aloft, ready to take aim at my virtue.

I caught her wrist. "I can do it myself," I explained, prying the water bottle out of her fingers with my other hand. Still holding her at bay, I sprayed down the front of my pants and blotted away the ice cream drip with my napkins. "See? All better." I let her go.

Terpsichore examined my work skeptically, then relaxed, turning to sit next to me. Exhaling slowly, she capped the Tide pen and placed it at the end of the row of objects across the table. I set the water bottle down beside it, but clearly I didn't do it right, because Terpsichore had to nudge it into alignment.

We sat there in silence for a while, Terpsichore's gaze fixed on the items in front of her.

At the counter, the haggard-looking coach was attempting to pay Spider with a sticky wad of paper bills. At his side, the kid in jersey number eleven was picking his nose with the bottom of a waffle cone. The coach drove the herd of children out the front door, leaving puddles of melted ice cream destruction in their wake.

"Outside the workshop," I began cautiously, "when you followed me down the street . . ."

Terpsichore's face twisted in discomfort as if she'd just eaten something sour.

I picked up her bowl of ice cream from the other side of the table and set it down in front of her. "You said you needed a best friend urgently. Why?" I asked. "What does that even mean?"

Terpsichore fiddled with her spoon and set it down. "My mother believes that because of my autism, I won't be able to form meaningful relationships or navigate nuanced social situations. I'm homeschooled, and if she had her way, I would get an online college degree or maybe not even get a degree at all and live at home with her until she dies." She picked up her stress ball and squeezed it in quick bursts. "Or I die, but it's statistically unlikely that she'll outlive me, unless I should develop some rare, fatal disease."

"So, you don't want to stay at home with her?"

She rolled the stress ball between her hands. "I want to study costume design and work on Broadway shows."

"And there's so much of that around here," I said.

She must not have picked up on my sarcasm, because she shot me an indignant glare. "There's none of that!" she said sharply. "I'm trying to convince her to let me attend Jackson High School in the fall as the first step to me going away to college. But she thinks I'll be a target for ridicule and that without friends, the bullying will irreparably damage my self-worth."

My mind wandered back to the great yellow tide, the echoing jeers, the cry of that hopeless violin. I shook myself out of it. "She's right."

"She's not!" Terpsichore began to return her various doodads to her magical Mary Poppins pockets. "I have plenty of self-worth," she mumbled.

"But no friends."

"I just need one," she insisted. "Not even a real one, just someone to pretend to be my friend in front of my mother. Then she'll have to enroll me."

I couldn't believe that she *wanted* the thing that scared me most. "I'd give anything to be homeschooled," I admitted.

"Because you have no friends?"

"I *do*," I replied. "One. She's, uh, confused right now. But she'll be back. I just have to be patient." I sat up straighter. "And show her that I'm thriving without her."

Terpsichore studied me curiously, like a specimen under a microscope. "You don't seem to be thriving," she decided.

I sulked into the corner. "I'm not. She just has to think I am."

"That's deceptive."

"So's your plan," I countered, using the remaining napkins to fan dry my crotch. "Finding someone to pretend to be your friend in order to convince your mom that you're capable of making friends. There's a lot of irony there."

The door opened, and I raised my head a little to see who'd come in.

"—can't believe how tan you got."

"No, really, it was amazing. And the boys there were so much better-looking. Tell her, Shae!"

Dear God. Shae Luden had entered the building.

Chapter Nine

My body was overcome by an involuntary reaction, like when an opossum gets spooked by a predator and it flops over paralyzed. Or when those fainting goats get yelled at and they seize up with their legs out and their round little bellies to the sky. Confronted with the threat of mortal danger, it turned out I too possessed a spontaneous survival mechanism that mimicked death. Without warning, every muscle in my body went limp, allowing me to melt down the seat and collect in a structureless heap under the table.

"Dolores!" Terpsichore demanded, shifting her feet out from under me. "What's going on?"

"It's Shae," I whispered. *"Please, don't let her see me!"*

Terpsichore stood up. "Where?" she asked, very much not whispering.

I grabbed her hand and yanked her back down. *"Please! Just pretend I'm not here!"*

Terpsichore looked down at me, her brow furrowed. "I'm not good at pretending," she admitted.

"Squeeze your stress ball; you'll be fine."

I could see their shoes approaching. I knew Shae's right away. She had on her favorite sneakers with the custom dye job. She got them last year. There were two other sets of shoes to match the pair of voices that quickly approached the counter: magenta high-tops and gray canvas flats.

"One of the proprietors is coming over," Terpsichore mumbled out of the side of her mouth.

"What?"

"He's mopping under the tables."

I writhed as far as I could against the wall and held my breath. Sure enough, the wide, long-handled mop appeared in front of me, swooped across the floor, and bumped hard against my leg. Then it pulled back and bumped me again, like a confused English sheepdog. Spider peered under the table. I put my finger to my lips and grimaced.

The man raised his eyebrows—he had sharp, arched eyebrows with two little slits shaved into them.

"Please," I mouthed, pointing to the teenage girls, who were standing in front of the register to pay. Spider glanced at the group. Seeming to understand the gravity of the situation, he gave me a quick little nod, removed the mop, and continued to the next table without a word.

I relaxed against the wall and stared at the underside of the booth. Just a little longer, and then they'll be gone.

"Hey, you!" The pair of gray flats was right in front of us.

Terpsichore stiffened, nearly popping her stress ball in a vise grip.

"I really like your outfit," Gray Flats continued. Magenta High-Tops flanked her other side. We were totally surrounded. "Where'd you get it?"

"I made it," Terpsichore answered.

"No way!" Magenta High-Tops exclaimed. "It's so cute. You're lying!"

Terpsichore swallowed. "I have no reason to lie to you."

The shoes shifted toward each other, then back to the booth. "Uh, okay. Anyways, I'm Lucie," Gray Flats announced. I knew right away it was Lucie Bernard, one of the girls who lived in Shae's neighborhood. A year ago, Lucie's parents pulled her and her brother out of school and shipped them to their grandparents' vineyard in France. I guessed she was back. "This is Emelia, and that's Shae." The custom sneakers skipped over.

"Sorry, I didn't know whether to get crushed pretzels or almonds." Shae's warm voice cut me like a knife. "Hi, what's your name?"

"TerpsichoreBerkenboschJones."

"What?" Shae asked.

Lucie laughed. "I don't think I caught any of that. You're going to have to slow that down."

A clump of soggy almonds fell on the floor in front of the table.

"Ugh," Shae groaned. "My ice cream is shedding all over."

"Leave it," Lucie said. "It's fine."

"No, that guy just mopped. I'll clean it up."

As Shae descended toward me, I prayed for the first time in my life. *If you are real, God,* I thought, *and you do care about me like that priest says, just get me through this interaction without being discovered. Intervene. In your merciful omnipotence, command a cockroach to scurry across the floor, push a dirty spoon off the cart, anything to make her look away before she—*

My heart was thumping in my throat as Shae's face dropped into view. Crouching, she used a napkin to pick up the fallen toppings, folded it in half, then ran it once across the floor. I was almost in the clear; all she had to do was stand back up.

Then she wrinkled her forehead, like she sensed something. Some unpleasant psychic disturbance. It was as if our years of sisterly devotion had stitched an extrasensory connection between us. I wondered if it was like those stories about twins, where one can sense when the other's in danger or hurt. Or dead. Mom had said Shae and I were like twins, hadn't she? I clenched my jaw. *Please, God, please. I'll never ask for anything again.*

Slowly, purposefully, Shae looked up. Our eyes met.

Okay, God. I see how it is. Mom was right about you. Almighty, my butt crack.

I cringed, waiting for Shae to say something. To address the bizarre situation unfolding around us—*Dolores? What are you doing? Why are you under the table?*

But she didn't say anything.

Instead, she looked back down at her hand, crumpled her napkin into her fist, and stood up.

"Say your name again," Emelia requested.

"*Tirp* like chirp, *sick* like ill, *ore* like the metal, *ee* like the letter. Tirp-sick-ore-ee."

"I'm never going to get that," Emelia confessed.

Lucie laughed. "Don't take it personally. Em's not the smartest," she explained. "Can't handle a word that's more than three syllables."

"I'm smart enough to know how to keep my bangs from separating."

"Ooh, shots fired." Shae laughed.

"It's the fashion in France."

"The fashion," Shae repeated. "Don't let her fool you. Lucie talks like she owns Paris, but really, she spent a year in some grubby little village in the middle of nowhere."

I felt nauseous. Why hadn't Shae said something? Why hadn't

she acknowledged me? How could she just pretend like I wasn't there?

"Um, Shae?" Terpsichore's voice was too confident, too loud. "Are you Shae as in Dolores's friend Shae?"

I smacked her shin under the table.

"Dolores?" Shae squeaked. "Dolores who?"

"Oh, please, everyone knows you were besties with the piddler," Lucie scoffed.

"That was ages ago," Shae insisted. "We were little."

"Piddler?" Terpsichore asked, moving her legs away from me. "What does that mean?"

"She wet herself," Emelia explained. "During end-of-year exams."

"It's the great regret of my life to have missed it," Lucie said. She burst into a song. "There once was a girl named Dolores, she pee-peed all over the floor-es. She slipped in the flood, and hit her head, thud, then she lay there and pee-peed some more-es!"

Tears turned my vision blurry.

"You must be new here," Emelia said. "Otherwise you would have heard about it."

Terpsichore tried to answer. "Actually—"

Emelia interrupted her. "You should come to this party Shae's hosting in, like, two weeks. You'll meet loads of people. There'll even be some junior and senior boys."

"Men!" Lucie corrected her in a husky voice. I heard her set something down on the table. "Put your number in my phone; I'll send you the details."

Terpsichore shifted in her seat. "Shae, I'd really like to know more about why—"

I dug my elbow as hard as I could into the toe of Terpsichore's suede ankle boot. Terpsichore kicked me in the stomach.

"Ow!" I shouted. Then I threw my hands over my mouth.

"Oh my God! Dolores?" Lucie asked, dropping to the ground with Emelia. "What are you doing under the table?!"

"She's thriving," Terpsichore announced.

I grimaced. Lucie looked the same as she always had, thin face and thin nose, with an expression like a mischievous fairy who'd pooped in your coffee. The only thing that had changed in France was that she'd come back with a bob. And boobs.

"Uh, hey," I said, scooting forward. Then I remembered the giant wet spot on my crotch. I tried to pull my shirt down to hide it, but the action merely drew their attention. "It's not what it looks like. I didn't . . ." I stumbled over my words, face getting hotter. "I dripped ice cream and tried to clean it and Terpsichore had a water bottle—"

"No worries, girl, I believe you," Lucie said. "Shae, you were down there scrubbing the floors like Cinderella; why didn't you say anything?"

Shae's jaw clenched tight. Every muscle in her neck bulged as she studied her ice cream like it held all the secrets of the universe. "I didn't see her," she said stiffly. She pulled on the other girls' arms. "Hey, let's go, my cone is melting, and Mom will be pissed if I get any in the car." Emelia stood up, but Lucie shook her off and turned her attention to me.

"You know, I'm glad we ran into you, Dolores," Lucie began, spooning ice cream lazily into her mouth, "because this whole thing at school with the pee and the ambulance, it's really no big deal. You can laugh about it now, right? We can laugh about it?"

I was trapped in Dante's *Inferno*. Each moment I descended to a deeper, colder layer of hell.

"Definitely," I whispered.

Lucie grinned. "Great, well, in that case, you should come to the party with Twirldippidy here, right, Shae?"

"It's not really a party." Shae shrugged. "I mean, I don't think she'd even want to."

"Of course she wants to," Lucie said, giving Shae a pointed look.

Shae sighed, meeting my gaze for the first time since she discovered me under the table. "You should come if you want to, Dolores."

I nodded, a glimmer of hope lighting in my chest. "Okay."

"Great," Lucie said, standing up. "See you guys soon."

The group of three made their way through the ice cream parlor and out the front door. I gave it to the count of fifty, then slowly squirmed back out from under the table into the seat across from Terpsichore.

My boothmate didn't say anything for a while. It was as if her brain needed time to process the situation. "I don't think we should go to that party," Terpsichore murmured finally, carefully stacking the discarded napkins on the table.

"We *have* to go," I said. "You don't understand. That's as much of an olive branch as Shae can offer me right now." I let my head hit the table. "Oh, God, that song Lucie sang! It's horrible. I have to do something about this whole situation before next fall!"

"Then you can go by yourself. I don't want to."

"That's not how it works. They invited me to come with you." I turned my face to the side. "You really want to go to high school?"

"I want to leave home someday," Terpsichore answered firmly. "I want to be independent. It begins with Jackson High School and ends with a Tony for Best Costume Design."

"A Tony," I repeated. Spider and Teardrop wheeled a full cart of dirty dishes across the ice cream parlor, studying Terpsichore and me with surreptitious glances as they went past. I sat up. "Go with me to that party, help me put this whole piddler business behind me, and I swear you'll start school in September."

"Really?" She seemed genuinely shocked at the offer.

"I'll be the best best friend your mom has ever seen," I vowed. "I've got years of experience."

She smiled so big her cheeks lifted her glasses up.

"No, don't you look at me like that," I warned. "If you ask me, you should forget about the whole thing and stay at home forever. But if you're sure."

Terpsichore nodded emphatically. From under the table, her phone started buzzing a cheerful calypso tune. She ignored it. "Why don't you tell Shae that you want to be her friend again?" she asked me.

"She's in too deep. At this point, she's got to think it's her idea," I explained. "And you can help. If she and the others think you're cool and you like me, then that gives her permission to like me too. It makes sense, I promise." I pursed my lips. "Are you going to answer that?"

"It's my mother," Terpsichore said grimly, leaving her singing phone in her pocket. "She's waiting in the car wondering where I am. I told her I was buying stamps."

"Pick up," I instructed.

She flinched. "I'd rather not."

"Seriously, pick up the phone."

"No." The tune ended abruptly, and she fished the phone out of her pants. "Look, it stopped ringing. Hey, what are you doing?"

I snatched the phone out of her hands and pulled up her texts. "Sorry . . . lost track . . . of time," I typed, reading the words out loud. "Ran into someone . . . I met . . . at the workshop."

Terpsichore slumped against the back of her seat. "I use complete sentences."

"I'm sorry, I lost track of time," I revised. "I ran into someone from the workshop. She lives downtown. We got ice cream."

Terpsichore scoffed. "She won't believe that."

I handed Terpsichore her bowl. It was just gummy bears in a fudgy grave at this point, sinking to the bottom of the glass like tiny bog bodies. "Hold this."

"Why?"

"Just do it," I instructed, scooting out of my side of the booth to sit beside her. I held her phone above us. "Okay, now smile."

Terpsichore pulled her lips taut and squinted.

"God, no, not like that, you look like a hostage."

"I never smile in pictures," Terpsichore said. "It feels disingenuous."

"You need to look like you're having fun. Just move your chin here . . ." I used my hand to tilt her head toward my shoulder. "Better. And open your eyes. More. More. Too much, go back to the last one. Perfect. Hold it, and look right there at the camera. Three . . . two . . . one." I brought the phone down so she could examine the results. "It's nice, isn't it?"

Terpsichore nodded. I went back to her texts.

"There. I sent the picture to your mom and said you'd be right out. And I sent it to me, too, so you have my number and I have yours." I handed her phone back to her and stood up.

"Shouldn't you come with me?" Terpsichore asked, slipping out of the booth after me. "To meet her?"

"Not yet; that's too much too soon. It's got to feel natural." I picked up Terpsichore's ice cream bowl and napkin pile. "Anyways, I need to get back. My brother wasn't exactly thrilled about me ditching him."

Terpsichore nodded.

"Hey, uh." I looked around to see if anyone was eavesdropping. "I have a bladder condition," I explained, setting the bowl on a cart and throwing the napkins away. "That's why I went to the bathroom a bunch of times at the workshop. It was flaring up that day."

Terpsichore's expression was unchanged by this news. "What's it called?" she asked.

"Interstitial cystitis. IC for short." I swallowed. "It's also why I wet myself last year." I held the door open for Terpsichore and followed her outside.

Terpsichore looked out at the passing cars. "Okay. My mother's parked that way," she said, pointing in the opposite direction of the print shop.

"Right. I guess I'll see you later, then," I said.

She nodded and turned away, her long strides quickly taking her around the corner of the building and out of sight. Just like that, gone.

I leaned against the brick and let out a long, slow exhale. Then I walked back to the print shop and pulled on the door. It didn't budge. I tried my keys but was surprised to find it was already unlocked. Cupping my hands over my eyes, I squinted through the window. Someone had used a broomstick to wedge the door shut. I banged on the glass.

"Mateo!"

My brother turned from where he'd been arranging a row of poster tubes. "*Can't hear you,*" Mateo mouthed, putting his hand up to his ear and shrugging. He was alone in the print shop.

I smacked the window harder. "Mateo, this is ridiculous—open the door."

"Ten minutes, Dolores," he called through the glass. "That's all I asked you for. *Ten minutes!*"

"I know, and I'm here now," I said, yanking the handle again. "I'll take over."

Mateo came to the door and shook his head. "It doesn't work like that."

"Why not?"

"It just doesn't."

"Where's Johann?" I asked. "He's sane. I'd rather talk to him."

"Me too," Mateo said. "But he left. Right after you did." My brother removed the broom and opened the door. "Go shower, Dolores. You're not allowed back here until you've soaped every nook and cranny." He slammed the door closed and rewedged the broom.

"You're an idiot!"

"Like this, Dolores," he said, doing increasingly lewd shower pantomimes against the glass. "Scrubbing all of this . . . And these . . . And this twice."

"Fine!" I shrieked. "I'm going. But this is the last time I offer to help you!"

"Oh no," he wailed, clutching imaginary pearls. "How will I ever get by without your grand philanthropic sacrifices? I shudder to think. Now go, there could be customers coming."

"There are never any customers!" I yelled. "Never!"

He picked up a poster tube and smacked it against the glass. "Don't be hyperbolic, Dolores. Go on, get."

Furious, I kicked the door as hard as I could, remembering too late that I was still wearing flip-flops. "You know what?" I shouted, hopping on one foot, holding the other one in my hands.

"What?" he screamed back.

"Johann's too good for you anyway!"

Mateo laughed at that, really laughed. "*Obviously!*"

Hobbling up the stairs, I realized that it had finally happened. Fragile, weak-minded, unibrowed Mateo had snapped. Although I wasn't sure I could take credit for it, I couldn't help but feel partially responsible, even if I didn't totally understand why.

After work, Mateo went straight to his room without eating. He played the *Cats* soundtrack at full volume on a loop for fourteen hours straight. At six a.m., as I returned from the bathroom to yet another encore of "Memory," I texted Terpsichore.

> Did Cats win the Tony for best costumes?

I could have looked it up myself, I guess. But I didn't. I waited a few minutes to see if she'd respond, and then decided she was asleep and set my phone back on the nightstand. Just as I was drifting off, it buzzed.

> Yes, the original production in 1983. John Napier.

The little bubble sat there on the lock screen, directly over the picture of me and Shae, obscuring our faces. I typed a response.

> Thanks

Chapter Ten

Me: Are you there, sir, it's me, Dolo— Wait, no, I'm not supposed to tell you my name.

Priest: You can if you'd like, my rat king friend. It's good to hear your voice.

Me: No time for pleasantries, sir. I need to ask you something.

Priest: Of course.

Me: If God is real, why doesn't he answer our prayers? Is it that he can't or that he chooses not to?

Priest: We're not pulling any punches today, I see.

Me: I'm serious.

Priest: Oh, I know. *Why do we suffer if God is good?* That's the big question, isn't it?

Me: I thought religion was supposed to be about answers, not questions.

Priest: It is for some people.

Me: How?

Priest: For some people, religion gives them a clear, compressed lens with which to view the world. Everything happens or doesn't happen according to God's decision. They feel like God's will is not for them to understand or agree with, but to humble themselves to.

They feel safe in the belief that everything in the world moves by the direction of a single unstoppable force.

Me: But not everyone thinks that.

Priest: No. Many believe God operates under a structured set of rules and covenants. We do one thing, God does another—actions and reactions laid out in Scripture or tradition or revelation.

Me: Bury St. Anthony, find your glasses.

Priest: If you like. For these people, the comfort lies in the belief that there is an exactly correct way to do something in order to bring about favor and miracles. You just have to find it.

Me: And is there?

Priest: I couldn't say. I've never buried St. Anthony.

Me: What do you believe, then?

Priest: I believe . . . that God loves you.

Me: Oh, please. Loves to laugh at me, maybe.

Priest: I won't deny that the divine has a sense of humor.

Me: That's it? That's all you've got? My body's broken, my family's a mess, I'm a community laughingstock, and God loves me?

Priest: That's pretty much the crux of it.

Me: That doesn't make sense.

Priest: Think of the saints. God loved them fiercely, and their lives were filled with suffering. Some of the worst, most violent kinds imaginable.

Me: If the goal here is to convert me, sir, you're not very good at your job.

Priest: Oh no, child, God is the one who converts people. I'm just here to sit with you. That's all.

Me: You're very frustrating, you know.

Priest: I have been told that, yes.

<hr>

Terpsichore and I texted a little over the next couple days. I even called on the phone once, purposefully interrupting a family dinner. The plan was to gradually acclimate her mother to the idea of us meeting up again, intentionally this time. It would have to be on her home turf, of course. I tried to picture what Terpsichore's house looked like, but I always ended up with something like Rapunzel's tower, with a first-grader-sized goblin roaming around the base of it—Terpsichore's problem-child cousin, Casimir. His name did sound like a mythical character who carried around a club and required any passersby to answer riddles three. Finally, Terpsichore got the go-ahead.

My mother will pick you up at 11:00 am tomorrow.

Could probably get a ride if you send your address

No. My mother wants to see where you live and find out if you come from a good family.

Good family?

The kind with no guns, large dogs, or creepy uncles.

We're good then

Excellent.

~~~~~~

That night I started looking through a book I'd checked out from the library—*Saints and Sacrifice: The Tribulations of Holy Martyrs*. It was old and thick, with a broken spine and crumbs wedged in the cracks between the pages. I admit it wasn't my typical reading material. I'd chosen it, though, for the full-page photographs of statues, woodprints, and gold-illuminated paintings of saints. A lot of the artwork depicted graphic torture, things I didn't even know you could do to a human being. The whole thing was more than a little stomach turning. Still, I stayed up way later than I should have to read it, and I had just started back up when Mom knocked on my door the next morning.

It was my mother's first day off from work in a while, and she seemed set on making a big deal of it, going so far as to have Johann take the morning shift at the print shop. She told me and my brother to get dressed and meet her in the kitchen for family breakfast. I picked my least dirty clothes from off my floor, brushed my hair, and took the spooky saints book with me to the table.

Dad was standing at the counter, popping the aluminum top off a frozen can of orange juice concentrate while Mom fished a plastic pitcher out from under the sink. It used to be our plant-watering pitcher, back when we had a nice array of ferns and spider plants around the apartment. But those were long dead now. She set it next to my dad and turned up the stove.

Mateo emerged from the hallway with an expression of someone who would much rather be unconscious. He meandered his way through the living room, stepped around the TV in its box, and picked up a crocheted afghan from the couch. He wrapped it around himself like a hooded cloak and sniffed the air.

Mom had a special way of making pancakes, not special in that it made them taste any better, but special in that I'd never seen another person approach the task the way she did. Instead of ladling out quarter or half cups of Krusteaz batter in nice little circles or Mickey Mouse heads or hearts, she poured the mixing bowl over the pan until the batter spread to the edges. Then she'd do that one or two more times. My mother swore these goliath pancakes were more efficient, but I'd yet to see any peer-reviewed material on the subject.

I opened my library book and leaned back, hoping that appearing busy would get me out of any dishwashing requests. Mateo walked over and lurked behind me.

"Who's he?" my brother asked, poking a picture of an oil painting. The illustration featured a young man in a loincloth tied to a tree. Beneath messy bangs, the martyr's eyes rolled toward the sky, arrows piercing his rippling abs and quads.

"St. Sebastian," I answered.

Mateo nodded, his finger still lingering on the page. "I like that one."

"Why?" Mom asked as she shoved one, then another spatula under her pancake blob with a little too much aggression. "What's there to like?"

Mateo shrugged. "I don't know, just something about him." He pulled a chair over to sit next to me, cocooning himself in the afghan.

"Well, get this," I said. "He's the patron saint of archers."

"Huh." My brother sucked his teeth. "Grim."

"You think that's bad." I flipped back a few pages. "That's St. Cassian of Imola, who was slowly—and I mean slowly—hacked to death by his students. Patron saint of schoolteachers." I flipped again. "St.

Lawrence, grilled alive, patron saint of chefs. And St. Bartholomew . . ."
I turned back to the beginning, looking for a very specific image of a
horrifying marble statue. "Aha, St. Bartholomew, flayed to death. Patron saint of tanners, bookbinders, butchers, and leatherworkers." I
shook my head. "It's like being hit by a bus and becoming the patron
saint of public transportation."

Mateo took the book from my hands. "Look at him," he said,
holding the picture close to his nose. "Just a muscly nightmare man
with a loose skin suit draped over his shoulder."

"No skin suits at the table, Dolores," Mom called, flipping the pancake. "And what's with the sudden fascination with Catholic saints?
Did Vera give you that book?" She raised her eyebrows as Dad carried
the pitcher over to us.

"No, it's from the library," I said, defensive. "I just thought it looked
interesting." No one knew about my regular visits to the church or my
conversations with the invisible priest in the wardrobe. And I didn't
plan on telling anyone either, because I knew they would ask me why
I went. And I didn't know how to answer that, really. It wasn't to clear
my head. I always left those talks more confused about things. My
last visit had me particularly muddled. *Think of the saints*, he'd told me.
How much God loved them or whatever.

I took the book back from Mateo. "I mean, maybe Tía Vera got me
thinking about it," I lied. "It's just super messed up, the ways that they
all died. Or didn't die, at least, not immediately." I shook my head. "As
far as I can tell, the angels can save these suckers from beatings and
burnings and gougings and drownings, but not beheadings. Beheadings seem to be final."

"So, like, zombie rules," Mateo deduced.

My dad sat down and swirled the pitcher of reconstituted orange juice. "*Mateo.*"

"Dolores, put it away," Mom scolded, bringing the monster pancakes to the table on a cookie sheet. She leaned across to set a fork in front of each of us. I dropped the book loudly to the floor.

"So, what's going on?" my brother asked, eyeing the breakfast spread suspiciously. "We're using name-brand paper plates. Is someone dying?"

Mom glared. "Don't be a smart aleck, Mateo. No one is dying."

Mateo reached over and tore apart a pancake with his hands. "Then why are we all here?" he asked.

"Because we're a family," Mom said, pouring herself a glass of juice. "And we're having breakfast."

"To be fair," I countered, stabbing a large pancake remnant and sliding it across the cookie sheet, "we never have breakfast."

"Well, then," Mom said. "We're making an effort."

Mateo held out the bottle of syrup and examined it like it was a skull and he was that character in *Hamlet.* "Why, though?"

Under the table, I felt the whoosh of Mom's foot hitting Dad's shin. "Because your mother says so," Dad added, suddenly becoming very invested in chewing his food.

"That's not what . . ." Mom rubbed her forehead. "Because we love each other."

Mateo's mouth shrank. "Do we, though?"

"Mateo!" Mom and Dad shouted his name simultaneously.

Mom pushed her chair back, the legs squealing on the linoleum floor. "How could you say such a horrible thing? How could you even think it?"

"Oh, don't look at me like that." Mateo took a bite. "I mean, wouldn't we all be somewhere else this morning if we had a choice?" He turned to me. "Wouldn't you?"

"I mean—" I had yet to mention that I fully intended to bail in less than a half hour.

"Of course not," Dad interrupted.

"Shut up and eat your pancakes," Mom hissed.

Although this command was directed at Mateo, everyone obeyed. For several minutes, the only sounds to be heard were grating chewing and plate-scraping noises. I bore it for as long as I could.

"St. Cecilia sort of survived a beheading," I began. "But only sort of because they didn't actually take her head off; they botched it. She lived for another three days, and her followers sopped up her blood in handkerchiefs to keep as relics." I paused, drizzling syrup over my remaining pancake crumbles. "There's quite a bit of that in this book. Blood sopping—"

Mom squinted at my brother. "What do you mean, you'd be somewhere else?" she insisted.

"Nothing," Mateo grumbled. "Forget I said it."

"Just leave it, Mom," I begged.

"No, I don't want to keep him here if he's miserable." She folded her arms.

As if mirroring her unconsciously, Mateo pulled his blanket tighter around himself. "I didn't mean it," he insisted. "Don't worry about it."

I swallowed. "Uh, the pancakes are very . . . porous today."

Mom shot me a look. Instinctively I tucked my legs up under my chair, out of foot-swinging range.

"It's a good thing," I added. "For the syrup. Never mind."

Dad cleared his throat and raised his unibrow. "I'm actually glad we're all here together."

"*Actually*," I mouthed at my brother. "*Actually glad.*" Mateo let out the smallest laugh, which he disguised as a cough.

"Because I have some news for everyone," Dad finished.

My brother sat up straight. "I knew it."

I felt my face twist to an expression of panic.

Dad took in our reactions and shook his head. "No, no, it's good," he promised. "Something that will help us get the print shop up and running again." He puffed out his chest. "You see, I'm going to be making a very lucrative investment in our future."

Mom snapped her neck to look at him. "You what?"

"I heard about it when I was helping one of Vera's friends," Dad offered. "Her daughter told me all about it. It's this company where you can be your own boss, work your own hours—"

"And where are you getting this investment capital?" Mom asked.

Dad had prepared an answer for this question. "That's just it, it won't really cost any money," he said. "She, the daughter, is going to set me up with all the start-up inventory in exchange for tiling her bathroom."

Mateo hid his mouth behind the afghan. "*Oh my God*," he whispered. "*Dad's selling Amway.*"

My father wrinkled his forehead. "No, that's not it, it's something else."

"Mary Kay?" I offered.

Dad sighed and patted the pockets of his jeans. "I don't remember, but I have it written down—"

"Diego?" Mom interjected.

Dad smiled. "Yes, my love?"

Mom shook her head. "You're not doing that."

"I've sort of agreed already," my father explained. "See, she doesn't have any money to pay me for the work I've already done for her, so this is what she's giving me instead. She said to think of it as an opportunity for unlimited revenue growth—"

Mom's voice was firm but emotionless. "Kids. Downstairs. Now."

"Yup." Mateo popped up from his chair and swished out the door. Cape-less and thus with significantly less spectacle, I trailed after him.

"You can't really fault him," I told my brother, following him down the stairs. "I mean, he trusts people. He's sweet. He's always trying to do the right thing." I thought about what Terpsichore had said about her father leaving when she was young. "There are worse dads."

"Never said there weren't." Mateo sat sideways on the bottom step, putting his socked feet up on the building and his back against the metal rails. "Didn't say *anything*."

I sat a few stairs up, facing him. His gaze was fixed on a crack in the mortar between two bricks. A long row of ants marched out of it. Mateo looked sadder than I'd ever seen him, even sadder than when he got the role of the Tin Man his senior year instead of the Scarecrow. Of course, there were no tears this time. But I was starting to learn that the older you got, the less tears worked as the measure for quantifying unhappiness.

"Are you okay?" I asked him.

"Of course," he answered, still watching the ants.

I tried to find the right words. "You know you could tell me . . . if you weren't."

He turned his head and gave me a purposeful stare. "Are you okay?" he asked.

"Point taken," I replied. I glanced at my phone. "Crap, it's almost eleven."

Mateo started sweating in the late morning heat. "You got a hot date lined up?" he asked.

I rubbed my back. "I'm going to a friend's house."

"Shae?"

"No, someone else."

"Someone else?" he scoffed in disbelief. "*Someone else?* I never thought I'd hear such anti-Luden blasphemy."

"Stop it, it's not a big deal," I said, stretching my legs out, trying to relieve the dull ache gradually encompassing my pelvis. "Her name's Terpsichore. We met at that sad kids thing."

Mateo nodded, remembering. "The day you threw all my flyers into the road."

I winced, partly at the memory, partly at my bladder. "Yeah, sorry about that."

"I'm not sure how much it matters now," my brother ruminated. "Do you need a ride?"

"No," I answered. "Her mom is picking me up. Apparently, she's a little . . . protective." The pain wasn't sharp or jagged today. Instead it was like I had a knotted muscle somewhere that I just couldn't reach. I wished I could pull apart my body like an anatomical model, layer by layer, until I found the culprit. Maybe then I could excise it. Or exorcise it. I blew a long, slow breath out my nose.

Mateo watched me, brushing his curls back from his face. "It hurts, doesn't it? Your bladder thingy."

I wrinkled my nose. No one had ever asked me that question. Not Mom. Not Shae. Not even the wheely crab man urologist. Unlike the list of cumbersome accommodations that IC added to those around me, my pain didn't impact anyone else. I'd told people about it, sure. But that always felt awkward, illegitimate. Like I was a lawyer trying desperately to sway a suspicious jury.

"Yeah," I said finally. "I mean, it's not quite as bad as being flayed alive. But it hurts."

Mateo nodded. "Now?"

"All the time," I answered. "But sometimes I can forget about it."

"I guess I understand that," Mateo conceded. He didn't elaborate. "Hey, I think that car has circled the block three times since we've been out here." He stood up. "Have you noticed it? That green one. What do you think they want?"

"What one?" I asked, squinting out at the road. "Oh no, that's her. She's early." I pulled myself up. "We should go into the print shop."

"Why?" Mateo asked. "You'll just have to come back out."

I dusted off the butt of my pants. "Because she wants to see what kind of family we are and where we live and stuff."

"Ew." Mateo thought for a second. "Wait, we don't live in the print shop."

"I know," I said, "but I don't want her seeing where we live. Just be normal. And ditch the blanket."

"Don't know that I can," Mateo said tying the afghan around his neck. "The blanket feels right. I think this is who I am now." He held the door open for me.

"You're an idiot is what you are."

"That is not very kind language, Mendozas," Johann called. He sat behind the counter, scribbling in a sketchbook. "You know I do not like it when you are fighting."

"She started it," Mateo said, walking back to meet him. "She's making fun of my blanket." My brother strained his neck to get a peek at what Johann was working on.

The German quickly snapped his sketchbook closed, putting his arm across it. "That is no good, Lola. You should not make fun of your brother."

Mateo sagged over the counter, deflated by the rejection. "See, Dolores? You should be nice to me."

"Fine, whatever," I muttered, glancing through the door. "They've parked. Just please act like a responsible adult when they come in. Please."

Mateo shrugged and pulled the blanket off, balling it up and tossing it behind the counter. "Okay, I hear you."

Mrs. Berkenbosch-Jones, as I had been instructed to call her even as a divorcée, looked very little like I'd imagined her. The woman was my height, maybe an inch or two shorter even, with a light brown pixie cut and wide, nervous eyes. Her round face and round build contrasted against her daughter's lanky, angular features. As Terpsichore trailed behind her mother, head hunched forward, I noticed that the two weren't entirely dissimilar. Their gold-rimmed glasses were identical and sat exactly the same way across their faces.

"Hi, Mrs. Berkenbosch-Jones," I said, smiling. Covertly I wiped my hand on my shirt, then extended it. "It's a real pleasure to meet you."

"You must be Dolores," she said, shaking my hand slowly as she studied me. "Yes, I recognize you from the picture. It's nice to meet you too." She glanced up. "And you two are?"

I turned around. "Oh, sorry, yes, my brother, Mateo. And that's Johann."

Mrs. Berkenbosch-Jones frowned.

Terpsichore leaned forward. "Don't worry," she told her mother. "They're gay." She looked up at the boys pointedly. "Right?"

Mateo blinked and then gave a thumbs-up. "Oh, uh, yup."

Johann glanced over at him and copied the gesture. "Ja."

Mrs. Berkenbosch-Jones relaxed and smiled. "Oh, well, that's okay, then. Nice to meet you as well."

I had trouble wrapping my brain around it. This woman hardly inspired the fear or frustration that her daughter seemed to feel. This was the person standing between Terpsichore and her dreams? It couldn't be. Her clothes looked like they were from Ann Taylor Loft.

Mrs. Berkenbosch-Jones pushed her glasses up her nose and craned her head to see past us. "Oh, is this it?" she asked. "I was really hoping I could meet your parents, exchange numbers, food allergies, blood types—"

"Yeah, sure." Mateo pointed upward. "Our parents are right—"

I coughed loudly into my elbow.

Mateo quickly changed his hand gesture into a neck scratch. "At work," he finished. "Our parents are both at work."

"Don't they work here?" Terpsichore's mom asked.

"Nope," Mateo answered. "They leave that special privilege to me."

"Well, Dolores." Mrs. Berkenbosch-Jones looked at me apologetically. "I'm not sure I feel comfortable bringing you back to our house without actually speaking to your parents."

"But—"

She barged on in spite of my protest. "I wouldn't want to upset them."

"Oh, don't worry about that," Mateo said. "They won't be upset."

Mrs. Berkenbosch-Jones swiveled to face him. "With some stranger taking their child to an undisclosed location?" she asked, with more than a hint of judgment in her voice.

Mateo nodded. "Seriously, they do not care."

That was the wrong answer. I made my eyes as big as I could. "Because—" I added in a leading, purposeful way.

"Because . . ." he repeated in that same cadence, "because they told me that I'm supposed to get all that stuff from you." He swallowed. "Like your phone number and address. Because I am a responsible adult. I clean the lint out of the dryer trap every single time."

"I see." Mrs. Berkenbosch-Jones wrinkled her forehead, then started to fish around in her purse. "Well, here's everything you need to know," she said, passing a four-by-six card to my brother. "I put all the information on a magnet so you can go ahead and keep it some-where accessible. Maybe on your fridge?"

"Very creative," Johann remarked. "Wow."

"Uh, sure, okay." Mateo scratched something on a scrap of blank receipt paper. "That's my number. And you obviously know where we live. I don't remember her blood type off the top of my head, but I think C rings a bell." He paused and handed Mrs. Berkenbosch-Jones the paper. "Yeah, C sounds right."

"We need to go." Terpsichore fidgeted with the ring on her thumb. "You left Casimir in the car. Children die that way."

"Terpsichore," her mother snapped. She looked back at my

brother. "He really is old enough to be in the car for just a moment," she assured us. "The windows are down. He has his tablet."

"He could be asphyxiating right now." Terpsichore's voice was cold and matter-of-fact.

"Terpsichore, I can see him through the door; he's fine." Mrs. Berkenbosch-Jones shook her head. "It really is nice to meet you, Mateo and Johann. You seem like a lovely couple. I just have a few more quest—"

"Oh, uh, we're—" Mateo stammered an interruption.

Terpsichore talked over both of them. "Casimir's death will create a permanent rift in our family," she told her mother. "You'll go to prison. I'll be an orphan."

Mrs. Berkenbosch-Jones sighed. "Okay, we're leaving. Please, feel free to check in at any point," she told Mateo. "And if someone can't pick her up, I'd be happy to get Dolores home before dinner."

"You'd better," he said, slipping into an old-timey pirate voice. "We run a tight ship around here." Johann furrowed his brow at Mateo in confusion, which only made things worse, because then my brother swung his arm over his chest and added, "Matey."

"Thanks, Mateo," I said quickly, herding the Berkenbosch-Joneses out the door. As soon as the mother turned around, I glared back at my brother and mouthed, "Matey?"

Mateo raised his hands, flustered, "I don't know!" he mouthed back. "I panicked!"

Chapter Eleven

The Berkenbosch-Joneses' car was okay, nice but not new. Through the window I could see a black-haired boy in a booster seat jabbing his finger viciously at an iPad. Terpsichore's mom clicked her fob while her daughter reached for the passenger side door.

Mrs. Berkenbosch-Jones cleared her throat. "Terpsichore, don't you want to give Dolores the front seat?"

Terpsichore flinched. "Then I'd have to sit next to Casimir."

"Exactly," her mother said.

"I don't want to."

"It's fine," I said, opening the door opposite the kid. "I don't mind the back seat." Casimir didn't look up as I slid in beside him.

The car was messy, messier than my parents' cars, which was saying something. There seemed to be a few years' worth of crumbs crushed into the carpet—car sprinkles, as Shae had called them when we were little. Under the driver and passenger seats I spotted unwrapped sticks of gum, an empty prescription bottle, a beat-up paperback romance novel with the cover nearly torn off, and lots of loose pennies.

"Die, you stupid flamingos!" Casimir shouted. I didn't understand what he was playing exactly, but it involved catapults and zoo animals.

Terpsichore plugged her ears and folded her legs up. Her mom leaned over and pushed her legs back down. "If the airbags go off, your knees will get launched right through your skull."

"You stupid antelope! Take that!"

"Cas, honey," Mrs. Berkenbosch-Jones said, looking in the mirror, "can you turn that down?"

The boy kicked against the back of the passenger seat and screamed louder than I thought possible for someone with lungs the size of fruit snack bags.

"Stop it, Casimir!" Terpsichore begged. "Be quiet!"

"Cas, why don't you show Dolores your game?"

"I don't want to," he said, dropping the tablet in the crack between his seat and the door. I could still hear the monotonous game music, just slightly muffled. "It's my game, not hers!" Casimir pouted, pressing his round cheek into the seat belt.

"That's fine. It's up to you. Terpsichore, knees down." Mrs. Berkenbosch-Jones sighed and gave a quick look over her shoulder. "So, Dolores, Terpsichore tells me you're going to Jackson High School in the fall?"

"Yes, that's right."

"You must have a very tight-knit group of friends already," she said. "Kids you grew up with. I imagine it would be quite isolating for someone just starting new."

"No, not really." I studied Terpsichore who was curled up sullenly against the door, her fingers in her ears. She seemed like a totally different person. "I think most people are probably looking to make new friends."

"Well, aren't you worried about that big campus?" Terpsichore's mom pressed. "Getting lost, not being able to find your class?" The woman shook her head. "I can just imagine the sea of teenagers all thrashing against each other in the hallway, the noise that must make, and the smell. The athletes, the smokers—"

"Well, that's only for a couple of minutes a day," I said, shifting uncomfortably. Casimir was now staring at me without blinking, looking a lot like the boy in The Omen. "Most of the time you're sitting in class."

"It's just . . ." Mrs. Berkenbosch-Jones frowned. "I wonder how the teachers will be. It's not like elementary or middle school anymore; they don't baby their students. And they get paid hardly anything, so there's no incentive not to abuse their power. I imagine they'll all be very strict." She flicked her turn signal. "Burnt out. Unaccommodating."

I was starting to understand Terpsichore's strange relationship with her mother. It wasn't that the woman was intimidating. It wasn't that she said any mean things outright. But all Mrs. Berkenbosch-Jones had to do was "wonder" a few things about lifeboats, and I was sure she could convince a rat to stay aboard a sinking ship.

"My brother had a great time in high school." I kept my voice defiantly cheerful. "And he was a terrible student. But I think his teachers still liked him pretty good."

"Well, you know, I'm sure he didn't have the same struggles other students might have," Mrs. Berkenbosch-Jones concluded. "Socially, I'm sure he's very savvy. You know, I don't envy you, Dolores, being a teenager in the public school system nowadays. Kids are just so cruel. They'll find any little weakness or eccentricity and twist it into . . ."

The weight of the woman's negativity gathered around me like a cloud, blurring my vision in a gray haze of gloom. I felt my mind wander.

EXTERIOR SUSAN B. ANTHONY MIDDLE SCHOOL, LATE AFTERNOON, FALL, THE YEAR BEFORE

We open on a shot of the building from the street, the long row of yellow buses honking and swerving around each other. The drivers shout curses out the open windows, banging on their steering wheels. Fortunately, the overlapping soundscape of teen voices, school bells, and traffic drown out any problematic language. The scene evokes the hustle and bustle of a New York City street, an intriguingly dangerous chaos that might chew our protagonist to bits if she's not careful. And where is she? There, leaned coolly against the brick building, the camera catches the suave eighth grader in a quiet moment of contemplation. DOLORES is dressed in a dark peacoat, ascot, and fedora as she chews a stick of gum with a sophisticated air. SHAE bounds over, bright-eyed, naïve, with big earrings and a voluminous blowout.

> SHAE (approaching)
> Dolores, there you are!

> DOLORES
> Here I am.

Dolores removes her fedora, holding it against her leg. She shakes out her hair.

> SHAE (gesturing around)
> Can you believe it? Eighth graders.
> For the next nine months, we'll run
> this place.

> DOLORES
> Don't get too cocky, Shae.

Dolores pulls the gum from her mouth and sticks it to
the wall with her thumb, adding to the muted mosaic of
brittle polka dots. A thoughtful viola riff accompanies
a close-up shot of Dolores's wise face.

> DOLORES (cont.)
> Fortunes flip on a dime in these
> parts.

Suddenly, Dolores winces and falls hard against the
building. She staggers forward with her hat arm thrown
over her lower abdomen, crumpling in pain. Shae reaches
to help her.

> SHAE (gasping)
> You're hurt!

Dolores smacks Shae's hand away with her hat and shakes
her head.

> DOLORES
> It's nothing I can't handle.

> SHAE
> But—

> DOLORES
> Listen, Shae. I can't let them see
> that I'm weak. Damaged. It makes me
> a target. No, I must go on as I have
> always done, or else I might risk
> both of our standings.

> SHAE (in tearful admiration)
> You're so brave.

> DOLORES
> I know. Now go, you'll be late for
> class.

                              SHAE
          But what about you?

                            DOLORES
          I doubt I'll ever make it on time
          again, not the way I am now. Not
          with my . . .

Dolores briefly gazes down the camera lens.

                        DOLORES (cont.)
          Affliction.

Poor Shae is becoming inconsolable, the shot closing in
on her expression of hysterical, trembling desperation.
The viola becomes more urgent, crescendoing to a cymbal
crash.

                              SHAE
          Then let me tell the teachers!

                            DOLORES
          No, dammit, didn't you hear what I
          said? No one can know! Better I be a
          truant than an invalid.

                              SHAE
          Oh, Dolores!

                    ~~~~~~~~~~

"Dolores. Dolores!"

"What?" I sat up and looked around. The car had pulled into a
driveway at the end of an average-looking cul-de-sac.

Terpsichore stood outside, holding my door open. "We're here," she said. Mrs. Berkenbosch-Jones wasn't in the car anymore. She was up on the porch unlocking the front door. Casimir jumped back and forth between paving stones, holding his recovered tablet precariously under one arm.

"Oh. Right." I undid my seat belt. "Your mom," I began, still trying to slow my heart rate. "Oh my God, is she always like that?"

"No," Terpsichore answered, looking down and spinning the ring on her thumb. "Sometimes she sleeps."

Chapter Twelve

Terpsichore led the way to her bedroom and pulled a key from her pocket. "Casimir stole my rotary cutter the first week he was here," Terpsichore explained, "and he made a rather bold alteration to the tip of his left thumb. Mom acted like it was the worst thing that could've happened, but with the amount of time the boy spends without pants, it's a miracle he didn't circumcise himself." She opened the door. "After you."

If Shae's room was a five-star resort and mine a seedy motel, then Terpsichore's was a comfortable Days Inn—cozy, family friendly, low crime.

"You know some people hang up posters," I said, staring up at the quilts that covered all the walls.

"I know," Terpsichore said. "But I've never found any posters of quilts."

I laughed. "Hah, that's funny."

"Is it?" she asked, raising one eyebrow.

I studied her face, trying to read her expression. "Maybe?" I shook my head. "It is very folksy, I'll give you that. Kind of like *Little House on the Prairie* meets *One Flew Over the Cuckoo's Nest*. Give me a padded cell, but make it whimsical."

She smiled at that. "Thank you," Terpsichore said, pulling a wooden chair out from a corner desk. There was a sewing machine on one side and a stack of books on the other with titles like *Get After That Garment*, *Historical Costuming*, *Sewing for Stage*, *Dreams of Seams*, and Susan Carlson's *No Fuss Tailoring for Beginners*. The books were bursting with colorful sticky notes.

I turned around. "Oh, yikes. Who's the scary headless lady standing over your bed?"

Her smile faded. "My dress form," Terpsichore answered grimly, sitting down. "And don't look at it. I'm deeply unsatisfied with my progress."

I squinted at the green dress pinned to the mannequin. "Why? It looks nice."

Terpsichore seemed to bristle at the word. "That's the problem," she said, leaning her elbow on the desk. "In my head the dress is stunning. But the best I can do is nice. I hate it." She rubbed the nails of her thumb and middle finger together. "It's . . . middling. Mediocre. A waste of beautiful fabric."

"You really shouldn't be so hard on yourself," I told her. "It's good. If I knew anything about clothes, I'd probably be able to tell you it's really good. But I wash my lights and darks together, if that tells you anything."

She glanced at me, breaking her melancholy trance. "You shouldn't do that without a color catcher."

"What's that?" I asked. "A Care Bears villain?"

"No. It's like a sheet that you throw in the washing machine with your clothes." Terpsichore sighed. "It absorbs any color bleed, so the light fabrics don't." She shook out her hands, like she was drying them off. "I just want to sew the things I picture in my head. Exactly how I picture them. The dissonance frustrates me."

"Yeah, I can see that. You're all flail-y." I shook my head. "Listen, you're probably not going up for your Tony anytime soon, so you've got a while to practice." I laughed. "I mean, you can't *actually* expect to be an expert at fourteen."

"I *can*," she shot back. The force of her conviction seemed to surprise her a little. She blushed and pushed her glasses up her nose. "I mean, I can *expect* it," she said, softer. "That doesn't mean I can . . . accomplish it."

"No one can accomplish it. It's mathematically impossible." I walked to a bookshelf full of different bins: thread, ribbons, patterns, pincushions, lots of other stuff I didn't recognize and most of it sharp. "You can outsmart your mother, sure, but Father Time—"

Outside the door, I heard Casimir running around the living room, dragging something extremely loud and rattly behind him.

"That would be the Crockpot." Terpsichore sighed, covering her ears. "He gets it out of the cupboard and pulls it around by the cord. He calls it Dogpot." She waited until the noise moved to the other side of the house and brought her hands back down. "Do you want to see something interesting?"

She stood up and crossed over to a dresser, then opened the top drawer, revealing a carefully folded line of cotton briefs and a stack of A-cup bras. Something about the location of the "interesting" possession made me nervous. What kinds of things did people keep in underwear drawers, anyway? Drugs? Weapons? Illicit materials?

"Here it is," she announced, pulling out a gallon-sized Ziploc stuffed with something woolen and ratty. And plaid.

"It's, uh, hmm . . ." I realized I was a little disappointed that the reveal hadn't been scandalous. "Sorry, Terpsichore, I don't really know what it is."

This didn't dull her enthusiasm. "It's made by hand from a Simplicity pattern that came out in the early 1940s," she said, pulling open the bag and laying out the contents on her desk: a matching jacket and skirt. "I got it at the same estate sale where I found my sewing machine, although the outfit significantly predates my machine, so they don't share a history." She held the jacket top up to the light. "Look, look how beautifully done it is. The flat-felled seams up the arms, the sharp corners on the cuffs. And inside, the beautiful lining and bias tape." She gazed at the ripped interior with deep admiration. "No one else would ever see that, Dolores, but she put it there anyway, just for herself." Unsatisfied with my apathy, Terpsichore took my hand and ran my finger around the edge of the collar. "Look at the top stitching here and down the lapel. And the welt pockets."

"Uh, yes," I said, worried that my hand was sweating all over the precious two-piece. "They're very welt."

Terpsichore laughed. I realized that I'd never heard her laugh before. She had a short staccato chuckle that almost sounded fake, but I knew instinctively that it wasn't. "That's just what they're called," she said. "It's not an adjective."

"I told you I don't know anything about clothes."

Terpsichore was still holding my hand. She guided it over the seam down the edge of the skirt. "You don't need to know anything to appreciate the pattern matching. Do you know how difficult that is?"

"Nope."

"It's very difficult," she said. "And time-consuming." Terpsichore dropped my hand and picked up the jacket with a wistful expression. "I think she was my sewing soulmate. The woman who made herself this suit."

I scoffed. "Okay, setting aside that you think your soulmate wore shoulder pads, how do you know she made it for herself?"

"No one would ever put this much effort into something they were going to give away," Terpsichore explained. "People are far too selfish."

Okay, so she had a point there. "Well, what are you waiting for?" I asked. "Put it on."

"It's not even close to my size. I swim in it." Terpsichore wiggled the metal buttons. "Isn't it sad? She died, and her family just cleared out her house and tossed this out." Her voice was indignant. "Can you imagine? It's like tossing out a sculpture or a painting."

A fraying painting, I thought, *that smells like mothballs and war rations.* But I wasn't going to say that out loud, not when it was clear how much Terpsichore valued the story she'd woven: the perfect seamstress whose rigorous attention to detail stemmed from the fact that she was a conscientious person and not completely anal-retentive.

"It's as if there's still a little bit of her here in the stitches," Terpsichore continued, folding the wool suit and sliding it back into the bag.

"If you like old clothes so much, why don't you want to do something with that as a career?" I asked.

"I thought about historical textile preservation," Terpsichore answered. "But I don't want to work in a museum with artifacts that no one ever really sees. What I love about the wool suit is that it tells a story, and that's what I want to do with all the things that I make— tell a story."

"So, theater costumes?" I asked, remembering her Broadway fixation.

"They're part of a character," she explained, "an extension of their identity. They tell you who the character is and what they've been through, and more than that, they make you believe it." She glared at the dress form. "If the designer can get it right, that is. The problem with the green dress is I don't know what its story is. I'm stuck."

"Do my clothes tell a story?" I asked, glancing down at myself.

"Everyone's do." Terpsichore said, still examining her work. I waited to see if she would elaborate on this answer organically. She didn't.

"So?" I prodded.

She sighed and looked back at me, eyes scanning me intensely from the neck down. "Well, if you were a character on a stage, I would think that the costume designer was trying to convey several things about you to the audience."

"Like?"

Terpsichore paused. "Well, for starters, you're poor."

I scoffed, slightly stunned by her frankness.

"What's so funny?" the girl asked, wrinkling her forehead.

"Nothing, sorry." I swallowed. "Please, continue."

"You prioritize comfort. Or you're depressed." She tilted her chin. "Maybe both."

"What else?"

Terpsichore leaned back. "You wear boys' clothes," she answered finally. "So, you're likely not hung up on traditional gender roles. This guess is also supported by your unshaved body hair—"

My face flushed, and I realized that this was actually a terrible game. "Let's change the subject," I interrupted, making sure my hedgehog armpits were fully tucked away.

Terpsichore adopted a polite, slightly practiced sort of voice. "What do you want to do when you grow up, Dolores?"

"Shae and I made a plan that we were . . ." I paused. "No, that we *are* going to backpack across Europe after high school."

"I meant along the lines of a job or vocation?" Terpsichore frowned, perturbed by my answer. "What are you passionate about?"

"Uh . . ." I looked around Terpsichore's bedroom, a shrine dedicated to her life's goal. She knew exactly what she wanted and all the steps to get there. "Shae's got all the great ideas, so she'll come up with something."

"Really?" she asked. "You have no thoughts about what you want. Just Shae?"

"Honestly? No, not really." I folded my arms. "I generally try not to think about what life will be like after high school."

"Why?" Terpsichore asked.

I examined the quilts on the wall, all the shapes stitched within them: flowers, houses, pinwheels, stars. "Well," I sighed. "I just get the feeling that I won't be very happy."

Terpsichore laughed again, but this time the staccato notes felt sharp like needles. "But isn't that up to you?" she asked.

I coughed, clearing the lump in my throat. "Where's your bathroom?"

"Right around the corner."

~~~~~~~

Bathroom #65: The Berkenbosch-Joneses' House. This cramped full bath is structurally unremarkable, containing a tub, toilet, freestanding sink, and storage closet. However, one is keenly aware that this restroom is dominated by a young child marking its territory. The large basket of malodorous bath toys, wooden step stool, and splatter of pee on the underside of the toilet lid significantly lower the overall experience. The toilet paper is midlevel quality at best, and there is a communal bar of soap that stays perpetually damp. One star.

~~~~~~~~~~

I opened the bathroom door to a large, threatening smile.

"Hello, Dolores."

I practically jumped out of my skin. "Oh, uh, hi, Mrs. Berkenbosch-Jones," I said. "You scared me." I took a steadying breath and reached back to flick off the bathroom light. "Do you need something?"

The woman positioned her body between me and her daughter's room. "I just wanted to pull you aside for a little chat."

"Okay." I looked around, hoping that Casimir might choose this moment to make an appearance. I pictured him careening around the corner with his Crockpet in tow. But unfortunately the little gremlin never showed.

Mrs. Berkenbosch-Jones lowered her voice. "Terpsichore has autism spectrum disorder." She spoke the words gravely, as if we were lingering outside the room of a cancer patient discussing how long they had left to live.

"Yeah." I shifted a little to see if I could maneuver around the woman. "She mentioned that. What about it?"

"Well, I'm just making sure." Mrs. B-J blocked my escape route. It was like we were engaged in some awkward playground standoff. "Do you know anything about autism, Dolores?"

"Not really," I admitted.

"That's okay, neither did I," she said breathily. "Not until Terpsichore got diagnosed. She was six, which is younger than a lot of girls on the spectrum, but she'd been having issues. After Terpsichore's father left"—the woman widened her eyes, highlighting the significance of the statement—"I'm sure she mentioned that as well. After he left, I threw myself into understanding the disorder. That's what my life is about."

I'm pretty sure she never asked you to do that, I wanted to point out. But that didn't fit into my perfect, polite best friend routine. And if I didn't help Terpsichore, I had no chance of getting to that party and ending up back in Shae's good graces. "That's very generous of you," I said, finally. "It must have been a difficult adjustment."

Her mother nodded, pleased by my response. "Yes, well, Terpsichore's brain works differently than most people's. But it's such a gift, I think. She's just so smart and creative and practical, all at the same time, don't you think?"

"Yeah, sure."

Mrs. Berkenbosch-Jones pursed her lips. "But sometimes, and this is why I'm telling you all of this, Dolores, social cues might be harder for her to pick up. She might not know if someone is making fun of her, or if she's asking a question that might be seen as inappropriate."

She paused, waiting for some kind of affirmation on my part. When I didn't offer one, she continued, with a darker expression. "So, I'm just letting you know all this," she said, "because it's my job to protect her from things she can't handle. She could really get herself into trouble."

"Uh, okay," I replied. Hoping that the conversation had reached a conclusion, I made another move for Terpsichore's door.

Mrs. B-J thwarted me again. "Have you ever been bowling, Dolores?"

"Yeah," I answered, trying to keep the annoyance out of my voice.

"Well, I'm sure when you bowl, you don't use the gutter guards, do you?" She shook her head and laughed. "No, you don't need them, right?"

"Um—"

"Well, Terpsichore's not like you." Mrs. Berkenbosch-Jones reached out and held my arms above my elbows. "She needs the gutter guards. She'll *always* need the gutter guards. Do you understand?"

Suddenly her grip was just a little too tight and her nails were just a little too sharp.

I squirmed. "Yup, I understand."

"I'm sure you do!" Mrs. Berkenbosch-Jones beamed, releasing me. "Now, let's get you a treat."

Chapter Thirteen

I returned to Terpsichore's room with a plate of cookies and a profound sense of confusion. "Hey, do you and your mom spend a lot of time bowling?"

Terpsichore was sitting at her desk again. "No, I hate bowling," she said. "It's far too loud and highly unsanitary. Do you think they disinfect the finger holes on the balls? No, never. The whole scheme seems designed to be some kind of experiment on disease incubation and spread."

I looked around for another chair, but there wasn't one. There was the twin bed against the wall, but sitting there felt wrong, suggestive of a casual intimacy that Terpsichore and I didn't have yet. Plus, something told me Terpsichore was the kind of person who really didn't care for cookie crumbs in her sheets. "See, I couldn't picture you as a bowler, either," I said, sitting down on the floor cross-legged. "Only your mom seems to think you intend to go bowling a lot."

"That doesn't make sense." Terpsichore blew away some colorful fuzz that had gathered in the metal whirlydoos of her sewing machine.

I shrugged. "Yeah, I'm not sure what she was talking about." I stared at the cookies on my lap, and fidgeted with the plate. Mrs. Berkenbosch-Jones hadn't said if they were flavored. Lemon, maybe?

"You can have those," Terpsichore said, fiddling with a dial.

"Huh?"

"I assume that's why you're hesitating," she continued, without glancing over at me. "You're wondering if you can eat them. You can." She clicked something on the back of the machine. "I looked up interstitial cystitis, which means that my mom looked up interstitial cystitis with me, because, you know, it was on the internet."

"You're not allowed to use the internet?" I asked, ignoring the fact that Mrs. Berkenbosch-Jones probably now knew more about my bladder condition than my own mother. "You're a teenager. Isn't that, like, some kind of crime?"

The light on the sewing machine turned on. "I'm allowed to use the internet all I want," she said casually. "As long as I'm supervised. Mom has everything password protected."

"But what about your phone?"

"It doesn't have internet access."

I took a bite of cookie. "You're Amish."

"Hardly!" she said. "I watch YouTube videos, I have a Pinterest, I can research whatever I want." She wound red thread through the machine, licked the end, and slid it through the eye of the needle. "And we have a TV in the living room; you saw it."

"Yeah, but—"

"My mother just doesn't want me groomed by some internet pedophile," she snapped. "Is that so difficult to understand?"

"Fine, whatever." I wiped my mouth. "But I can't imagine living like that."

"You know, there's only anecdotal evidence to support the IC diet, anyway," Terpsichore said casually. "No actual scientific studies. And even the subjective evidence varies drastically on what foods might cause discomfort and what might not. Some people notice little to no difference following the diet or ignoring it."

"What?" Cookie crumbs sprayed from my mouth, but I didn't care. "Says who?"

"The Mayo Clinic," Terpsichore continued. "The preferred treatment approach seems to include various therapies, pain management strategies, and medications. But I assume you know all of this."

"No. I don't," I said. I wiped my mouth on my arm. "I guess I thought . . . I don't know what I thought. My urologist didn't tell me anything about that. He didn't tell me anything, period." I put my hands over my face and groaned. "God, he wouldn't even say 'period!'"

Terpsichore pushed her glasses up her nose. "You have a chronic illness. You really should take time to understand and research your diagnosis."

"Is that what you do with autism?" I asked.

Terpsichore flinched. She turned in her chair to face me. "Autism is not an illness, Dolores." She spoke the words in a slow, enunciated way as if explaining it to a child. "It's a neurological difference, with a lot of unique presentations. Tons of people have had it that were never diagnosed. It's not wrong; it doesn't hurt me or anyone else. It's just a deviation."

I thought about the tone Terpsichore's mom had used in the hallway, like it was some kind of disease. "But don't you wish you didn't have it?" I asked.

She rubbed her hands along her pants. "It's the way my brain works, how it understands the world," she explained. "If I had a different brain, I would be a different person. And I, this me, would be dead. So, no." She turned back to the machine but didn't touch it.

"That was a stupid question that I asked you," I said. "Wasn't it?"

"Yes, very," she answered sharply.

I nodded. "I'm sorry," I said. Then I lifted the plate slowly as a peace offering. "Cookie?"

"Two, thank you."

~~~~~~~

Terpsichore spent the rest of my visit flitting between projects I didn't understand. She puzzled over the green dress some more, drawing on the fabric with chalk. Then she went to the table and started sketching something. She used scissors to cut the drawing out, then took some fabric off the shelf.

We only talked a little bit during this time, mostly about what she was doing. She'd start explaining and then trail off in the middle of a sentence, her face becoming focused. She didn't treat me like an intruder, though, so I felt okay just sitting against a wall for a while watching her work. Eventually, though, my butt fell asleep and my bladder really started to hurt, so I texted Mateo to come get me.

"My brother will be here in a few minutes," I announced, standing up. Terpsichore was leaning over to stare out the window. "Uh, thanks for having me over."

She didn't answer. Instead, she squeezed around the desk so she could look down into the yard. "It's Casimir," she said. "His mother would be furious at him for starting that fire."

"Wait, what?" I crossed the room. "Like, a literal fire?"

"It's not a metaphorical one," Terpsichore mused.

I maneuvered behind her to look out the window myself. Casimir was squatting calmly with a grill lighter held aloft as he watched a steadily burning box of tampons. "Terpsichore, you've got to go handle that!"

"Why?" she asked, leaning away from me. "I'm not babysitting him."

"That doesn't matter!" I protested. "He could hurt himself."

"Mom!" Terpsichore shouted, plugging her ears. "Casimir needs you in the backyard."

I heard Mrs. Berkenbosch-Jones's voice from the other side of the house. "Tell him I'll be right there!"

"That doesn't . . ." I groaned.

Terpsichore flipped the lock on the window and shoved it open. The breeze blew the smell of smoke into the room. "Casimir, step back from the fire."

The little kid shrieked like a banshee and kicked the smoldering box against the house, sending a flurry of little red embers into the air. "You're! Not! My! Mom!" he screamed.

"He'll definitely lose his tablet for this," Terpsichore mumbled.

I could hear the back door open. Mrs. Berkenbosch-Jones must have broken an Olympic record for her sprint toward the little arsonist.

"Look, Dolores, the wet flower beds put it out," Terpsichore said. "Problem solved."

While I was trying to verify that the fire was indeed no longer burning, Terpsichore slammed the window shut, spun around, and then . . . *the crash.*

I swear it happened in slow motion like the replay of a fatal race car collision. And even though the moment stretched on forever, decades, really, I was entirely powerless to stop it. My knee bashed into hers. My cheek made full contact with the top of her neck and chin. And worst of all, my right hand plowed straight into her left boob.

Her braless left boob. Why wasn't she wearing a bra? Her damn drawer was full of them!

"Oh my God, I'm so sorry," I babbled, jumping back in horror. "I didn't mean to . . . I mean I was just trying to see out the window . . . and then you . . . I didn't . . . I just . . ." The words trailed off to a single pained note escaping through my gritted teeth.

Terpsichore stared at the ground in shock. I couldn't blame her. I'd once seen a bird look like that right after it flew into a window, all quiet and stunned. And then it died.

"I think I've hit my social limit today," she said without emotion. "Your brother's almost here?"

"Yeah, right around the corner." I realized that she'd already begun ushering me out of the room. "You're not mad, are you?"

Terpsichore ignored the question. "I'll expect a phone call tomorrow. We can go over details of our next get-together then." She bit her lip. "I know it happened at the same time, Dolores, but me asking you to leave has nothing to do with you touching my nipple through my shirt." She paused. "Maybe not nothing, but still very little. The groping contributed only a trivial amount."

Panicking, I tried to come up with a word, a phrase that would acknowledge her statement and help us move past this ridiculous incident like mature adults.

I swung my arm in front of me in my best here-we-go gesture. "Righty-o, uh, *matey*."

And just like that, I was staring at the closed front door of the Berkenbosch-Jones residence. Hanging my head in shame, I caught sight of the scratchy brown welcome mat under my shoes.

ONLY GOOD TIMES HERE, it promised.

~~~~~~~~~~~

Mateo picked me up in Mom's car. "Have a nice playdate?" he asked.

I flopped into the passenger seat and put my forehead on the dashboard. Mateo pushed a button by my ear, and the glove box smacked open, hitting me in the face. "Ow! What was that for?"

"Nothing." My brother reached into the glove box and pulled out an envelope. "Vera left this for you."

I took it. It was heavier than a letter and bulged out a little at the bottom. "What is it?" I asked.

Mateo pouted his lips like a duck. "Does it look like I opened it?" He shifted the car out of park.

I rolled my eyes, ripped the envelope down one side, and cautiously slid the contents into my palm. It was a silver bracelet strung with blue glass beads. Each one had a white and black bullseye pattern on it. "It's pretty," I said, holding it up to the window. "I don't know why she'd give it to me, though. My birthday was over a month ago."

Mateo hit a stop light and glanced over. Then he laughed. "El mal de ojo!"

I glared. "What does that mean?"

"The *eeevil eye*," he said in a whistling, ghostly voice.

"Why'd Tía Vera give me the evil eye?" I asked.

"No, stupid, she didn't give you the evil eye." He slowed down as a car merged in front of us. "The bracelet protects you from it. The evil eye is when people are thinking bad thoughts about you, cursing you. Got a lot of enemies, Dolores?"

"Very funny, Mateo. I'm not falling for that."

"No, I'm serious," he insisted. "I bet Vera thinks that's the root of your bladder problems." He smiled. "You know, she gave me one too when I got a C in world history. Ha! Mom was so pissed."

I held up the bracelet. I could recognize the eye shapes now, there in the glass ogling me. Of course, it was some superstitious crap. "That's so disappointing," I groaned. "And I liked it, too."

"Then wear it!" Mateo said.

"But it's stupid."

"Be careful, Dolores," my brother warned. "You're starting to sound like Mom."

He knew that was a low blow. "Fine," I said, wrapping the bracelet around my wrist. "I'll wear it. It won't help anything."

"Not with that attitude." Mateo glanced at me. "So, how'd it go with not-Shae friend?"

"She's really only a sort-of friend," I clarified.

"Quite the vote of confidence."

"No, I don't mean it like that," I said, struggling with the clasp on my bracelet. "I'm trying to help her with something. See, her mom thinks she's this vulnerable useless thing that can't hack it in the real world. Like a Fabergé egg."

"Is she a Fabergé egg?" Mateo asked.

"I mean, maybe?" I put one side of the bracelet in my mouth. "But it feels wrong not to let her jump off the wall and see if she shatters," I mumbled. "If that's what she wants to do, I mean."

Mateo squinted. "I think you're scrambling your egg metaphors there, Humpty Dumpty."

"Ha ha." I dropped the bracelet from my mouth, giving up. Mateo pulled down the alley by the print shop.

"We're here," he declared. "Home again, home again, jiggity—"

I squeezed my eyes shut. "*Igropedherboob.*"

"What?!"

"It was an accident. I think we're still friends, though." I opened my eyes and looked at my brother. "Do you think she has to grope my boob for things to be even?"

Mateo's mouth hung open. "Nope," he said decisively, unbuckling my seat belt. "I'm not engaging with you on this. Get out of the car."

I opened the door but didn't move. "You know, earlier, I think Johann was hiding his sketchbook from you because he was embarrassed. Not because he didn't want you to see it. It might be possible that he does like you back. You never know."

Mateo pushed me. "Out, Dolores."

"I'm just saying." I sighed and held out my bracelet to my brother. "Help me?"

"Ew," he said, clasping it around my wrist. "It's all drooly. There. Go. Shoo."

~~~~~~~~

That night, I sat up reading the scary saints book in my bedroom. It turned out I'd been partly wrong when I told Mateo that no one survived beheadings. It wasn't survival per se. St. Denis was the most famous example. He'd been so good at converting pagans that the Roman governor arrested him and two of his friends and had them all beheaded on the highest hill in Paris. Unfazed, St. Denis picked up his still-talking severed head and walked with it for miles, giving a sermon the whole way. And then somewhere en route, when his head had had its say, both parts of him dropped to the ground, dead. This happened to enough saints that there was a term for them as a group—*cephalophores*. Head carriers. After the sword or axe or what-ever, these men and women would pick up their heads and continue on with their mission until it was completed. They all had different motivations: finish the psalm, preach the sermon, reach the confes-sor, the tomb, the church, or even throw the head downstream as a relic for the faithful. They all had a purpose so compelling that they couldn't rest until it was done. Imagine.

That got me wondering, though, about the two other guys with St. Denis. Why didn't they pick their heads up and walk down the hill too? It didn't seem fair that some people had this great conviction that propelled them on and others just lay there and bled.

Dad knocked on the open doorframe.

"Hey, Dad," I said, blinking. All of a sudden, my eyeballs felt like they had rug burn. I looked at my phone. It was two in the morning.

"You doing okay?" he asked softly.

"Sure," I said, closing the book and setting it on the ground.

"Good, good." He nodded, then lingered there, like he was waiting for something.

"And how are you?" I asked.

He waved his hand. "I'm good, mija."

"Did you get Mom on board with your entrepren—"

"Oh, not yet, but she'll come around to it."

"Hmm," I said. I lay down on my side, still facing the door. "When you were my age," I asked, "what did you want to be? When you were older?"

His eyes lit up. "Your age, well, I wanted to be a movie star. But that changed. Then the dream was bartender. Then long-distance truck driver, ranch hand. Vera wanted one of us boys to go the clergy route, of course."

"Of course," I repeated.

"But I knew I wanted a family." He ran his thumb along his jawline. "Really, that's the only thing I've ever known for sure. Kids who grew up with a mother and father, parents who were always around." He shrugged. "That's when I decided on a family business. I didn't care what it was, so long as we could be together all the time."

I sighed. "It's a nice idea."

"Your mom thought so too." He tilted his head. "Why do you ask, mija?"

"No reason," I answered yawning. "A ranch hand, really?"

Dad laughed. "You can't picture it? Me in a cowboy hat and spurs?" He mimed straightening the brim of a Stetson. "You must remember I was thin then, like Mateo. And I had all my hair. I was very handsome."

"It's true," Mom said, appearing in the doorway beside him. "He was very handsome."

"Was?" Dad asked playfully.

"What did you want to be, Mom?" I asked.

She shook her head. "You'll laugh at me."

"No, I won't," I promised, sitting up just a little.

"I wanted to be a pilot," she said.

"Really?"

She nodded.

I wrinkled my forehead. "But you never said anything about that."

"You never asked," she replied, pulling her hair up into a claw clip.

"Anyway, it didn't work with how we wanted to raise you two. Not that it was having kids that stopped me. Truthfully, I wasn't smart or determined enough to actually go for something like that." She gave a half smile. "I just really liked the idea of it. And the outfits. I thought they were . . . sharp." She reached for the doorknob. "Go to sleep, Dolores."

"Good night, mija," Dad whispered.

I heard the door creak closed, but I didn't see it. I was already somewhere else, standing at the top of a hill holding a needle and thread. Approaching from the other side was a long line of people I knew, all holding their heads under their arms: Mom, Dad, Mateo, Vera, Johann. They marched up to me and held their heads out, demanding that I reattach them. But just as soon as I'd stitched each one back on, the head fell off again and tumbled down the hill with the body running after it. I had almost given up when a decapitated Shae approached me. But she was holding two heads, one happy and warm, the other cold and distant. I didn't know what to do, so I tried to stitch on both, but there wasn't enough room on the neck, and eventually the heads went rolling down the hill with everyone else. But Shae's body just stood there, like it was waiting for something.

Terpsichore appeared. "Don't look at her," she instructed. "I'm deeply unsatisfied with my progress."

Decapitated Shae was wearing the green dress from Terpsichore's room, stuck with pins like a voodoo doll.

"She's all wrong," Terpsichore continued, pulling out a pair of sewing scissors. "Nothing like how I imagined." She lunged at Shae's body with the blades, but the body ran, tripping over the green dress. In its blind panic, the headless form barreled into me. I lost my balance and we both fell backward, not to the bottom of the hill, but into that twisting dark oblivion at the end of a nightmare, a big black tunnel of stomach-churning nothingness.

Chapter Fourteen

Me: So, what do you think it means?

Priest: I'm afraid dream interpretation wasn't a big part of my seminary training.

Me: That's kind of pathetic, no offense. Even Psychic Layla at the crystal shop on the corner can tell you what a dream means.

Priest: Did you try asking for her help?

Me: Apparently she's got a twenty-dollar minimum.

Priest: I see. Well, perhaps your dream was just a dream.

Me: I guess. Hey, Catholics don't believe in divorce, do they?

Priest: There are Catholics all over the world from innumerable backgrounds. I imagine there's a wide variety of opinions on the subject.

Me: I feel like you're avoiding the question.

Priest: Absolutely, that is correct. Why do you ask, daughter? I assume you're unmarried.

Me: My parents.

Priest: Are they divorced?

Me: No, but . . .

Priest: But?

Me: It's something my brother said the other day. About our family maybe not loving each other or something. How we would all run if we had the chance.

Priest: Do you believe that?

Me: I've never told anyone this, but I used to have this silly little thought that if something bad happened to my parents, my best friend's family would adopt me. Their lives are so glamorous. They have a lady come in and take their dirty laundry and return it all ironed and folded. She even puts it back in the drawers.

Priest: That does sound glamorous.

Me: The thing is, what if it wasn't a silly little thought? What if, deep down in my subconscious, I wanted something bad to happen to my family? What if I'm part of the reason my parents are so unhappy— that instead of being a good daughter and trying to make everyone get along, I was secretly plotting their deaths in some terrible and tragic accident? Oh my God! What if I've given my family the evil eye?

Priest: Okay, hold on. First, do you think that by behaving or believing a certain way, you can *make* people get along with each other?

Me: I mean, I could try.

Priest: But ultimately people will make their own decisions, correct? Independent of your actions?

Me: I guess.

Priest: Do you really believe you can wish someone into difficult circumstances, whether consciously or subconsciously?

Me: I don't know.

Priest: I'll put it this way. Do you think the divine creator of the universe would hand a fourteen-year-old that kind of power?

Me: What about St. Joan of Arc? She was fourteen.

Priest: Are you worried you might be a saint?

Me: Well . . . no.

Priest: Good. I like you much better as yourself.

Me: So, what about praying? Are you saying that doesn't do anything? Is that what you believe?

Priest: I believe . . . that God loves you.

Me: Another cop-out.

Priest: Maybe.

~~~~~~~

As promised, Lucie sent Terpsichore the information about Shae's party.

"What are the words *exactly*?" I asked, lowering my voice. I hated talking on the phone in the apartment. The walls were basically papier-mâché, but less structurally sound. More like the stuff wasps' nests are made out of, which is mostly bug spit, I think.

"'Hope you can make it,'" Terpsichore read. She sounded bored.

"This is important," I told her, stumbling over the war zone of my floor to reach the closet. "Now, is there an exclamation point at the end or a smiley face?"

"Neither," she answered. "It's a GIF."

I flicked through the hangers looking for something party appropriate. "A GIF of what?"

"It appears to be one of those inflatable tube men they have outside of car dealerships." Terpsichore paused. "It's lime green."

"Okay, so is it, like, sort of dancing or, like, really dancing?"

"Dolores," Terpsichore sighed. "I can't possibly decipher the indifferent gyrations of inanimate objects."

"Then send it to me!" I insisted.

"No."

"Please?" I tried a different tactic. "How about this? I'll let you use my computer to look up anything you want. No parental controls."

Terpsichore was quiet for a moment. "Fine," she said quickly. "There."

I pulled my phone away from my ear. "Okay, so it's really dancing. That's good."

"If you say so." In the background, I could hear Terpsichore's mother whispering something, trying to weasel her way into our conversation.

Time to drop the subject of high school parties. "Do you think your mom would be okay with us hanging out again soon?" I asked loudly. "She's really cool, and I had such a great time at your house."

"I'll check." Terpsichore turned away from the phone, but I could still hear her. "Mom, would you be okay with Dolores and me—"

Mrs. Berkenbosch-Jones interrupted, "Oh, of course! She seems like a lovely girl."

"She's invited me to her house this time," Terpsichore said.

My jaw dropped. This was a straight-up lie. I had done no such thing.

"Are you sure?" Terpsichore's mom seemed uneasy at the prospect. "What if you get overwhelmed? Or have an anxiety attack? What if you need—"

"Then I can just call you to come get me," Terpsichore answered. "Right, Mom?"

"Well, I guess." Mrs. Berkenbosch-Jones sounded unconvinced.

"Today?" Terpsichore asked. "Five o'clock?"

I shook my head. "Hold on, I never said—"

"I'll see you then."

"Wait—" The phone beeped.

I looked around my bedroom, seeing it with fresh eyes. There was a stack of dirty dishes on my nightstand. The scum on the bottom of the bowls had given birth to fuzzy silver creatures that smelled like . . . I sniffed a cereal mug, then doubled over, heaving. Ham, it smelled like ham. I retched into the unlined trash can.

Mateo flung open the door. "Geez, Dolores, tell me you're not dabbling in bulimia."

I shook my head. The fluffy little mold invaders had tickled their way up my nose and were tap dancing on my uvula.

My brother went pale. "You're not . . . pregnant, are you?"

I wiped the sweat off my face with my shirt. "No, you idiot. Not unless I'm the Virgin Mary."

Mateo exhaled and relaxed against the doorframe. "Whew. Well, then—"

"How have you let me live like this?" I demanded, gesturing around my room.

"How have I?" My brother scoffed. "How have I? Let's have some accountability here, little lady. How have you let yourself live like this?"

I took stock of the laundry and garbage that covered the floor. "It just never seemed that gross until now."

"When I opened your door, a cockroach ran out," Mateo said. "Not in. Out. Like it was seeking asylum."

"Help me?" I asked.

"Of course not." Mateo gave a patronizing smile. "I'd never forgive myself for taking away your rock-bottom moment. This is a learning opportunity." He held his hands out to clap on each word. "Grow. Through. What. You. Go. Through."

"Mat-eh-o," I whined.

"Do-lo-or-es," he mocked, turning to go down the hall. "I believe in you. Girl power!"

I looked at the clock. I had two hours until she got here. Two hours. It had taken a month, more than that, to get my bedroom to this point, and I had all of one hundred twenty minutes to make it no longer a biohazard. It was impossible.

But what was the alternative? Risk Terpsichore seeing me for the pathetic garbage human I was? Never. I grabbed a bunch of empty laundry baskets, paper towels, trash bags, and every kind of chemical I could find under the sink. Then I dragged it all back down the hallway, like a rat to its nest.

Mom walked by about an hour later in her blue janitor uniform. "Will you look at that," she said, doing a double take.

"What?" I spat, using a dustpan to plow through the field of crap next to my bed.

"Nothing, I'm just—"

"Just what?"

Mom put her hands up, surrendering. "Just nothing. As you were."

"Oh, uh, wait." I grimaced, realizing that I probably shouldn't have been so snotty before asking for a favor. "Terpsichore is coming over. That girl from the workshop. Is that okay?"

"Sure," Mom replied. "Yeah, that's fine. Dad and I'll be around this evening too."

"You guys don't have to be here," I said. "It's not, like, a thing."

"We can make it a thing," she offered.

"Please, God, do not make it a thing."

"I think we should make it a thing," she said decisively. "I'll go talk to the boys, see if they have plans."

"Why?" I asked. "Why would you do that?" I threw a shoe aggressively into a pile across the room.

"It'll be fun," Mom insisted. "Family game night. We used to do those all the time when Shae came over."

And now Shae doesn't want to talk to me, I thought, shoving paper plates into a garbage bag.

"Come on, Dolores, it's been ages." Mom tilted her head. "We used to have such a good time."

"Look," I said, using my wrist to brush the hair out of my face. "I can't do much to stop you at this point, can I?"

"That's true," she replied. "Want me to throw something in the washer for you?"

I pointed to the three full laundry baskets I'd lined up against the wall. "Those."

"Okay, well, that offer extended to one load, so I'll just take this here . . ." Mom picked up the smallest basket and backed out of the room, "And I will leave you to all of . . ." She circled her palm in the air. "That."

~~~~~~~

I don't know exactly how it happened. I must have bent the laws of time and space, made a deal with the devil, stepped into the Twilight Zone, but somehow by 4:57 p.m., my room was returned to a semi-normal state. Okay, so my mattress didn't have bedding, but nobody's perfect, right?

The staircase vibrated against the brick as Terpsichore and her mother made their ascent. Of course, Mrs. Berkenbosch-Jones would accompany her daughter inside; I was prepared for that. I'd stationed my mother in the living room to greet them while I wedged the two remaining laundry baskets full of dirty clothes in the closet.

I could hear my mother greet the pair at the door. "Hello! Come on in. I'm Abigail, and this is my husband, Diego."

"Hello!" my father chimed.

"It's so nice to meet you both," Mrs. Berkenbosch-Jones said. "Dolores is a wonderful child."

Mom's tone was skeptical. "Oh, well, I'm glad you think so."

I hightailed it up the hallway before my mother could throw any further shade on my character. "Hello, Mrs. Berkenbosch-Jones!" I called brightly. "Thank you for letting Terpsichore come over on such short notice." I cast a covert glare at the guilty party. "Really, it was such short notice."

"Hi, Tirp-sick-or-ee, is it?" Mom glanced at me for validation. I nodded. "It's so nice to meet you!"

Wordlessly, Terpsichore held out a dripping grocery-store bouquet.

"Oh, uh, flowers?" Mom asked.

Terpsichore frowned. "My mother made me."

"*Terpsichore*—" Mrs. Berkenbosch-Jones snapped.

"It feels excessive," Terpsichore continued.

"They're lovely. I'll just put them in some water." Mom ducked into the kitchen and raised her voice over the sound of the running faucet. "I understand you met Mateo and Johann."

"Yes, I did." Mrs. Berkenbosch-Jones waved at the boys, who were sitting on the floor in front of the coffee table, sort of blocked in by the TV box.

"Hallo!" Johann responded. Mateo lifted his water bottle in a toast.

Mom returned, wiping her hands on her pants. "Well, we're just settling in for a game night if you would like to join us." She picked the tin of dominos off the kitchen table. "Do you know Mexican Train?"

"My mother doesn't like games," Terpsichore answered quickly.

Mrs. Berkenbosch-Jones hesitated. "Well, I could—"

"She left my cousin in the car," Terpsichore interrupted. "It's very dangerous to leave a small child in a hot car."

I was beginning to notice a pattern in the way Terpsichore got rid of her mom.

"The car is not . . . Never mind." Mrs. Berkenbosch-Jones reached for the doorknob. "Thank you all for the offer, but no. I'll be back at eight thirty, if that's okay?"

"Sure, sure," Dad answered. "We'll be here!"

"Great." The woman lingered in the doorway. "Terpsichore. *Terpsichore.*"

Terpsichore snapped her head up at attention. "*What?*"

Mrs. Berkenbosch-Jones gave her daughter a meaningful look. "Be safe."

"Yes, Mother," the girl replied. Then taking hold of the knob, Terpsichore swiftly, firmly, closed our front door.

"'Be safe'?" Mateo repeated. "Does she expect us to offer you black tar heroin?"

Mom and Dad returned to the kitchen to finish dumping dollar store chips and off-brand Chex mix into plastic bowls. I couldn't fathom who they were trying to fool with all this frippery. We weren't chip-bowl people. We were hardly even meal-plate people. In the last month, I'd seen Mateo eat a whole quesadilla off the floor. Our family was about on par with free-range chickens.

Terpsichore stood at the window watching her mom drive away. Satisfied, she sat down on our sofa, then made a panicked noise as she sank down into the frame.

"It's okay, it does that," I explained. "You can't just sit. You have to sort of roll onto it and disperse your weight. Like on thin ice."

Terpsichore threw her arms out.

"No, no, don't struggle," Mateo warned. "It'll swallow you right up if you struggle."

"Dolores?" Terpsichore whimpered.

"Here." I gave her my hands, which she gripped so tightly both our knuckles turned white. "Hey, what's your deal, anyway?" I asked, yanking her to her feet. "You told your mom I invited you over. I thought you couldn't lie."

"I'm autistic, Dolores, not Pinocchio." Terpsichore shook herself off and straightened her glasses, which had gone wildly askew in the ordeal. "I hate your sofa. I will never sit there ever again."

"It's really not that bad when you learn its quirks," I said. "But I see your point. You can have the recliner."

Terpsichore shook her head emphatically. "I don't want any of your upholstered furniture to touch me." She sat on the floor across from Mateo and Johann. "You can ask me again in a little while, but I probably won't say yes then either."

My parents came out of the kitchen. "Okay," Mom announced, setting snack bowls on the coffee table, "we've got Cheesy Waveys, Nacho Triangles, Cereal Jumble, and Chocolate Sandwich Thins. Plus, some other things I found lying around."

"Tell me honestly, Mother dearest," Mateo entreated. "How long have those peanuts been at the back of the pantry?"

"I don't know, Mateo," she answered. "How long have you been a smart-mouthed windbag?"

Mateo laughed and blew a kiss. "I got it from my mama!"

Terpsichore glanced between my mom and brother nervously, as if waiting for someone to throw a punch.

"No, no, it's okay," I explained, sitting down next to her. "See, my family is a lot like the couch."

"It's a liability?" Terpsichore asked.

"No, I meant they've got some quirks. But you get used to them."

The girl shook her head. "Are they fighting?"

"No, no, they're, like, at their best right now, actually," I answered. "Plus, you'd know if they were fighting."

Mateo drummed his hands on the table. "Alright, let's get this started."

"I have not played Mexican Train," Johann said. "How do you do it?"

"With dominos," my brother answered, grabbing a fistful of Cereal Jumble. "It's just a matching game with some light strategy." Mateo picked up a domino and held it out across the table. "Alright, Tirp-sick-or-ee, I have a very important question for you. When you look at the domino, do you see numbers, colors, or shapes?"

Terpsichore wrinkled her forehead. "I don't understand."

"Mom sees numbers," Mateo explained, examining the tile. "She looks at this and sees a five, whereas I see color first—gray-blue. Dolores here sees an X."

"Why is this question important?" Terpsichore asked.

"Well, Terps," my brother answered, "I believe you can tell what kind of person someone is by what they see first."

"I see the number," Johann said. "What does that mean?"

"You are driven by logic," Mateo answered. "If you see color, emotion is what motivates you. And if you see shape . . ." My brother looked up at me and grinned. "That means you like to smell your own farts, right, Dolores?"

I flipped him off. "Grow up, Mateo."

"That doesn't seem to fit thematically with the other two," Terpsichore observed.

"I'm just teasing! People who see shape are more communal," Mateo said, turning to me. "You see things in terms of the people around you. The big-picture stuff."

"That's nice, Lola," Johann said, stretching his long legs under the coffee table.

Terpsichore picked up the domino. "I see a blue five in an X shape," she said, rubbing it between her thumb and forefinger. "What does that mean?"

"It means we should start playing," Mom answered, carrying a chair in from the kitchen. Dad settled into the recliner, sighing heavily as he put his feet up.

"Don't fall asleep, Dad," Mateo said. "Mom will kick you out of the game. She's ruthless."

"I won't fall asleep!" Dad promised, closing his eyes. "Why don't you start explaining the rules, Abigail?"

"I should probably warn you," I whispered to Terpsichore. "My mother is insanely competitive. The local humane society permanently banned her from their monthly charity bingo nights."

Chapter Fifteen

Terpsichore hung with us the first four rounds before the shouting and accusations of cheating had her covering her ears. That was longer than Dad managed, though. He was out like a light before we'd even finished turning the dominos over on the coffee table.

"I think I need a break," Terpsichore announced, standing up. "Can I have your computer, Dolores?"

I studied the dominos in play. "What?"

Terpsichore shifted her weight impatiently, rolling out one ankle and then the other. "You told me I could use your computer."

"Oh, yeah, right. Hold on." I pulled myself up. "Hey, Johann, make sure none of these jokers look at my tiles. I'm actually in the lead for once."

Mom and Mateo glared at the German. Johann made a nervous, noncommittal noise in the back of his throat.

"Okay," I said, walking to my room, pointing back and forth between Mom and Mateo. "If either of you look, I will gouge your eyes out, so help me, St. Lucy!"

"Take your time!" Mom called after me. "No rush!"

When I returned a minute later with my laptop, I put it on the side table a safe distance away from the game. Dad started to snore.

"Your brother looked at your tiles while you were gone," Terpsichore reported dutifully, pulling up a chair. "Your mother asked what they were, but he didn't say."

"C'mon, Terps," Mateo groaned. "Why'd you do me like that?"

"Because *she's* a *good* person," I said, typing in my password. "As promised. All yours."

"Are you working on a project, Terpsichore?" Mom asked, setting a domino down.

"That was my spot!" Mateo protested, bumping his elbow into the TV box. Dad snorted in his sleep and lolled his head to the side.

"It's a journey of self-discovery," Terpsichore answered. I could see the reflection of the screen in her glasses.

"That's nice," Mom said. "We could all use more of that." There was a beep from the kitchen closet. "Oh, Dolores, that's your laundry done if you want to switch it over."

"No, I don't want to switch it over," I said, placing two tiles on the line in front of Johann. "In fact, I think I'll stay right here, to make sure none of you betray me."

"Dolores doesn't separate her dirty clothes." Mateo smirked, like this was top-tier gossip. "That's why all her stuff eventually ends up beige. She's a heathen."

"Terpsichore said you don't even have to," I snapped. "You can use this thing in the washing machine called a color catcher."

"What's that?" my brother asked, setting a domino down. "Sounds homophobic."

Johann smirked a little at my brother's joke and played a tile.

"It's not homophobic," Terpsichore said. "It's like a dryer sheet."

Dad jolted awake. "Did we start?"

"Don't worry about it," Mom said, scanning the table for moves. "Nothing? Nowhere for a two?"

"You mean green?" Mateo shook his head. "No, believe me, I would have found it by now."

Mom pinched her mouth small and drew a tile.

"Really?" I picked up a domino. "I already have this one. This game is bull."

"Your face is bull," Mateo mumbled.

"Wait," Dad said, leaning forward to study the splintering lines of tiles. "Did you skip my turn?"

From that unlucky draw, things quickly went downhill for my score. Two rounds later, my lead had turned to a dismal last place.

"El mal de ojo," Mateo joked, when Mom tallied the scores.

"Can't be," I told him. "I've got the merchandise."

My mother glared at the bracelet on my wrist, but didn't say anything to directly acknowledge it.

Then, after she'd been totally silent for almost half an hour, Terpsichore addressed the room. "The internet is wasted on you, Dolores," she mused. "The whole wealth of human knowledge perpetually at your fingertips, and this is what you choose to look at?" She flipped my laptop around to face the table.

Mateo threw his hands in front of his eyes. "Ah! Porn!"

"Shut up, Mateo!" I turned back to my family, cheeks flushed with embarrassment. "It's not porn. Dad, it's not porn."

My father scratched his chin and looked at the ceiling. Just my luck he managed to stay awake for this moment. "Really, Dolores," Dad mumbled. "That's none of my business."

"It's not pornography, no," Terpsichore said, finally. "It's a quiz called 'Unlock Your Passion.'"

Mateo snorted. "Okay, I'll admit I was joking, but that actually does sound like porn." He put a domino down.

Mom's face was grave. "Dolores," she said, "you are way too young to be unlocking your passion."

"Yeah," Mateo added. "Keep that jazz locked up until you're at least fifteen."

"Mateo!"

Dad cleared his throat and lowered the footrest on the recliner. "Uh, I'm going to the kitchen for some water; does anyone need anything?" He stood up. "Johann?"

"Yes, please." Johann, sensing the importance of assigning the man a task, scanned the coffee table, then held out the only empty bowl. "You could take this back with you, Mr. Mendoza."

"Of course," Dad said, his face relieved. "Happy to help." Something told me he'd stay out of the room for a while.

"And I believe it is now my turn," Johann continued, picking up one of his dominos. "I will go right here, I think."

"*I swear to God, Mateo*," I whispered, once Dad was out of earshot. "I am going to murder you."

"Interestingly enough," Terpsichore said without looking up from her unrestricted googling, "fratricide is the first death in the Bible."

My mother raised her eyebrows. "Are you religious, Terpsichore? Dolores mentioned you were homeschooled, so I didn't know if it was one of those . . ." She trailed off, looking for the right word. "Those, uh, situations. Oh look, there's a spot for my double three."

I put my head on the coffee table. "Mom!"

"What? I don't mean to say it like it's a bad thing, I just think it would be helpful to know if that was her particular background."

Mom shrugged a little. "And if we needed to hide our matches and Judy Blume books."

Terpsichore continued her typing. "No, my mother and I aren't religious," she answered. "But I like to be informed on cultural references, and in a predominantly Judeo-Christian country—"

"Is it my turn?" Mateo interrupted.

"Dolores's," Mom said.

My brother rolled his eyes. "Hurry up, Dolores!"

"Give me a second!" I chewed on my bottom lip. "Are there really no open fours?"

Across the room, my computer made a dinging sound. Terpsichore looked up at me over the screen. "Dolores," she said, "you got a message."

I'd forgotten that my laptop was synced to receive my texts. I patted down my pants pockets, then remembered I'd left my phone charging in my room. "Who's it from?" I asked. "Because I'm not standing up if it's spam; my legs are asleep."

Terpsichore pushed her glasses up her nose. "It's from Shae."

My stomach dropped. "Seriously?"

She nodded and started rubbing the edges of her nails together.

I stumbled to my feet, gasping at the pins and needles that spanned from hip to toe. "I'll be right back," I said.

"Why don't you answer it later?" Mom called, watching me limp down the hall to my bedroom. "Terpsichore's mom will be here soon."

"It won't take long!" I grabbed my phone from the bedside table where I'd plugged it in to charge.

Are you coming on Saturday?

My heart thumped in my chest. It was the first text Shae had sent since the day of the workshop—that terrible "love you" that zapped around my brain like a silver marble in a pinball machine.

I stared at the words. Why was she asking? There was no way to know her tone. At first, I read it as tender, almost apologetic, like when she'd accidentally run over my foot on her Razor scooter when we were eight. But what if she didn't mean it to be kind? What if she meant to be unfriendly and detached, like how she'd been at the ice cream parlor?

I didn't see her, she'd told Lucie. Like I was a bug or a stain or a no-loitering sign. A squirrel that darted out in front of the car she was driving. I didn't see her.

<hr />

EXTERIOR LUDEN LAKE HOUSE DOCK, NIGHT, THREE SUMMERS
EARLIER

The camera slowly pans over the still, black lake, the
dark water reflecting a host of aggressively twinkling
stars. SHAE, age eleven, is still played by her
fourteen-year-old counterpart, but with the addition of
braces and pigtails. She sits on the end of the dock,
holding a pair of sharp silver scissors above her head.
The blades glisten menacingly in the moonlight.

                           SHAE
            It's time.

The camera rotates, revealing a wide-eyed DOLORES,
seated in front of her best friend. Dolores puts the
back of her hand to her forehead.

                         DOLORES
      I can't!

                          SHAE
      You must! Do you truly think you can
      enter womanhood without first leaving
      something behind? We aren't children
      anymore, Dolores. We're middle
      schoolers!

          DOLORES (clutching her hair)
      But—

                          SHAE
      You promised. Swore it on our
      sisterhood that you would let me do
      this.

                         DOLORES
      I swore.

Dolores braces herself, taking a long slow breath as
Shae points the scissors toward her face. As soon
as Shae makes the first exaggerated snip, Dolores's
eyes roll in a faint. She falls backward to the dock
unconscious. Her hand dangles over the edge to leave her
fingers trailing in the water. As we watch the ripples
travel, we hear the crisp snip, snip, snips of the
blades. Dazed, Dolores blinks her eyes open.

                          SHAE
      It's done.

Facing away from the camera, Dolores slowly rolls over
to study her reflection in the lake, hidden from the
audience. Shae appears at her shoulder.

SHAE
Dolores reinvented. Isn't it
perfect?

Dolores is silent. Slowly, deliberately, she turns to
face the camera. She is wearing an uneven wig, bangs
chopped to pieces, unsymmetrical, backcombed to create a
horrifying tiara. She lets out a bloodcurdling scream—

~~~~~~~~

"What did she say?" Terpsichore was standing in the doorway to my bedroom, staring at the place where the linoleum in the hallway gave way to beige carpet that was once white.

"Huh?" I shook my head, processing her question. Then I glanced down at my phone. "Oh, uh, right. She was just asking if I would be at the party on Saturday." I shrugged. "I guess that's good? Don't you think?"

"'Saints and Sacrifice.'" Terpsichore read the title of the book on my nightstand. "Unusual nighttime reading."

"Is it?" I asked, putting my hand on the back of my neck. "Honestly, I haven't actually read any of it besides the picture captions." I worried this made me sound stupid and quickly added, "But there are actually a lot of pictures, so . . ."

Terpsichore didn't weigh in. She was too busy studying my bedroom, her eyes scanning back and forth from wall to wall like she was hunting for Waldo. "Why don't you have any sheets on your mattress?" she asked, gesturing her chin in the direction of my unmade bed. "Is it a bladder thing?"

It took me a second to figure out what she was asking. Then I blushed. "No, no, God no," I stammered, "Just doing laundry. Regular laundry." I laughed defensively. "I don't wet the bed."

Terpsichore raised her eyebrows, her glasses sliding a little down the bridge of her nose. "I don't care either way, Dolores. I was just asking." She crossed over to the baby animal calendar on my wall, which had permanently stagnated on March of this year—a group of particularly smug-looking ducklings.

"I care," I said. My face was starting to feel hot. "I really don't want you to think that I do that."

"Why?" Terpsichore flipped through the months methodically until she reached June. "It doesn't make you better than anyone who does." She looked over her shoulder at me, suddenly grinning. "It's a kitten in a flowerpot. That's cute."

"I know it doesn't make me better than anyone," I lied.

"Good." Terpsichore turned around. "I like your room." Her voice was decisive.

"Really? Uh, I mean, thanks." I shook my head. "Shae was never very impressed. She always said it was brown and cluttered."

Terpsichore straightened her glasses. "Your room is a reflection of you."

"Brown and cluttered?"

The girl frowned and did a little half eye roll. "It's sentimental and functional," Terpsichore explained. "But neglected."

Down in the alley I could hear a car pull up the gravel. I glanced at the time on my phone. "That's probably your mom."

"Almost certainly." Terpsichore looked back at the calendar kitten and smiled. "It's so cute."

"Hey, why don't you take it, then?" I said. "It'll just stay on that page until January anyway."

Terpsichore thought for a moment, then shook her head. "How about this?" she offered. "If you continue inviting me over at regular intervals, I'll keep your calendar on the right month."

I didn't answer for a second. "Maybe . . . ?"

"Aw, that's so sweet," Mateo poked his head in my bedroom and wrinkled his forehead. "Dolores, did you hear that? You might not recognize it, because you're basically a goblin hermit at this point, but she's offered you *kindness*. The appropriate response is 'thank you.'"

"Oh my God, shut up, Mateo." I groaned.

My brother held his arms over head, stretching his shoulders on the doorframe. Granted, he had to stand on his tiptoes to reach the top beam. "I like this," Mateo said, nodding benevolently at us. "The energy in here feels healthy. You have my blessing."

"Why aren't you bothering Johann?" I asked through gritted teeth.

Mateo lowered his voice. "He went to the bathroom."

"Our bathroom?" I asked. Bathroom #1 in the T.U.R.D. A solidly one-star experience. "You let him use *our bathroom*?"

"What's wrong with your bathroom?" Terpsichore asked.

"I had no choice!" my brother lamented, ignoring her question. "I'm never going to see him again." Mateo leaned his head on his shoulder and gave us a woeful, bittersweet smile. "I've given up on finding happiness for myself. But you two, I can live vicariously through whatever this is. *Ow, Dolores!*"

"I told you to shut up!"

Mateo hopped on one foot, "Your heels shouldn't be that pointy! You're a freak of nature, you know that? A weird little goat-hoofed—"

"I should probably go meet my mother at the car," Terpsichore said, squeezing past us. "I'd rather she not walk in on this situation. Or be tempted to use the bathroom, apparently."

"Bye, Terps." Mateo watched Terpsichore start down the hallway, then he turned to mouth at me, *"Are you going to hug her goodbye?"*

"Why would I hug her?" I mouthed back.

"Because you're friends."

"She doesn't want a hug."

"Did you ask?"

The front door opened, then closed, and we could hear Terpsichore's footsteps going down the staircase. "Everyone needs a hug sometimes, Dolores," Mateo said judgmentally.

There was a flush from the bathroom.

I lowered my voice. "Johann's going to need a hug after finding the light dusting of pubic hairs on the underside of the toilet lid."

Mateo shook his head. "You're so uncouth."

I stuck my tongue out at him and slammed my door closed. Then I pulled out my phone.

> Yes I'll be there

Staring at the text, I felt like it was lacking. So, I added the GIF of the green dancing tube man. Then I clicked Send.

Shae's answer came almost immediately.

> Ok

Chapter Sixteen

"Repeat all that back to me," I said, holding the phone against my ear. I'd snuck down to the alley in my pajamas to take this early-morning strategy call. It was paramount that no one in the Mendoza sardine can could hear my conversation.

"I'm supposed to tell my mother that I'm spending the night at your house on Saturday." Terpsichore's voice sounded pessimistic. "I'm not supposed to mention that we're attending a party that evening."

"Right," I confirmed. "She's definitely going to get squeamish if you use that word." I sat down against the wall. "Even though it's a pizza-and-spin-the-bottle situation. Not, like, keg-stands-and-property-damage."

"I really doubt she'll agree to a sleepover, Dolores."

I brushed my hair back. The traffic had started to pick up on Main Street as people made their ways to work. Strangers in cars going about their lives. "We can't leave the party early. Isn't there anything you could do to convince her?"

Terpsichore paused. "I'm not sure. And maybe that's a good thing, as I still don't want to go. If my mother finds out I lied to her about where I was, I'll never be allowed out of the house again."

"What if I spent the night at your house first?" I asked. "Then it won't seem so weird when you bring it up to her, right?"

"I suppose," she conceded.

"Great! Pull one of your wall quilts down for me."

"I won't be doing that," Terpsichore said firmly. "They're very carefully mounted. Casimir might have some blankets you can use."

A terrifying prospect. "I'll bring my own stuff," I told her. "See you soon."

~~~~~~~~~~

"Hey, I need a favor," I said, flipping the light switch in Mateo's room.

My brother retreated into his comforter like a threatened turtle. "Turn off the light. God, what time is it, even?" He pulled his phone into his hovel. "Six fifteen? You're waking me up at six fifteen? Are you insane?"

"Johann was still here when I went to bed." I raised my eyebrows suspiciously. "What time did he leave?"

"I don't know. Late," Mateo mumbled. "Early."

"Harlot."

"We were *literally just talking*, Dolores."

"Floozy."

"You're a child."

"Trollop."

"Are you . . ." Mateo pulled his blanket off his face to glare at me. "Are you finished?"

"I need you to be my alibi for Saturday," I said, lowering my voice. "All you have to do is tell Mom that you're taking me and Terpsichore to the movies. And maybe bowling after."

"What will you really be doing?" Mateo asked. Static and sleep had done otherworldly things to his hair. Even his unibrow had gotten involved.

"Going to a party Shae's hosting. We got invited." I tried to keep my voice cool and casual. "You drop us off, pick us up, we all go home, and no one's the wiser. Bring Johann to keep you company."

Mateo blinked at the glow-in-the-dark star stickers on his ceiling. "I'm too old for these hijinks."

"I don't see why it's a big deal." I folded my arms. "You went to a billion parties in high school."

"Yeah, but they were hosted by friends," Mateo explained, digging his thumbs into his eye sockets. "People who I liked, who liked me."

"Shae likes me," I said, pulling my phone out of my pocket. "She *loves* me. I can show you the texts."

Mateo's eyes popped open. "I swear to God, Dolores, if you invade my personal space, I will drop your toothbrush in the toilet."

"Fine, if you're going to be a baby about it." I put my phone back. "And your friends can't have liked you that much," I told him. "They never come back to see you."

"I can tell you're trying to hurt me, Dolores." Mateo rolled onto his side. "But I understand how it works. Just because we're not close now doesn't mean we weren't back then. People move on."

"Will you take us or not?" I asked.

My brother lifted his head. "You're not going to drop this, are you?"

"Mateo, it's important. Everyone thinks I'm a joke after what happened. They wrote a song about it."

"Fine, just go. Let me sleep!"

~~~~~~~~

Mom was standing in the kitchen in her janitorial uniform with her hair unbrushed. She set a clean filter in the coffee maker. "You're up early."

I went to the living room and pulled one of the kitchen chairs around the TV in the box, between the sofa and recliner, and back to its spot at the kitchen table.

"Can I sleep over at Terpsichore's house tomorrow?" I asked, sitting down.

"Sure, I don't care," she answered dismissively. On the counter, the coffee had started to dribble into the pot. The crisp, soothing smell was enough to lure my brother, stumbling, out of his cave. He was still wearing his clothes from last night.

"You look awful," Mom observed.

"Thank you."

"What were you up to last night?"

"Nothing! We were just talking, honestly, you people . . ." He scooped a plastic cup into a bag of grocery store ice in the freezer.

Mom sighed and stirred her coffee with her pinkie.

"Where's Dad?" Mateo asked, pouring coffee into his cup. The ice crackled.

"Getting dressed," Mom answered, passing my brother the creamer. "I've told him that today is the day he's going to collect the money from that pyramid scheme lady. He did all that work; he deserves to get paid."

Mateo took a sip of his drink, then winced. "Wow," he said, swallowing. "Getting paid for doing a job. What a novel idea."

"It's different with family," Dad said, appearing from the hallway. "Business ownership is the American dream."

"So I've been told," Mateo said. He poured another stream of creamer into his cup and started whistling "America" from *West Side Story*.

"Shut up about your hard-knock life, Mateo," I said. "At least you can drink coffee." *And alcohol*, I added in my head. *And everything else your normal bladder lets you handle.*

Mom pursed her lips. "You know, if you're unhappy at the print shop, Mateo, we can always trade. You can go scrub floors and pick up steroid vials, and I can sit behind a desk all day handing people their print orders in little white boxes . . ." Mom trailed off. Someone was coming up the metal stairs outside.

The door swung open. "Ay, mijos, you shouldn't leave the door unlocked," Tía Vera scolded. "Not with those two cholos running the ice cream shop next door."

"Vera!" Dad exclaimed, crossing the room to greet her.

Mom's expression stiffened. "Vera, what an unexpected entrance." She gestured to the counter. "Can I get you anything? Coffee? Snack cake?"

"No, don't go to any trouble," Vera said, waving a small padded envelope. "I can't stay long. *El Corazón Palpitante* is on soon, and the pianist Juliana is about to wake up from her coma to find out her hands have been stolen by the evil surgeon Don Carlos." My aunt pushed the envelope into my hand. "I just came to drop this off for Dolores."

"What is it?" I asked.

"Open it," she instructed. "It arrived today . . . from the internet."

Inside was a little glass vial with a rubber dropper cap. I read the label out loud. "St. Vitalis of Assisi oil."

"I prefer canola," Mateo mumbled into his coffee. "Higher smoke point."

"Bah, you don't cook with it," Tía Vera said, taking the vial from my hand. "You use it on your belly." She unscrewed the cap.

"Tía, look." I held up my wrist, bracing myself for my mother's glares. "I'm wearing the bracelet, see? Isn't that enough?"

"No, this will also help," she insisted, filling the dropper and lunging at my abdomen. I scrambled backward. The oil was yellow and had a strong clove scent.

"Don't, Vera," Mom said, exasperated. "It'll stain her clothes."

Vera put the dropper back in the bottle and set it on the counter. "Use it. Every day. Promise me. Promise me, mija."

"Okay, okay," I said. "I promise."

"My perfect sobrina deserves a miracle." Tía Vera sighed and then glanced over at my brother, who was leaning on the counter half-asleep and chewing on a generic zebra cake. "Mateo," she said. "Mateo."

He glanced up at our aunt, blinking heavily.

"Why are you so tired?" Vera asked. "You're a young man. Where is your energy? You have that kissing sickness? The Epstein-Barr?" She shook her head.

I laughed. "You have to actually kiss someone to get mono."

"Oh my God! The only thing I'm sick of is everyone constantly being in my business," he snapped, picking up his coffee and zebra cake. With that, he stormed out of the apartment, the door slamming closed after him.

"Well, okay, then," Dad muttered.

Vera put her hands in the air. "You know, he doesn't get this from our side of the family."

Mom's mouth shrank. "Don't even start—"

I could hear the thunk, thunk, thunk of my brother's shoes on the metal stairs. Then there was a faster, louder, ascending thunk-a, thunk-a, thunk-a. The door opened just wide enough for Mateo to stick his curly head back inside. "Uh, I feel like that came off aggressive," he explained meekly. "Really, I was going for passive-aggressive."

My mother nodded. "Thank you for clarifying."

Mateo winced. "Okay, cool. Because I don't actually want to be outside, so, yeah." He slunk back in the apartment, down the hallway, and closed his bedroom door softly behind him.

"Try not to look quite so smug, Dolores," my mother cautioned. "You share your DNA with that boy."

I shuddered. "Ew. Don't remind me."

~~~~~~~~

Me: So, I think that catches you up on everything.

Priest: I see.

Me: I've got four days until I have to make it right, prove to Shae and everyone else at that party that I'm not just this one, embarrassing event. That I'm a person, not the punchline of a joke, not a freaking limerick.

Priest: You're putting a great deal of pressure on yourself to change the opinions of others. Is that something you realistically can control?

Me: Don't throw that therapy crap at me. Just think of it as missionary work. Going in and converting people to my perspective. You can't act like that's far-fetched, sir, not from where you're sitting.

Priest: If you're referencing the colonialism of the Catholic Church, just because we did it, doesn't make it right. And I hope you don't intend to commit genocide in order to get your point across.

Me: Of course not. I'm just going to . . . Why do you always do this?

Priest: What, daughter?

Me: Make me feel like I'm doing something stupid. I've got a plan. I already told you, I'm not going alone, I've got Terpsichore. She's my ticket in.

Priest: Do you think she wants that?

Me: I think she wants to help me. Like I want to help her.

Priest: And if you restore your childhood friendship to its former glory, what happens to this girl then?

Me: She'll have gotten what she wants too, and we can part ways. You're making this a bigger deal than it is.

Priest: Well, it sounds as though you've thought this through.

Me: You don't approve. I can tell from your voice.

Priest: Does my approval matter to you?

Me: No . . . It's just . . . It's not really you.

Priest: It's what I represent.

Me: You know, if there is a God, I would want that, I don't know, being, force, whatever to agree with what I was doing. So God could grease the wheels, I guess.

Priest: And if the wheels are jammed and squeaky?

Me: I was happy when I was friends with Shae. Doesn't God want me to be happy?

Priest: God doesn't promise anyone happiness. Think of—

Me: That's right. The *saints*. Quite the cheerful freaking bunch. I've got to go, sir.

~~~~~~~~~~

That evening when I went to pull my overnight bag out from under my bed, I found that it was all dusty. When was the last time I'd slept over at Shae's? Surely it hadn't been that long ago. I sat on my bed and tried to remember.

~~~~~~~~~~

INTERIOR LUDEN MANSION, NIGHTTIME, TEN MONTHS PRIOR

The camera takes us through the opulent textures of
the Ludens' world: marble floors, wrought-iron railings,
silk curtains. Maids in long black dresses with fluffy
white bonnets and aprons glide up and down the double
staircase, buffing and scrubbing to the sounds of
a jaunty harpsichord. We follow one MAID to SHAE's
bedroom. She opens the door to reveal a king-sized four-
poster bed draped in extravagant fabrics and tassels.
Shae and DOLORES are sitting side by side, propped up
against the many decorative pillows, eating bonbons from
a gilded box.

                        SHAE
        There you are, Glenhilda, the fire's
        gone cold! We could catch our death
        in this big room.

Shae claps her hands. The maid ducks her head and
obediently tends to the hearth across from the bed. The
fire makes fire sounds as she pokes it with one of those

twisty metal sticks. Dolores watches the maid leave,
then turns to her friend.

                    DOLORES
          You really have no idea how lucky
          you are.

     SHAE (distractedly tugging her diamond necklace)
          Hmm? Oh, I suppose.

Shae throws herself backward onto the pillows, sending
the box of expensive chocolates tumbling to the floor.
The dark shiny shells of the scattered candies reflect
the fire's glow. Dolores frowns.

                    DOLORES
          I was still eating those. What's the
          matter, Shae?

                    SHAE
          Nothing. Everything. Oh, Dolores,
          it's all too much to explain. But
          maybe . . .

                    DOLORES
          Maybe?

                    SHAE
          Maybe I could explain it better if
          your dashing brother were here.

Dolores gasps as a drum sounds dramatically.

                    DOLORES
          Mateo? You know his heart belongs
          to Johann, the handsome German
          artist. My brother's love for him is

unrequited and yet unyielding. Plus,
you're a girl.

                    SHAE
          But think, Dolores! If Mateo and I
          were to marry someday, then you and
          I would be sisters for real.

Dolores stands, needing to clear her head. She holds
on to a carved pillar of the four-poster bed. Her
fingernails dig into the wood. Facing the camera, she
scolds her delusional friend.

                    DOLORES
          Impossible. Get over your silly
          schoolgirl crush.

                    SHAE
          Fine. But I can't sit here a moment
          longer.

Shae stands, moving purposefully to the closet. She
tosses expensive dresses and blouses to the ground with
growing frustration. Dolores follows her. Confused, she
tries to pick up the discarded wardrobe.

                    DOLORES
          What are you doing?

                    SHAE
          Lucie down the street is throwing a
          going-away party. She would let us
          in. And she always has boys there.

Dolores laughs. Shae freezes, turning to look back
at Dolores over her shoulder with simmering anger.

She pushes past her friend and returns to the main
bedroom, throwing herself onto her bed. Again, Dolores
follows.

> DOLORES
> Wait, I thought you were joking. Are
> you serious?

> SHAE
> So what if I was?

The camera lingers on Shae's pout. We follow her gaze
to the far side of the room, where a spot of wall
is entirely dedicated to the commemoration of the
two girls' friendship. Ticket stubs and mementos,
photographs, locks of hair. The pictures come alive,
creating a montage of memories played over a tender
soundtrack. We can see the girls as they were when they
met (still played by their current selves), four-year-
olds in preschool, picking each other's nose. We watch
them grow older as they learn to ride bikes. They build
a papier-mâché volcano. They go on picnics in the park.
They ride a roller coaster. They get their first periods.
Shae sits up abruptly, ending the music and emotional
slideshow. She speaks slowly, weightily.

> SHAE
> Don't you ever get tired of this,
> Dolores?

Dolores shakes her head. She rushes to hold her friend's
hand as she kneels at her bedside.

> DOLORES
> Tired of what? Of you? Never. You
> know that.

>   SHAE (weakly)
>   But we've known each other forever.
>   How do you know there aren't better
>   friends out there for you?

Dolores pulls her friend's hand affectionately to her
cheek.

>   DOLORES
>   You're hysterical. Stop worrying.
>   I'm not going anywhere. I promise.

~~~~~~~~~

We had stopped having sleepovers. I couldn't remember exactly why, but I felt like it was connected to my bladder. My diagnosis. I mean, nights were always the worst, just lying in bed staring at the ceiling trying not to think about the fact that I had to pee. Even when I dehydrated myself, the symptoms were still there. I had to explain all this to my mother after I fell asleep with an electric heating pad down my pants and woke up with toasted genitals. Mom said I was lucky I didn't barbecue myself and take the apartment with me. She made me switch to a hot water bottle after that, but those didn't work and weren't worth the hassle. None of this suited a sleepover.

I yanked at a stuck zipper on my duffel bag. What if I did something to embarrass myself while I was at Terpsichore's? What if I couldn't sleep? What if I didn't play my part as model best friend well enough? What if there was something inherently bad about me that had made Shae stop—

That was enough spiraling, I decided. No point thinking about it now.

Chapter Seventeen

Mom dropped me off at the Berkenbosch-Jones residence the next day. Casimir was pushing one of those red-and-yellow Fisher-Price toddler cars up the driveway. The wheels of the plastic coupe made a loud, scraping sound against the concrete. It definitely wasn't a pleasant noise.

"Hey, Casimir," I said as I passed him, carrying my duffel bag over one shoulder.

"Get out of the way!" he yelled. "I'll run you over!"

Terpsichore sat on the porch looking miserable, her fingers in her ears. The front door was open behind her, and I could smell something sweet baking inside. "It seems Casimir is playing road rage."

I picked up her abandoned stress ball from the step next to her and sat down, my overnight bag on my lap.

"He's loud and leaky, and he smells like cheese, and his hands are *always* sticky," Terpsichore continued, shuddering. "It doesn't seem possible that one person could encapsulate all the worst sensory experiences, but he does. He really does."

I'd noticed that the more time I spent with Terpsichore, the less she actually looked at me. Her piercing, unwavering gaze was reserved now for her hands, or her feet, or the top of her knees. Any eye contact between us had almost disappeared entirely. I was relieved. "Is there anything you like about having him here?" I asked, squeezing the stress ball.

Terpsichore thought for a second. "Mom buys juice now. She never bought juice before. Too much sugar."

The two of us sat for a while without speaking, watching Casimir play. The boy was actually too big to fit inside the red car, so he opened one of the plastic doors and shoved one leg inside, placing a hand on the steering wheel. Then he sort of shuffled along while making engine noises.

Inside the house, a timer went off, and Terpsichore popped up to her feet as if she'd been sprung from a toaster. "Mother, it's been ten minutes," she announced, heading inside. "I'm coming in now."

Shifting so I could see through the door, I heard Mrs. Berkenbosch-Jones's voice in the kitchen. "Terpsichore, hold on, I have to take these out of the oven." The alarm was still beeping.

"I said I'd watch him for ten minutes." Terpsichore ignored her mom and headed for her bedroom. "It's been ten minutes."

Mrs. Berkenbosch-Jones poked her head out of the kitchen to see me sitting on the porch. She forced a smile. "Dolores, could you—"

I nodded. "Sure thing, Mrs. Berkenbosch-Jones, I'll watch him."

The woman disappeared and the alarm stopped.

When I turned my body back around, Casimir was standing on the walkway, watching me. "You smell bad," he said, swinging a matted brown teddy bear around by one of its legs. "You smell like you ate a giant poop for breakfast."

"Joke's on you, Casimir," I said. "I didn't eat breakfast."

He stuck out his tongue at me and blew a raspberry in my face. Then he bounded back into the house. Terpsichore wasn't kidding. The kid *was* leaky.

"Thank you, Dolores," Mrs. Berkenbosch-Jones said, appearing behind me in a flour-speckled apron. "Terpsichore doesn't seem to understand the supervision Casimir requires. But she'll learn, I suppose. His mom doesn't get back until January."

I stood up, grabbing my bag.

"Why don't you—" she continued, holding the door open for me.

It was my turn to hit her with an impromptu monologue. "Hey, I was thinking about how excited I am to start at Jackson in September," I interrupted, stepping inside. "Ninth grade, remember?"

"Yes, of course," Mrs. Berkenbosch-Jones replied. She wiped her hands on her apron. "That's so nice. I hope it's a good thing for you."

I took a breath. "Well, I just think it would be really fun if Terpsichore and I could start high school together." I clarified, "At Jackson. I know she'd fit right into the drama department, with all her costume and sewing skills. She's so talented, she'd make tons of friends. My brother had a great time there."

Mrs. Berkenbosch-Jones's brow furrowed. "Oh, that's sweet of you to say, Dolores. But Terpsichore is much too fragile." The woman shook her head. "No, she'd never be able to handle public school."

I couldn't believe how unreasonable Terpsichore's mother was. "But I—"

"It's not going to happen, Dolores," she interrupted firmly. "I'm sorry if that disappoints you, but I'm not going to change my mind just because you want to exploit her gifts for the school's theater club."

My throat felt tight. "I didn't—"

"Dolores." She put her hand up to stop me. "I'm happy you've taken such an interest in being my daughter's 'friend.' I think it's very generous and compassionate of you."

Generous and compassionate? I wanted to ask, *What's generous and compassionate about it?* But the words dried up on my tongue and left a sour taste like bad milk.

"But she's *never* going to Jackson," Mrs. Berkenbosch-Jones continued, glaring over the metal rims of her glasses. "And if I hear one more word about it, I'll have to reconsider whether you're a good influence in her life."

I stood there, holding my duffel bag against my chest like it could shield me from this woman's infuriating condescension. It felt like she'd sucked the air out of my lungs, vacuum sealed them, and thrown them on a freezer shelf for later. I'd never met a person like Mrs. Berkenbosch-Jones, someone who could straight up dismember you with a single look and all without ever raising her voice.

"I hope I've made myself clear," she added.

I thought back to that day at the ice cream parlor. I'd promised Terpsichore I could convince her mom to register her for school. That was our deal. That was why she was risking her freedom to go with me to the party on Saturday. But that was before I'd met Mrs. Berkenbosch-Jones, back when I thought the task would simply be proving Terpsichore could make a friend. Now I knew I wasn't going to be able to keep my end of the bargain.

"Perfectly clear," I said, forcing a smile. "No worries."

~~~~~~~~

After dinner, a portion of which Casimir crushed into the tablecloth, Terpsichore and I went back to her bedroom.

"Come up with your story for the green dress?" I asked, noticing that the mannequin was now in the middle of the room.

"Maybe," she said, kneeling in front of it. "I'm not sure." She rolled the hem between her fingers.

I sucked my teeth. "Do you, uh, do you want any help?"

Terpsichore laughed, and the sound made my cheeks flush red with embarrassment.

"Right," I said, gritting my teeth. "I guess I wouldn't actually be much help if I don't know anything about sewing. It was stupid of me to offer."

Terpsichore tilted her head, her expression suddenly serious. "Do you want to learn?"

I shrugged. "I mean, sure, I guess."

She walked over to her desk and picked up a pair of scissors. "Do you like your T-shirt?" she asked.

I stepped away from the blades. "What?"

The girl shifted her weight impatiently, buckling out her ankles. "It's too big for you, Dolores. Do you like it?"

"No, not really. It was Mateo's."

Terpsichore held out her free hand. "Take it off, and give it to me." When I hesitated, she rolled her eyes. "You said you wanted to learn."

Still uncertain, I pulled my shirt over my head, then stood awkwardly in my sports bra. "But what am I going to wear?"

She took my T-shirt. "You'll wear this when we're done with it. Except it will be better this time." It was nice of Terpsichore to say *we*, even though I was pretty sure she would be the one making any actual alterations. With her scissors, she cut along all the seams of the T-shirt until she was left with nothing but beige scraps in various sizes. "Sewing clothes is about making flat shapes three-dimensional," she explained. "So, if you take everything apart at the seams, you get these flat shapes." She opened a drawer and pulled out a measuring tape. "When you make a change to the flat shapes, it changes what the three-dimensional product looks like afterward. Arms up." Without warning, Terpsichore's arm encircled my torso as she wrapped the measuring tape around my chest. I jumped.

"Arms down," she instructed, studying the number where the tape overlapped. Which meant she was staring directly at my left boob. My nipple, unused to contact, had decided to make an appearance. It didn't go unnoticed.

"Your hands are cold," I lied, inwardly dying of humiliation.

She pulled the tape back. "Sorry."

I folded my arms in front of me, tucking my fingers into my armpits. "So, uh." I gestured with my chin to the desk. "What's next?"

Terpsichore shook her head. "Right, yes. Next, we use your measurements to make the garment fit you." She placed a ruler along one of the cotton pieces and marked it with a pen. "Which means we'll need to leave some room for it to fit comfortably and a little more for the seams. The bottom is the worst part; it's much too long on your short torso."

"Oh."

Terpsichore gathered the pieces and took them to a white machine with four cones of thread on top of it. I followed her. "I'll sew this on my serger to get the seams done cleanly," she said, sitting down and flipping the machine on. Slowly she fed it the pieces of T-shirt, which it chewed with noisy urgency. I stood behind her chair and wondered why the sound of the serger didn't bother her. She cut the threads, freeing the shirt, and turned it right side out. "There," she said, holding it out to me. "Put it on."

I studied her work with wonder in the bathroom mirror. "It looks so different," I said coming back into her room.

"I'd hope so," she said, blowing fluff out of her chompy machine.

When we changed into our pajamas, I held my joggers out to her. "Do it again. And explain it slower this time."

Terpsichore showed me how to measure myself accurately and how to pin fabric together and even had me cut the pieces apart along the seams. But she said I wasn't ready to use the serger yet. Just like the T-shirt, the joggers were magically transformed from my brother's hand-me-down to something that seemed like it belonged to me.

"You're really good at this," I told her, sitting down on the floor against her bed.

She turned the machine off. "I know."

"I wish I was good at something," I said, folding my legs into my chest. "I mean, the only thing I've got going for me is a local bathroom guide."

Terpsichore sat down next to me. "What's that?"

"I write where the bathroom is and what kind of stuff it has in it and then I give it a rating from one to five stars. Like a critic writing for a fancy magazine." I put on a haughty voice. "Bathroom number thirty-six: Chinese Palace: This well-kept restroom maintains the theme of the restaurant's decorations with red and gold wallpaper, a waterfall sink, potted bamboo, and a black tile floor. The unforgivable flaw, however, is that instead of a row of stalls that come out from the wall, there is a column of stalls where by one enters to the side of the toilet and uses the bathroom directly in front of or behind someone else. This gives the occupant the unsettling feeling of being on the world's worst train. One star." I shrugged and dropped the accent. "Stuff like that."

Terpsichore was staring at me with captivated interest. "That's very useful information, Dolores," she said.

"It's mostly a joke, really," I explained. "It's just something I started doing when I got diagnosed. It made me feel better, I guess."

"It sounds helpful." She rubbed the edges of her fingernails together. "I hate using public restrooms, because I never know what to expect. And I abhor automatic flush toilets."

"Yeah, those always lower the rating by half a star."

"Please, would you give me a copy?" she asked.

"I mean, sure." I leaned my head back against the edge of the mattress. "No one else knows I do that, by the way. Rate restrooms."

Terpsichore shook her head. "Why don't you tell them? It makes you infinitely more interesting."

I frowned. "I just feel like people would think it's weird."

"Everyone uses the restroom," she said excitedly. "The combination of your subpar bladder and your research-oriented mind places you in a rare position to chronicle your experiences for the betterment of countless neurodivergent people or people with mobility issues or even people like you who urinate frequently." She held her hand up. "Imagine, a whole community sharing bathroom ratings all over the country. It could be a movement."

I laughed. Terpsichore looked over at me confused. "What's so funny?"

I rubbed my forehead. "No, it's stupid."

"Tell me."

"Just, you calling it . . . a bathroom movement." I snickered.

"I don't get it."

"I told you it was stupid." I yawned and glanced at my phone.

Somehow it was already one a.m. "It's past my bedtime, so I'm going to make me a nest right here"—I pulled a blanket out of my duffel bag—"and go to sleep."

Terpsichore clicked her nails some more before she spoke. "You can sleep on my bed with me," she said, slowly. "As long as you take the side by the wall and we don't share a blanket."

"Okay," I said. "But I'll probably have to get up a bunch of times to pee."

"That's okay," she replied.

Terpsichore's bed was small. With the lights off, it was too dark to see each other, but I could feel the outline of her body next to mine, the way her silent breath just barely shifted the covers. Shae and I had shared a bed, a king-sized one with a pillow barrier between us. It was a totally different feeling lying next to Terpsichore. I tried to stay completely, totally still so that I wouldn't wake her up. Then, in the darkness, I heard a stifled laugh. It was silent again, and then, not half a minute later, there was that laugh a second time.

"What's so funny?" I asked.

Terpsichore rolled over to her back. "I just got it," she whispered. "*Bathroom movement.* Like bowel movement, right?"

That made me laugh, which made her start up again. We descended into a fit of hushed giggles. Every snort or *shhh* made things worse, and by the end of it, there were tears on my cheeks and all the muscles in my face hurt.

"Imagine how helpful the guide will be at the high school next year!" Terpsichore said, when she had finally regained the ability to speak. "I hate the idea of using an unvetted bathroom. You're very clever, Dolores."

Suddenly I didn't feel like laughing anymore. I shifted against the wall. "Thanks," I said.

"What rating did you give my bathroom?" Terpsichore asked.

"One star." I said it apologetically, although internally I was extremely relieved she'd changed the subject. "It's not your fault, though."

"I know." I heard her sigh. "Casimir has no aim."

Chapter Eighteen

I woke up to Terpsichore standing hunched over me, backlit by the morning sun. Her legs, which straddled my body, stuck out at odd angles from her long floral nightgown. With surprising strength, she rubbed her knuckles into the middle of my chest.

I gasped. "Ow! Oh my God, what are you doing?"

Startled, Terpsichore fell down onto my stomach, knocking the wind out of me. "You're alive," she said, panting slightly. She took a long inhale, as if to steady herself from some terrible fright. "You weren't breathing."

"Of course I was breathing," I choked out. She was deceptively heavy for someone so thin.

Terpsichore shook out her hands. "It didn't look like it."

"What?" I coughed.

My eyes had unblurred enough to make out the relieved expression on Terpsichore's face. "Your skin was cold, and your jaw slacked in a rather unsettling way. Then your phone started ringing, and you didn't even flinch."

I moved my hand over my chest. I was sure I must be developing one hell of a bruise under my T-shirt. "What did you do to me?" I asked.

"Sternal rub," Terpsichore explained, reaching for her glasses on the nightstand. "It's a technique used by emergency professionals to revive someone from a state of unconsciousness."

"Great," I squeaked. Terpsichore's sharp tailbone dug into my bladder. "Are you going to keep sitting on top of me?" I asked, trying to wiggle myself out from under her.

She was quiet for a moment. "No," she said finally and slid over to one side like she was dismounting a horse. She shimmied her night-gown back around her ankles and got off the bed.

"You should be grateful," Terpsichore added, crossing over to her chest of drawers. "I could have done worse. Historically doctors used to drive needles under patient's toenails to make sure they were really dead so they wouldn't get buried alive." She pulled on a pair of pants.

"What a comforting image, Terpsichore, thank you." I sat up and rubbed my eyes.

Terpsichore pulled her nightgown over her head. Although she was generally turned away, I could see that she was naked from the waist up. I averted my gaze. Mostly.

She didn't seem concerned about modesty, though. Instead, she stared into one of the wall quilts and thoughtfully unfolded a tank top. "Pain is what tells us we're alive," Terpsichore said finally. "Isn't that interesting?"

"It's morbid," I scoffed, rubbing the IC ache between the top of my hip bones.

Terpsichore glanced back at me over her pale shoulder. "That's what your name means," she said. "Did you know that?"

I dug my thumbs into my spine. "Know what?"

"Dolor," Terpsichore continued, softening her mouth around the edges of the word the way that Dad and Tía Vera did. "It's Latin for 'pain.'"

I shrugged, watching as she pulled the tank over her head and tucked it into the waistband of her pants. "Well, not all of us get to be Greek goddesses."

The bedroom door opened, and Casimir poked his sweaty little head inside to look at us. And no wonder it was sweaty. The kid was wearing a heavy winter coat even though the weather had been in the upper nineties all week. "Can I have your scissors, Terpsichore?"

"No," she answered in an uninterested voice.

He scrunched his face. "It's not for crimes," he said, hanging on the doorknob and swinging back and forth. Something about his jacket looked funny to me, but I couldn't put my finger on it.

"You can use some of the safety scissors my mom got you."

"Those don't work," he groaned, knocking his forehead against the edge of the door. He wiped his face down the wood until his nose was pressed flat. "*Tirp-sick-or-ee-ee-ee*," he whined. Just then, something started moving, writhing around *Alien*-style inside the chest of his coat.

"You didn't." Terpsichore's eyes widened.

The little boy stood up straight, pouting his lips. "It's nothing." Realizing quickly that his cousin wasn't buying it, Casimir made a calculated lunge back out the door.

Terpsichore caught his floppy sleeve. "You put Mrs. Reyes's hen back in her yard this instant."

Like a lizard ditching its tail, Casimir unzipped his coat and slithered out of Terpsichore's grip. When he did so, a large yellow chicken flapped unhappily to the floor, blinking and fluffing and getting its bearings. Taking advantage of the chaos, Casimir, now half-naked, ran through the house, leaving the poor disgruntled fowl abandoned at the base of the dress form.

"Despicable hellion," Terpsichore sputtered, clicking her fingers. "Impish little changeling!"

The bird ruffled its feathers and made a nervous trilling noise, its nails clicking on the hardwood. My phone, tucked into the outer pocket of my duffel, started to ring. The chicken pecked at it enthusiastically.

"That must be my ride," I said, using my foot to scoot the hen away from my bag. "Are you okay if I head out?" I asked. "Sorry it's so abrupt."

Terpsichore picked up the abandoned coat and threw it over the bird. "Yes, I can handle this."

I stood up. "So, about Saturday," I told her, grabbing my duffel bag. "Mateo and I will come get you."

Terpsichore crouched down and put her hands on either side of the warbling lump, lifting it up. "It depends on what my mother says."

"But you will try to convince her, right?" I backed out the door. "I mean, you're the one they really invited."

Terpsichore sighed. "Yes, Dolores," she said, sounding slightly aggravated, "you've mentioned that."

~~~~~~~~~

When I went outside, I was surprised to see who was behind the wheel of the Corolla. "Hey, Dad," I said, walking around the car to pop the trunk.

My father turned around as much as his gut and seat belt would allow. "Wait, mija, don't—"

"I'm just putting my bag . . ." I trailed off as I accidentally exposed the secret my father was so anxious to hide. The trunk was absolutely full of cardboard boxes, each one with a weird, swirly logo stamped on all six sides. I slammed it shut and got in the passenger seat, duffel bag on my lap.

Dad cleared his throat and turned on the radio. "Mom's helping Mateo with a big order at the shop," he said, shifting the car out of park. "So I offered to come get you. Some one-on-one time." He smiled at me sheepishly. "You're growing up too fast."

"What's in the trunk, Dad?" I clenched my jaw. "Is that the stuff from the pyramid scheme lady?"

He forced a laugh. "You say that like I've got something illegal in the car."

"I wish you did," I said. "You can sell illegal stuff. A couple of kilos of weed. Black market organs. Unpasteurized cheese. There's a demand for that kind of thing." I shook my head. "Mom said you were going to get the money from her."

"Don't worry about it, Dolores." Dad clicked the turn signal.

We drove in silence for a while. I rested my knees against the dashboard and rounded my back into the seat of the car. What would a bladder go for? It was possible to live without one, to upgrade to an external urostomy bag without nerve endings. It couldn't hurt me if I got it removed, right? And why not profit off of the rude little flesh balloon? Why not send it to be a medical specimen in a research hospital? Or maybe some artist would buy it for a moody modern piece about medicine's apathy toward female pain. Hell, I didn't care if it ended up stuffed with oatmeal and onion, the defining element of a super-expensive cannibal haggis. Rich people in horror movies loved weird crap like that.

"Everything is okay," my father reassured me.

I looked back at him. "Does Mom know?"

He pursed his lips. "She knows I got compensation for the work," he answered. "All I have to do now is find someone who wants to pursue a vocation selling holistic skincare. It's all natural ingredients, you can put it anywhere on your body, you can even use it on dogs, cats—"

"Oh my God," I muttered.

"It is real money, mija. Just with a few extra steps." He shrugged. "Even cashing a check has extra steps."

"Dad—"

He pulled up the alley. "I'll tell your mother all the details once I've got the money in hand." His chuckle took in too much air and sounded more like a series of gasps. "Then this will just be a funny story." When I didn't reply, he pulled out his wallet and handed over four one-dollar bills. "Here, why don't you go get some ice cream cones for you and your brother."

"It costs more than that," I told him.

"Really?" He flicked through his wallet until he found a five. "There, how about now?"

"I can't help feeling like you're buying my silence," I said, taking the money.

He raised his unibrow in indignation. "No, I would never! Just—" He glanced up at the apartment. "Just keep it to yourself. You wouldn't want some little misunderstanding to get blown out of proportion. You know how your mother is. She doesn't get the vision. But you do, right mija?"

My father's upper lip was sweating through his stubble. It could have been the heat, but it also could have been fear. My intestines knotted up. "Sure thing, Dad."

Dad beamed. "You're such a good girl, Dolores."

He was wrong.

~~~~~~~~~

The young mom with the stroller was at the ice cream shop again. This time, though, she had the baby tied to her chest with a big, stretchy piece of fabric. The infant's fuzzy little head stuck out of the top, tucked right under the lady's chin. She was standing at the far end of the counter, flirting with Teardrop while he swapped in a new metal bucket of Hazelnut Hurricane. I realized they switched their flavors around pretty regularly. Gone was Terpsichore's Brownie Fudge, replaced by Movie Night and Maple Bacon.

"Hey, you!" Spider called from behind the cash register. I looked around, sure he must be hollering at someone else. "Yeah, you! Your family, next-door neighbors!" he said. "Mendozas, right?"

I winced. "Uh, okay."

"We moved in here two years ago, and none of you guys ever come see us." Spider shook his head. "Just you that one time. Hiding under the table."

"Yeah, sorry about that."

"We're good," he reassured me. "But what is it? Your family lactose intolerant or something?"

"No, we're just broke," I confessed. "And we're generally pretty thoughtless. Collectively."

Spider chuckled at that. He didn't seem quite so scary up close. "Okay, Mendoza," he asked. "Whatcha want?"

"Two vanilla cones," I answered. "One with chocolate drizzle, one without."

"Sure thing." He pulled out the cylinder scoop and grabbed two waffle cones off a stack. "Straight vanilla," he began, glancing up. "You're a purist. I respect that. And our vanilla is the best out of all those other ice cream shops. Maybe the best vanilla out there. A lot of work went into making it perfect." He drizzled one of the cones with chocolate from a clear bottle. "Ice cream, it's our passion, you know? We're always trying to make it better. But you get that—your family must feel that way about . . ." He paused. "Paper thickness. And decals. What with that being your livelihood."

"We couldn't care less about paper thickness," I said. "Dad heard about a printing business that was closing and bought all the equipment because it was going for cheap." I watched Teardrop and the lady with the baby. He'd said something that made her laugh. "None of us knows anything about printing, not really. I'm pretty sure we're terrible at it."

Spider wrinkled his forehead. "We're looking to get some stickers, like, with our logo. Do you do stickers?"

I shrugged. "Couldn't tell you. I don't actually work in the print shop. Mom always said I was too clumsy to be around pressurized blades." I paused. "I can send my brother over, though. He's the manager."

"No, don't worry about it. I'll drop by." Spider handed me an ice cream cone, and I held out the cash. He shook his head. "It's on the house."

I put the money in my pocket and took the second cone. "Thanks."

"Any time."

~~~~~~~~

Terpsichore's text came late that night.

> My mother agreed to Saturday. She was reluctant, but I promised her that you were a good friend, that your family was safe, and that I would be a responsible house guest.

A minute went by, and then:

> She really can never find out about the party.

I typed quickly, as guilt ran its fingers up my spine.

> Great! And don't worry, she'll never know.
> See you at five!

I put my phone on the nightstand and lay back until I was staring up at the popcorn ceiling. If I unfocused my eyes, the cottage cheese bumps morphed into familiar shapes: a bear, a face, a turtle humping a shoe.

My intestines felt bubbly. I thought about going to see the invisible priest again, now that I was probably (definitely) doing something that counted as sinning. Not having grown up going to church, I didn't totally understand the concept. So the word sin had always sounded kind of sexy to me, like shoplifting nail polish or sneaking a swig of vodka or getting a hickey. The little shoulder devil in those cartoons seemed driven by things that felt good. He wanted you to have fun. That's why he was so hard to resist, right?

Manipulating Terpsichore didn't feel sexy or salacious. It felt

gross. But what was the alternative? My friendship with Shae de-
pended on this. And what were the chances of Terpsichore's mom
actually finding out, anyway?

~~~~~~~~~~

It was a bad night. Between hourly bathroom trips and a lingering
spiritual malaise, I got about as much sleep as Ebenezer Scrooge on
Christmas Eve, but without the preachy specters and redemption arc.
There was nothing left to do. I'd laid out my clothes already, tweezed
myself bright red and dolphin-smooth. I'd secured an alibi and transportation. The prep work for the next day was finished. But I still felt
entirely unprepared.

In this same oxymoronic way, Saturday seemed to pass at a glacial
pace, but by the time I was dressed and sitting in the car, I wished it
hadn't gone by so fast. It must have shown on my face.

Mateo glanced at me in the rearview mirror. "Cheer up, Charlie,"
he sighed, pulling onto Main Street. "You look like you're off to a
funeral."

Johann turned his head to look over the passenger seat. "What is
wrong, Lola?"

"Nothing," I said, forcing a smile. "Don't miss the turn, Mateo."

"Are you not happy to be seeing your friend?" Johann asked.

"Yup, pleased as punch, can we talk about something else now?"
I swallowed and straightened the hem of my skirt. "What about you,
Johann, what's going on with you and your social life? You dating
anyone?"

Mateo hit the radio button so hard I wondered if it would get stuck like that. "Sorry, we can't hear you, Dolores," he called, turning the volume up. "What did you say?"

"Nothing!" I shouted over the music.

Johann glanced at my brother with an uncomfortable, almost guilty expression. None of us said anything until we pulled into the driveway of Terpsichore's house.

Mrs. Berkenbosch-Jones and Terpsichore were waiting for us, leaning against the back of their car. Terpsichore was wearing baggy linen pants and a T-shirt, with a tote bag tucked under her arm. The woman motioned at my brother to roll down the window. "Hello, Mateo, Johann, Dolores."

"Hi, Mrs. Berkenbosch-Jones," I said, leaning forward. "Thanks so much for letting Terpsichore come over."

She nodded, but her face looked uncertain. "I've talked with your mom on the phone, let her know that I can come and pick up Terpsichore at any point if needed. Any point."

"I'm sure it'll be fine," Mateo said. "Ready to go, Terps?"

Terpsichore scrambled into the back seat next to me. "Yes, please." She buckled her seat belt over her weirdly bulky pants and shrank down out of her mother's gaze. "Now."

"Be safe!" Mrs. Berkenbosch-Jones called, hugging her arms against her chest. "Make sure you text me before you go to bed!"

"Sure thing," I called.

The woman stood in the driveway watching us until we pulled out of sight. Only then did Terpsichore exhale.

"That's not what you're wearing, is it?" I asked, leaning over to her.

"Dolores!" Mateo scolded. "Is that a nice thing to ask your friend?"

"I just meant—" I stammered. "It's different from how she normally—"

"Don't worry," Terpsichore said, setting her tote bag between us. "I was scared that my mother would suspect something if I got too dressed up. I could get away with some eyeliner, but not much else." Still in her seat belt, she shimmied out of her pants. "I can change on the way."

Johann covered his eyes.

"Nuh-uh!" Mateo called, hitting his hand against the steering wheel. "No. Underage. Girls. Stripping. In. My. Car."

Terpsichore wrinkled her forehead. "It's your mother's car, though, isn't it?"

"Not the point, Terps," Mateo said. "We are on a major thoroughfare. Do not be taking your pants off."

"She's wearing other clothes underneath," I explained, rolling my eyes.

Mateo looked in the mirror. "Oh, okay," he said, relieved. "A sort of quick-change-in-the-wings moment. Well done, then."

"That's exactly what it is," she said, maneuvering around her seat belt to remove her shirt. "I've taken my inspiration from Rodgers and Hammerstein's *Cinderella*, the end of the first act. The two most beautiful gowns of the show—concealed in corsetry, ruffles, and capes— materialize effortlessly from the actors' costumes." She stalled, her arm tangled between her sleeve and seat belt. "Obviously, I don't have the budget for such a smooth transition from 'plain country bumpkin.'"

"Not a lot of rhymes for *pumpkin*, are there?" Mateo observed. "Really creates a problem for the lyricist, I imagine."

"Poomp-kin," Johann repeated, enunciating each syllable playfully. "I like that word very much. Poomp-kin. *Poomp*-kin. Poompkin." He looked back at us. "Oh, that is a very nice dress!"

"Thank you," Terpsichore said. "It has pockets."

"That's *the* dress!" I exclaimed, suddenly recognizing the emerald velvet spilling across her lap. "The one from the dress form."

"Yes, it is." The girl slipped off her sneakers.

"Looking good, Terps! That one is red-carpet-worthy for sure!"

Mateo was right. In the sleeveless shin-length gown, she looked like a famous movie star who'd been kidnapped and shoved barefoot into the back of our filthy Corolla. Maybe there was real merit to this girl's crazy ambitions, after all. Someone had to make the costumes for musicals and plays and stuff, right? Why *not* her?

"It's amazing," I told her. "But I don't get it, I thought you hated that dress."

Terpsichore flushed with pride as she flattened out the skirt. "I did. Then I finally found a story for it." She pulled a pair of gold kitten heels out of her tote bag. "Do you have the address, Mateo?" she asked.

"Don't need it," he answered, looking over his shoulder as he changed lanes. "Been driving to the Ludens' since I got my permit. Could do this route with my eyes closed."

"Please don't," Terpsichore begged.

"I am so excited for you." Johann beamed. "Your first young adult party. What a memory."

"Did you go to lots of parties in high school, Johann?" I asked.

The German nodded. "Yes, I guess so."

"You must miss all your friends, being in another country," I said. "You must think about them all the time."

Johann tilted his head, his scruffy bangs flopping to the side. "It is not like that, Lola. I do not have time to miss them all the time. I have work, and school, and people here in America who I also care about very much." He turned toward my brother in the driver's seat, but Mateo was motioning for another car to merge in front of us and didn't notice. "Things are different from when I was your age."

I wrinkled my nose. Was I the only one in my immediate circle who had experienced true friendship? Maybe that was why my brother and mom and everyone else were so dismissive about me and Shae. They couldn't understand.

"Are Shae's parents going to be home?" Mateo asked, pulling off the highway and down the winding road that led up to the Ludens' house.

"Probably," I answered. "I'm pretty sure."

"You're pretty sure," he repeated suspiciously, parking the car. "That's not super comforting, Dolores."

"I mean, what was I going to do?" I scoffed. "Ask? How pathetic would that sound?"

My brother rolled his eyes. "Fine, just get out of the car before I have time to think about it."

"Thanks, Mateo," I said, opening the door and stepping out onto the curb. I glanced back. Terpsichore was frozen, staring at her lap as she rubbed the velvet fabric between her fingers.

"Uh, hey, Terpsichore." I cleared my throat. "We're here."

My brother turned around to look at the girl in the back seat. "You know," he said gently, "you don't have to go in if you don't want to." He gave me a pointed look. "Don't let my sister bully you into anything. She can be a little intense sometimes."

I made a face at him.

Terpsichore bit her lip and glanced back at me.

"I mean, we came all the way here," I said.

She didn't move.

I swallowed. "It'll be really good preparation for school next year."

The line made my throat tense like I'd inhaled a sleeve of saltines.

She nodded and undid her seat belt.

Chapter Nineteen

"It'll be great," I told Terpsichore as we walked up the paved path to the large front door. "Nothing to be nervous about. People are going to love you."

"You think so?" Terpsichore asked, spinning her ring.

"Yeah, of course." I pushed the doorbell. "You're interesting and talented and gorgeous. Plus, you're new, so there's no history or drama. What's not to like?"

She looked around the porch uneasily. "Dolores, I—"

The front door swung in, and I heard a gasp. "Dolores!" Mrs. Luden exclaimed. "Oh my God, it's so good to see you again!"

"Hi, Mrs. Luden," I squeaked as the tiny woman in a silk blouse and white slacks crushed my rib cage in a hug. She practically carried me through the door, engulfing me in bleached-blond hair and a cloud of expensive perfume.

"I've been asking Shae all the time." Mrs. Luden's voice had its signature drawling slur. "'How come we never see Dolores anymore?'"

I patted the woman's arm until she released me. "I know, I know, it's been a while." I looked around the familiar front room. The warm wood paneling, the funky geometric paintings, the Sputnik chandelier. "Sorry, uh, this is Terpsichore. She's going to Jackson with us in the fall."

Mrs. Luden didn't seem to hear me, and babbled on as she steered me into the kitchen. "Mr. Luden is out, as usual, so it's just me here, coordinating the caterer and letting kids in. There's so much knocking at the door, it feels like Halloween. Oh! Dolores, are you and Shae going trick-or-treating this year? Tell me you're not too old. I couldn't bear it." She refilled a wineglass that was sitting on the granite countertop.

I shrugged. "I guess we'll see."

Terpsichore took in her surroundings, her eyes wide and observant behind her glasses. "You have a beautiful home, Mrs. Luden," she said. "I like the midcentury furniture."

"Mmm..." Mrs. Luden swallowed her wine and gestured around the room. "It's all original. The famous architect Hans SomethingorOther designed this for his oldest daughter. We got the house at auction after she died, furniture and everything." Mrs. Luden shook her head. "It's a sad story, actually, how she . . . passed." She smiled at Terpsichore. "Isn't it divine, though?"

"Yes." Terpsichore crossed her arms behind her back to fidget with her ring. Her body seemed stiff, uneasy. "Very lovely."

Mrs. Luden turned to open the fridge. "Well, why don't you two run along down to the basement? That's where all the kiddos are." She pulled out a crystal platter covered in cut vegetables and held it out to me. "And could you take the crudités with you, Dolores? I just hate to go down and interrupt."

The platter was cold and heavy, but I smiled and balanced it between my arms. "Of course, Mrs. Luden, I'm happy to help."

"Ah!" The woman sighed and put her hand on my cheek. "You always were just the sweetest thing. I wish all of that politeness would rub off on Shae one of these days." Mrs. Luden pulled away and took another drink of wine, and murmured, "God knows the girl could use it."

I shifted the veggie tray. "Um, thank you, Mrs. Luden. I'll see you later."

The sounds of music, voices, and laughter coming from the game room got louder as we descended to the basement. "Does Shae's mom frequently drink alone?" Terpsichore asked, when we were most of the way down the stairs.

"I guess so." I was too focused on not dropping the platter on the hardwood to give a thoughtful answer. The Luden house was entirely devoid of carpet, and every surface was polished to a mirror shine.

"Is she an alcoholic?" Terpsichore asked.

"Wine doesn't really count as alcohol," I explained, raising my voice to be heard over the party noise. "That's what Mrs. Luden always told us growing up."

Terpsichore squinted. "That sounds like the reasoning of an alcoholic." We stepped off the staircase.

"No," I said, feeling defensive. I'd always liked Mrs. Luden. "You don't get it. She's just fun. Not like our moms."

"Your mom is fun," Terpsichore replied.

I rolled my eyes. "Oh, please."

"Please what?"

"Nothing, it's just an expression."

Terpsichore looked around. "You know, this isn't at all how you described the house."

"It isn't?" I asked absently.

"No. I was picturing *Downton Abbey.*"

"Huh." I knocked on the door to the game room.

"What's the password?" It was a boy's voice, although I could hear suppressed female giggling and whispers in the background.

Terpsichore's forehead wrinkled in concern. "I don't know any password. Do you know a password, Dolores?"

"Let us in," I shouted. "We brought food."

"That's the password." The door swung open, revealing a boy I recognized from middle school, Harvey Slate. He was short and stocky with curly blond hair. "Oh, hey, it's Dolores on the Floor-es," he said, his expression surprised.

I winced at the rhyme. Terpsichore winced at the noise. The game room had teeth-rattling surround-sound speakers that had been hooked up to strobing colored lights in the ceiling. I hoped no one in the basement was epileptic.

"There was a rumor you died," Harvey continued.

"Nope." I forced a pained smile. "Still kicking." Terpsichore glanced at my feet and took a quick step away from me.

Harvey pouted, leaning against the doorframe. "Okay, this is, like, super weird, because I could have sworn I donated to a GoFundMe for your funeral." He glanced at Terpsichore. "I don't recognize you. What's your name?"

Terpsichore fluttered her fingers along her neck, like she was fighting the urge to plug her ears. "TerpsichoreBerkenboschJones."

Harvey pulled the door all the way open, letting us through. The room was dark except for the strobe lights and the LEDs along the crown molding. "Okay then, Dolores and friend are here," Harvey announced, picking something off the tray. "And they brought . . . tiny cucumbers."

Lucie Bernard appeared behind Harvey's shoulder. "You're the one with a tiny cucumber," she said, shoving him out of the way. "Hello, Dolores—" She paused. "And girl whose name I can't pronounce."

"You can call me Terps," Terpsichore offered.

Lucie nodded. "I can manage that."

Something about the interaction made my skin prickle. It was my brother who called her Terps. And why should she get a cool nickname when I had to be the kid who peed herself to death?

Lucie motioned over to a group of girls who were standing around the pool table. "You guys, this is who I was telling you about, the Project Runway chick. Terps."

Emelia bounded over. "Oh my gosh, you came!" she said. "Did you make this dress too?"

Terpsichore seemed more than a little uneasy, circled by the gathering flock of buzzing teens. "Yes." She spoke reluctantly, as if she was confessing a crime.

The girls talked over each other.

"It's stunning."

"You look so hot."

"That is the most beautiful dress I have ever seen."

"Are those—" Emelia squinted at the side of Terpsichore's skirt. "No way. It doesn't."

"Pockets?" Terpsichore explained, lifting the hem of her dress. "They go down to here. I reinforced the waist so I can fit a full-size water bottle down each side."

"You're a genius!" Emelia exclaimed.

I leaned over to Lucie. "Do you know where I should put this?" I asked, holding out the veggie plate. My hands were starting to sweat.

Lucie jutted her chin toward the back of the room. "Sure, over there at the bar. I'll go with you; I could use a drink."

The Luden game room had its own bar with a sink and a pebble ice maker and a fridge for mixers. The liquor stayed locked up in the cupboard, though. Shae and I used to take turns playing bartender as kids, making sugar-rimmed Shirley Temples and taking shots of straight lime juice or simple syrup. I hadn't grown up with parents who drank anything other than beer, so it was always exciting to see what fun tricks Shae learned from watching her mom.

I set the crudités down between a plate of macarons and a tower of tiny sandwiches. Lucie went behind the bar and opened the fridge. "Want a drink?" she asked, holding out a green bottle to me. I must have looked nervous, because she laughed. "Relax, it's Martinelli's," she said. Then under her breath, she added, "Unfortunately."

I shook my head and squinted out at the shadowy faces in the basement. There were about twenty-five kids all together. Some were playing video games on the giant TV, others were sitting on the couch, some were shooting pool or throwing darts. Although I recognized almost all of them from Susan B. Anthony, there was a notable absence. "Where's Shae?"

Terpsichore and Emelia walked over to us, leaving behind the entourage of fans. "Is there anything that's not carbonated?" Terpsichore asked Lucie.

"Tonic water?" Lucie offered, shifting bottles around in the fridge.

"No." Terpsichore went to see for herself.

"Ginger beer?" Lucie shook a plastic bottle. "This Coke looks pretty flat."

"I see cranberry juice." Terpsichore reached over Lucie's head, ignoring general guidelines regarding how close you should put your armpit to someone else's face. "I'll drink that."

Lucie set a pint glass on the bar. "Help yourself."

Emelia grabbed a sandwich. "Have you seen Shae?" I asked her.

Emelia got a mischievous look on her face. "Oh, Shae's spending seven minutes in heaven," she said, wiggling her eyebrows.

Terpsichore took a drink of cranberry juice, then immediately dribbled it back out of her mouth into her glass. "It's unsweetened," she said. Her dark red lips made her look like a vampire. "Seven minutes in heaven?"

"It's a game," I explained.

"A kissing game!" Lucie sang. "Well, kissing plus, if you're feeling adventurous."

Terpsichore's expression was grave as she set her pint glass back on the bar. "I am not feeling adventurous."

Lucie laughed.

"That's totally fine," Emelia said, picking up a radish carved to look like a flower. "Participation is optional, right, Lucie?"

"You can also just go in and talk," Lucie said. "Share some secrets. Show each other your feet."

Emelia's phone buzzed in her pocket. She pulled it out and knocked loudly on the closet door behind the bar. "Come on out, lovebirds, time's up."

The door opened, and some of the guys across the room started cheering. Shae and a boy whose face I couldn't see well fumbled awkwardly out of the closet, dislodging some cleaning supplies and accidentally freeing a Roomba.

"Shae!" I said. She must not have heard me over the music and the robotic vacuum, because she and the boy kept walking over to the couch. "Shae!" I shouted.

"Did you hear me, Dolores? I asked if you wanted in?" Lucie was typing something on her phone. "I'll add your name to the drawing."

"Fine," I said, gritting my teeth. "Whatever."

She and Emelia went back to the pool table. Behind the bar, the Roomba had gotten tangled up in a mop and was attempting to drag it around.

"Poor thing," Terpsichore murmured, kneeling down to rescue it.

"Shae!" I shouted again, waving my arm over my head. "I don't understand. Why isn't she coming over? I'm sure she saw me that time."

Lucie glanced over at us. It was dark, so I couldn't tell for sure, but it looked like she rolled her eyes. I clenched my jaw.

Terpsichore carefully pulled the ends of the mop out of the vacuum's rotating cylinder. "What do you mean?" she asked. "Shae's acting the same way that she did at the ice cream parlor."

"No way," I said. "She was totally different then."

Terpsichore stroked the back of the Roomba. "Dolores, what are you talking about?"

~~~~~~~~

INTERIOR ONE FELL SCOOP ICE CREAM PARLOR, DAYTIME, TWO WEEKS EARLIER

We open on a close-up shot of DOLORES's face—an exaggerated expression of panic, her manicured hands

gripping her rouged cheeks. As the camera slowly
pulls back, we can see that our protagonist is huddled
underneath a metal table. Her heavy breathing mixes with
the low drone of the timpani as she waits in terror.
Finally, the camera turns, and we understand who she's
hiding from—LUCIE and EMELIA. The two girls have bold,
backcombed hairstyles and sharp stiletto heels that
click on the floor like the raptor claws in *Jurassic
Park*. Emelia has a pronounced beauty mark under one
eye, while Lucie wears a bejeweled eyepatch. Both wear
dark lipstick. They approach a table where TERPSICHORE,
demure and trembling, twiddles her thumbs. A saxophone
wails.

                    LUCIE
        Hey, you! What's with your outfit?

                  TERPSICHORE
        I made it.

                    EMELIA
        You're a liar!

                  TERPSICHORE
        It's true.

The camera returns to Dolores. She turns, hearing
a third set of approaching footsteps. Her face is
silhouetted and obscured by the shadow under the table.

                    SHAE
        Hey, her outfit is cool. Leave her
        alone.

Halfway through her line, we see SHAE for the first time.
She's dressed in the same slinky, rhinestoned catsuit as
the other two girls, but hers is gray instead of black.

Her light makeup and flowing hair give her a softer
appearance, furthered by the gentle trill of a flute.
Lucie shoves Shae so hard the ice cream cone flies out of
Shae's hand.

                         SHAE
          Oh, no!

The cone falls in slow motion, finally splattering across
the floor to a cymbal crash. Dolores's face is splattered
with fudge. We hear the next lines of dialogue from
under the table.

                         SHAE
          Lucie, you made a mess!

                         LUCIE
          Just leave it. That thug will mop it
          up.

                         SHAE
          No, I'll get it.

Shae kneels on the floor with a big wad of napkins.
Dolores winces. Shae looks up, and their eyes meet in
a moment of surreal understanding. Dolores puts a finger
to her mouth. Shae nods stoically in understanding,
refusing to give her friend's hiding spot away—

~~~~~~~~~~

"She stood up for me," I remembered. "It was the other two who were
being awful. Shae was just trying to hel—"

     "That's not at all what happened," Terpsichore interrupted, look-
ing up at me in disbelief.

The percussion in my head was louder than the music playing over the speakers. "What?"

Terpsichore held the Roomba out to me. The lighting made her face look red and angry. "She was rude to you," the girl said. "She hurt your feelings. She ignored you."

I took the vacuum and looked over at Shae. She was laughing on the couch with that boy. "No, it wasn't like that . . ."

Terpsichore stood up. "I don't know why you're so attracted to her," she said, glaring at the floor.

"Attracted?" I repeated angrily. "I'm not attracted to her. She's been my best friend since we were in preschool! And what gives you the right to say anything about it?"

Terpsichore shook her head. "There are other people you could be friends with."

"What, like Harvey the cucumber guy?"

"At least he's acknowledged your existence. And he donated to your funeral expenses." She wrung her hands aggressively. "I don't understand you. And I don't understand how they can offer unsweetened cranberry juice. I'm going to go watch the billiards." She turned to leave, then looked back. "And I'm taking the Roomba with me," she muttered sullenly, snatching the robot. "It's not safe with you. You might forget about it, leave it to get stepped on."

"Terpsichore—"

"Hey, Terps!" one of the girls called. "Come on over!"

Terpsichore turned and marched toward the table.

I didn't follow her.

Chapter Twenty

Hours passed. I sat behind the bar, drinking expensive bottled water, chewing on de-threaded celery sticks. Shae was on the other side of the room with her boy toy, being all touchy and flirty and making every possible effort not to glance in my direction. Eventually my pelvis started to hurt, and I had a creeping pressure at the corners of my eyes. It was miserable.

Terpsichore seemed to be having an altogether different experience. Although she never initiated conversations, people gravitated toward her and her dress-with-pockets and her emotional support Roomba. It wasn't that she had suddenly revealed herself to be a majestic social butterfly. She stayed away from the rumbling speakers and fiddled almost constantly with her ring or her dress or her fingers. I watched her grit her teeth every now and then as she put her hands on her neck, like she was fighting the urge to plug her ears. She rolled her ankles and made too-intense eye contact and sometimes she would be the last person to laugh at a joke. Terpsichore wasn't effortlessly sophisticated in the fairy-tale way her looks and her dress would suggest. There was so much effort. But she never gave up.

Watching Terpsichore made my throat feel like it was closing up in anaphylactic shock. But I couldn't stop. I hyperfixated on every little gesture, every tell I'd learned came from her feeling uncomfortable, the smallest fidget or frown. I was scared she would embarrass herself. I was jealous that she hadn't. Immediately I regretted that thought—God, Dolores, what a horrible thing to feel! I gritted my teeth until my fillings ached. Terpsichore had put the most on the line tonight. She deserved this win. Deserved every win. She was a legitimately good person. Too good for you, Dolores. I swallowed and scanned the room.

Somehow I'd lost track of Shae.

The realization was shocking. When did she leave? How long had she been gone? How had I missed her sneaking out the basement door? The air was suddenly hot and close. The music from the speakers reverberated through me, into my bladder walls crumbling like Jericho. I had to get out.

The stairs. I went up on my hands and knees, desperate to escape the party. The texture of the wood under my palms summoned the ghosts of little Shae and Dolores. I could picture them laughing, racing up from the dark basement, shrieking in delighted terror. They ran in front of me, their bare feet squeaking as they skidded around the landing and climbed up the next flight of stairs. I staggered after them, hunched, unable to keep up.

Shae's was the first door on the left: solid pine with shiny brass hinges. I knew exactly what noise those hinges made, the rattling creak that accompanied our midnight ice cream excursions. I knew the first thing I would see when I opened that door. The wall: pictures of me and her tacked just above her desk. A decade of our memories, proof of our sisterhood. I needed to see it. Mom was wrong, Mateo was wrong, Terpsichore was wrong. Those two square feet would put everything back the way it was supposed to be. I opened the door.

It smelled like fresh paint and a lotion I didn't recognize, one we hadn't bought together at Bath & Body Works. I stepped forward, tripped on a new rug, and lost my balance, falling flat on my face.

"Dolores!"

Shae was sitting on her bed all cuddled up with that guy from earlier. I could see what he looked like now: a scrawny teenage boy in too-baggy jeans with sort of wavy red hair and the beginnings of a mustache. He raised his head a little to look at me. "Dolores? Oh yeah, you're the kid who peed on the floor last year, right? I heard about you. You totally derailed the standardized testing." He held up his fist in solidarity. "Way to stick it to the man."

Shae smacked his hand down. "Shut up, Declan." Her voice was furious. "Jesus Christ! What are you doing in my room?" From the way her mouth was all red and her lip gloss was smudged, I could tell that they'd been making out.

But I didn't really care about that. "You took it down," I said, studying the empty space above her desk. "All of it. Every single picture."

Shae brushed a loose strand of hair behind her ear. "Oh my God, Dolores, this is so not the time! Can you please just leave?"

"He can leave," I said, pointing to the guy with his arm around my best friend. "But I'm not going anywhere. Not until you answer my question."

"I'm not going to make him leave," Shae said. She turned to look at him. "Do you want to leave, Declan?"

Declan gulped and glanced between us. "Uh, I'd rather not leave . . ." he stammered. "I mean, if that's cool with y'all."

"Great, then I guess it's the three of us." Shae folded her arms in a pout. "So, tell me, what was your question?"

I stood up. "Why are you ghosting me?"

Shae rolled her eyes and glared at the ceiling. "I'm not ghosting you. I told you, it was just for a little while—"

I shook my head. "No," I interrupted. "You said that being around me would make you a laughingstock. That was a lie. No one at this party, none of your 'cool' friends, not even this dude," I said, pointing to the redhead, "no one is treating me like an embarrassment but you!" My phone buzzed in my pocket.

Shae's bottom lip started to tremble. "I'm not treating you—"

"You dumped me!" I said, "Erased me. Without any explanation."

"I gave you an explanation—"

"You lied to me, Shae! You lied!" I didn't realize how loud my voice had gotten, until I saw Declan wince, perhaps regretting his decision to stay. But it was too late for him to leave now. "I was your friend for ten years," I said. "I don't even remember a time without you! My whole childhood, it was just us."

Shae exhaled slightly, then opened her mouth. "I didn't—"

My breath came in gasps. "No, listen! I was there for you through *every* moment, right there, supporting you like a sister. And you just threw me out without a second thought, and I want to know why, Shae! Why?"

"*Because I outgrew you!*"

The words sucked all the air out of the room, like we were in a spaceship and someone had opened an airlock. Shae put her hand over her mouth, as surprised by her outburst as I was.

I stepped backward until I hit the wall. "What?"

Shae slowly pulled her hand down, letting it fall on Declan's knee. "I . . . I outgrew you."

"But . . ." I doubled over, sure I was going to be sick. "But, I . . ." Tears started to roll down my nose onto the floor. "But . . ."

"See?" Shae groaned. "This is why I didn't tell you! Come on, Dolores, don't be like that. *Dolores.*"

I felt my way back toward the hall. "Uh, hey," I heard Declan call. "Could you, uh, close—"

I kicked the door as hard as I could, slamming it shut. I hoped the whole house would rattle and fall like Jenga pieces. But it didn't.

I'd hardly stepped back into the game room door when Emelia appeared next to me and pulled my arm. "Guess what? You got picked for seven minutes in heaven!"

I couldn't comprehend what she was saying. Surely she saw the tears? The total devastation on my face? Apparently not. Before I could put up a fight, I was unceremoniously shoved into a closet, shut in a cell of pitch-black oblivion. It was only the sounds of someone else breathing that let me know I wasn't alone.

Then I heard the voice.

"Boo."

"*Lucie?*" I whispered, wiping my dribbling tears on my shirt.

"What did you say?"

It was too loud for her to hear me. "Lucie, is that you?"

"Yup."

"I don't know what you want." I sniffled. "But I'm really not having a good time, so if you could manage not to sing me a rhyming ditty about my misery, that would be great."

Lucie shifted, knocking something over. "Look, Dolores, I put our names together." She paused. "Not for gay stuff. But because there's something I want to say to you."

I winced, bracing myself. "What is it?"

I could hear Lucie take a breath. "All those things I said," she began slowly. "When we were at the ice cream place. I only said them because I didn't know you were listening. I don't know why Shae didn't say anything; there's no way she didn't see you crouched there. And believe me, I gave her hell for letting me come off like such an absolute *tête de noeud*."

"It wasn't a big deal," I said, digging my thumbs into the top of my hip bones. "It's fine."

The sharp edge returned to Lucie's voice. "Okay, I get that you're trying to play it off. But that makes you sound like a total doormat, Dolores."

I was glad it was dark so that Lucie couldn't see my jaw drop. "A *doormat?*" I repeated.

"You should be angry!" she insisted. "At least a little bit . . . I mean, definitely forgive me, but be *angry* first!"

I thought about the way that I'd pictured Lucie at the ice cream shop. The rude, eye-patched villain in a catsuit. *That's not at all what happened*, Terpsichore had said. Everyone exaggerated stories in their heads, but what if I did more than exaggerate? What if there were other memories I'd warped beyond recognition? "Why are you being nice to me?" I whimpered.

Lucie groaned. "Oh my God, I'm not being nice, Dolores!" I could hear her lean against the wall. "See, this is exactly what I was talking about. This isn't nice. This is the bare-freaking-minimum of me not being a *terrible* human being. That's it." She sighed. "If you're mistaking this haphazard, dark-closet apology for friendship, someone has really screwed with your head."

"That's not . . . I didn't . . ." My brain felt like it had been stuffed with cotton balls. "It's just . . ."

"Come on, Dolores, pull yourself together!" Lucie punched my arm, hard. "Sure, you're a sucker, a chump, a patsy. But you're also . . ."

"Pathetic?" I offered, my throat hoarse.

"No, well, I mean, the peeing on the floor thing was truly pitiful, I'll admit, and I won't lie to you, people will talk about it forever." She shrugged. "But, like, you couldn't control that, right? It's like getting your period the day you wear white shorts. Sure, it's humiliating, but it happens. Okay, you'll probably be Dolores on the Floor-es for the rest of high school, but it doesn't mean anything. It's just a joke. No one's going to ruin your life because you wet yourself. This isn't a John Hughes film." Lucie opened the door. The tears in my eyes made the rainbow LEDs swim.

"But—"

"No one's saying you can't join in the reindeer games. So stop moping." Lucie shook her head, studying me for a second. "Here's the thing," she said seriously. "If you're pathetic, it's because of how you let people treat you." She shoved me out the door. "Now, get out of my way, I've got to take a leak."

I stumbled out of the closet, crashing into a tower of green velvet. My phone buzzed again in my pocket. I ignored it.

"Dolores, what are you doing?" Terpsichore pushed me back to standing, her hands gripping my shoulders as she studied my face. "Are you crying?"

Crying wasn't the word. I was somewhere north of hyperventilating, but south of dry heaving. I tried to answer, but my voice came out like a whistle.

"I can't hear you." Terpsichore frowned. "Hold on, let's go upstairs."

I followed her out of the game room, spitting and sputtering like a dying car engine. In the stark light of the basement hallway, Terpsichore could see me for the first time. She jumped. "Dolores!" she exclaimed as the door swung closed behind us. "Your face! It's so . . . swollen."

Groaning, I put my hands over my burning cheeks and collapsed onto the stairs.

Terpsichore sat beside me, putting one hand cautiously on my back and pulling a pack of Kleenex out of one of her bottomless pockets. "What's wrong? Why are you upset?" Her expression became pained. "Is it something I did?"

I shook my head. I could feel my phone buzz *again*.

Terpsichore held out the Kleenex, but then she hesitated. "Uh, there's a lot of drainage happening, Dolores. I'm not sure the best way to . . ." She held the tissue with two fingers and used it to tap around my face. "There, there." She winced as she pulled back to examine her work. "Well, that's not even made a dent in it. Would a sanitary napkin be better?" She pulled out a plastic-wrapped pad. "It's heavy flow."

I laughed, in spite of myself, but the laugh came out more like a cough and the cough sprayed snot and saliva all over her, absolutely drenching her glasses. Embarrassed, I scrambled up the stairs to the nearest bathroom.

Chapter Twenty-One

Bathroom #10: The Luden House, Main Level. The ground floor of the Ludens' home has two bathrooms, but only the bigger one ever gets used. Thus, this single, solitary half bath tucked around a corridor is a true mark of extravagance. Its existence is superfluous, a toilet for no one. Perhaps it is this excessiveness, this impracticality, that makes it so unique. The geometric tile, sage green cabinets, mirror, and polished black hardware remain perpetually sparkling. Under the sink sits a stack of matching cotton towels, unused. This bathroom makes one feel unworthy, as if to merely step into the room would defile it. Five stars in theory, as this reviewer has never had the audacity to place fuzzy butt cheek to gleaming porcelain.

~~~~~~~

I'll have to update my review, I thought, flushing the Ludens' forbidden toilet. *At the end of the day, it's just a pot to piss in.* Taking a long, shaky breath, I washed my hands, then pulled a towel from under the sink, soaking it in cold water. I held it to my face, hiding from my puffy, tomato-red reflection. Then I wadded the towel into a ball and threw it against the wall. It made a satisfying squelching sound. Dammit, I still felt like I had to pee.

My phone was buzzing yet again. Aggravated, I pulled it out of my pocket to see DORKFACE flashing on my screen. At least it covered the boat picture.

"What, Mateo? What do you want?"

My brother's voice was exasperated. "God, why don't you answer your freaking phone?"

"That's what I'm doing!" I hissed. "And I'll hang up—"

"No, wait," Mateo stammered. "Johann and I, we, uh, well, we kind of stuck around in the neighborhood. In the car."

"Why?"

"Just listen to me. Does Terpsichore's mom drive a green Subaru? With the little puzzle piece decal?"

"*Yeah.*" I said the word reluctantly, as if my hesitation could derail the train that was headed right for us. I knew. I knew what my brother was going to say before he said it. When I opened the bathroom door, Terpsichore was waiting only a few paces away, wiping my snot off her glasses with a microfiber cloth.

"She's here," Mateo said.

The next thirty seconds felt like a nightmare, little snapshot moments stitched together by adrenaline. Feet racing down the hallway. Sound of the front door opening. Not fast enough, not fast enough. Careening into the foyer as that voice, that grating, awful voice—

"Terpsichore! Terpsichore, I know you're here! Come out this instant!"

I froze. The woman looked livid, like a cartoon character who was about to blow steam out of her ears. It went against every natural instinct to approach someone possessed by such fury. What could Terpsichore and I do, anyway? We were just kids. I glanced at the double doors that led to Mrs. Luden's bedroom, but I knew it was no use. I learned a long time ago that Shae's mom went to bed at nine o'clock and she didn't wake up until noon the next day. Her insomnia meds ensured there was no reviving her to talk down Mrs. Berkenbosch-Jones adult to adult, mother to mother.

"Terpsichore!" she screeched. "Now!"

Her daughter swallowed. "Mom what are you doing—"

"Oh my God, Terpsichore. What are you wearing, where did you get that?"

Terpsichore squared her shoulders. She looked like Anne Boleyn approaching the swordsman: defiant, dignified, resigned.

"Are you drunk? Did you take something? Was it pills? How many?"

I could hear the door to the game room open, music pouring out as a group of curious teenagers bounded up the basement stairs to see what the commotion was. Mrs. Berkenbosch-Jones was grabbing Terpsichore's arms, no doubt studying them for track marks.

"How could you do this?" the woman wailed.

"Get off me—" Terpsichore begged, trying to wiggle free from her mother's increasingly tight grip. "No, don't do that!"

Lucie was the first to emerge from the basement. "Hey, lady," she called loudly. "The girl said not to touch her."

There were mumbles of assent from the gathering teens.

"I will have you know that I am this girl's mother," Mrs. Berkenbosch-Jones spat, "and she is in a whole heap of trouble."

Lucie stepped closer, puffing out her chest like she was ready for a fight. "I don't care who you are, Karen. She told you to let her go."

I don't know that anyone had ever talked to Mrs. Berkenbosch-Jones in such a tone, let alone a mouthy teenager. She was momentarily rendered speechless. This gave the rest of the party time to weigh in.

"Let her go," someone called.

"Yeah, leave her alone!" echoed a few others.

"She didn't do anything!" I said, finally able to articulate a comprehensible sound. "There aren't any drugs here. Just crudités and Martinelli's, I swear."

Mrs. Berkenbosch-Jones dug into Terpsichore's arm with her fingers and shot daggers at me. "How dare you!"

"Mom, stop it," Terpsichore begged, trying to tug free. "Dolores brought me here to help me make friends for when I go to school in the fall."

Mrs. B-J pulled the front door open wider. "I know I made myself clear, Dolores. I told you last time you were in my home that I would never, *ever*, be sending my daughter to school."

Terpsichore froze mid jerk. "What?" she asked. She looked over at me, shaking her head. "That's not true. Dolores would have told me."

Seeing the pain in Terpsichore's amber eyes, I felt guilt the way I felt the sores in my bladder. It cut through me, settled deep into my bones, rotting me.

"Terpsichore, I—"

Her mom took advantage of Terpsichore's shock and pulled her outside into the hot, stale air. I ran after them, flanked by at least half of the kids from the basement. A couple even pulled out their phones to film the terrible scene. The little heels of Terpsichore's shoes caught in the aerated lawn, and she fell onto her knees, digging the front of her dress into the grass. Her whole body shook as Mrs. Berkenbosch Jones dragged her, half crawling, back to the car.

"Whoa. Her mom is crazy," Harvey muttered.

Lucie never stopped yelling. "Come on, lady! You're hurting her!"

"Please, Mrs. Berkenbosch-Jones," I begged. "It's not her fault."

Mateo and Johann hopped out of the car and jogged over to meet us. "Mrs. Birkenstock," my brother said in his best let's-all-be-reasonable voice, "I'm sure there's been a misunderstanding. They were just being kids." He pointed toward the street. "Look, we even parked out front to keep an eye on things."

Mrs. Berkenbosch-Jones turned on my brother. "You're a grown man!" she insisted, her voice dripping with loathing. "Terpsichore is a little girl with a disability, and you're taking her to a party at night? What were you thinking?"

Mateo shook his head in disbelief. "But she's—"

"I should call the police on you for kidnapping." She pushed past my brother. "I just might!"

Mateo's lips gaped open. He reminded me of a catfish fighting for life on a dock, gasping at the sky unable to fathom how his mouth had gotten him into such a dire situation. "I—" was all he could manage to say. Over and over again, "I—I—I—"

Johann put his arm out to steady my brother. Mateo practically fell against him.

"Please, ma'am," Johann begged. "Please think about it."

"I've thought about it plenty," Mrs. Berkenbosch-Jones answered curtly, opening the passenger door for her daughter. "And the more I think about it, the more sinister this whole thing seems to me. Get in the car, Terpsichore."

Her daughter quietly obeyed.

"You don't have to go with her, Terps!" Lucie called. "You stay right here if you want to."

"Terpsichore, I'm so—" I hung on the open car door. "I didn't—" But she never looked up at me. She just folded in half with her head in her hands, like a black hole collapsing in on itself. Mateo grabbed my elbow and pulled me toward the Corolla.

"Car, Dolores. Come on."

I strained my neck looking back. "But, she—"

My brother opened the door to the back seat. "Nothing you say is going to make things any better for her," his voice gruff with tension. "It's time to go. *Now*."

I cried the whole ride home, cried so hard that all my senses muddled together, going in and out of focus like the streetlights. I was vaguely aware of a conversation going on in the front seat between Johann and Mateo. Every now and then, a word or phrase made it through the haze: unreal, *cannot be serious, supposed to*. But already my brain was taking me out of the moment, pulling me into the twisting landscape of my unreliable memory.

~~~~~~

INTERIOR LUDEN MANSION, NIGHT, TWENTY MINUTES PRIOR

The camera opens on Shae's extravagant, overfurnished bedroom. The space is dimly lit. A vintage record player in the corner croons out a saxophone solo. SHAE, dressed in scanty lingerie, sits on the lap of a shirtless redheaded DECLAN.

~~~~~~

No! That wasn't right at all!

"—my whole life—" I heard Mateo say as the car jolted onto the highway.

I pulled on my hair and tried to focus.

~~~~~~~~~~

The bedroom is fully lit. There is lo-fi music playing on
the crappy speaker of a cell phone. SHAE, in a T-shirt
and miniskirt, sits next to a fully clothed, gangly
DECLAN. He's grotesquely unattractive, with a creepy,
wispy mustache.

~~~~~~~~~~

No, no, he was a regular freaking kid. Just a normal teenage boy. *Stop
it, Dolores! Why can't you just remember?*

"What will you do?" Johann asked, turning to look at my brother.

Mateo inhaled sharply. "It makes you think—"

~~~~~~~~~~

SHAE, in a T-shirt and miniskirt, sits next to a fully
clothed, gangly DECLAN. She looks up in shock as her
bedroom door bursts open. DOLORES slips on a rug and
lands in a heap on the floor.

                          SHAE
            Dolores! What are you doing in my
            room?

                        DOLORES
            How could you do this to me? How
            could you just abandon me when I
            needed you?

                          SHAE
            Because you're crap.

                        DOLORES
            No! I was a *good* friend to you,
            Shae.

> SHAE
> You're not a friend. You're not even
> a person. You're a freaky little
> barnacle, and I've spent the last
> year trying to scrape you off of me,
> but you *won't let go!* Get out of
> here, Dolores! Take a hint!

> DECLAN
> Yeah, loser, get lost!

Dolores stumbles against the wall, then staggers out
the door down the hallway. On the landing she passes
TERPSICHORE, held hostage by a figure cloaked in dark,
brooding mist: MRS. BERKENBOSCH-JONES. The woman's eyes
are entirely black, and her voice is modulated to a low,
cackling bass. She drags Terpsichore down the stairs by
her hair, the captive teen struggling the whole way.

> MRS. BERKENBOSCH-JONES (autotuned)
> Look at her, Terpsichore. She lied
> to you!

> DOLORES
> It wasn't really a lie! I didn't
> mean to!

> TERPSICHORE
> You're selfish, manipulative! I never
> want to see you again! I hate you,
> Dolores! I hate you!

~~~~~~~~

No, no, no! You *stupid idiot!* Think, Dolores, think! I thumped my head
against the window. What did she say? Before her mother took her
out the door, what did she *say?*

```
TERPSICHORE (with mascara running down her cheeks)
     I was a good friend to you, Dolores.
     And you set me up! My mother will
     never let me leave the house again.
     You've made me a prisoner!
```

~~~~~~~

My brother's voice was halting, unsteady, as he spoke to Johann. "Why do I . . . I mean, why don't I? Maybe that's the question."

No, no, no! Terpsichore didn't say anything at all. It was all her eyes. They'd looked devastated.

~~~~~~~

```
DOLORES staggers into the hallway, following TERPSICHORE
out of the game room. Terpsichore turns around.

                    TERPSICHORE
          Dolores, your face! It's so swollen!

Dolores is beyond the point of being able to speak.
She is sobbing so hard she's practically gagging. She
leans down onto the staircase. Terpsichore hurries over,
putting one hand on Dolores's back as she pulls a packet
of tissues out of her pocket.

                    TERPSICHORE
          What's wrong? Why are you upset? Is
          it something I did?

Dolores shakes her head. Terpsichore reaches out to
dry Dolores's blubbering, but realizes that it is a
losing battle. She makes a valiant attempt anyway. Her
expression is soft and affectionate, with the slightest
hint of humor, as she tries to lift Dolores's spirits
```

by dabbing the tissue all over her mouth and nose and
forehead.

                    TERPSICHORE
          Uh, there's a lot of drainage
          happening, Dolores. I'm not sure the
          best way to . . . There, there.

                    ~~~~~~~~~~

I caught my breath. I'd done it. I'd finally done it. I'd pulled some au-
thentic snippet from my useless, histrionic brain. Something honest
and unpolished and pure.

   Playing over the travesty of the evening, I couldn't be sure of what
everyone said. Or where we were when they said it. But I was absolutely certain that Terpsichore Berkenbosch-Jones had been a true
friend to me. And that I had let her down.

Chapter Twenty-Two

Mom was sitting on the recliner when we got home. "How was bowling?" she asked, setting the book down on her lap.

I took off my shoes. "We weren't bowling. I lied."

"Dolores!" Dad exclaimed, appearing from the bathroom. He raised his unibrow. "You lied?"

"Like that means anything coming from you," I spat.

"What's that supposed to mean?" Mom stood up and squeezed her way around the TV box.

"Nothing." I fell back into the crease of the couch, hoping it would swallow me whole, digest my soft meaty bits, and puke up my bones. Like an owl.

"Where were you?" Dad asked, changing the subject.

My brother tossed the keys on the counter. "Getting me ten to twenty in prison." He shook his head. "And not sexy Fosse prison with fishnet tights and punchy jazz numbers, no. Prison prison. Where criminals don't chassé their feelings away." Mateo squeezed past my father and retreated into his bedroom to sulk.

"What?" Mom turned back to me for an explanation. "Dolores, what is he talking about?"

"I really don't think it would hold up in court," I said, wiping my face on the inside of my shirt. "He's being dramatic."

Down the hall, I could hear Mateo let out a mirthless laugh. "You know, oddly enough, this time, I'm not hyperbolizing. Honest to God, I am underselling the evening, if anything."

Mom turned back to me, worry lines chiseled into her face. "What the hell happened?"

"Terpsichore and I went to a party at Shae Luden's house," I mumbled. "Mrs. Berkenbosch-Jones found out and threatened to report Mateo for kidnapping."

Both my parents started shouting at once, a chorus of "Oh my God," and "Why would you do that?" and "How could you be so stupid?" and "What were you thinking?"

"Well, obviously the two of you are grounded," Mom said finally, once she'd calmed down enough to speak at a reasonable volume. She held her hand out to me. "Phone."

"Figured as much," I said, slapping mine into her palm.

"Mateo!" Mom called. "Phone!"

My brother stuck his head out of his bedroom. "Uh, actually, no."

"No?" My mother's eyes widened.

"You know what," Mateo said, leaning against the doorjamb with his arms folded. "Tonight, I was rather terrifyingly reminded that physically, psychologically, in a court of law, I am an adult." He shook his head. "So, no, Mother, Father, I am not grounded. I am old enough to be punished by the consequences of my actions, thank you very much."

"Mateo . . ." my mom warned.

"Ooh, whatcha gonna do, boss?" he asked, rolling his eyes. "Fire me?" He pulled his door closed.

This meant that my parents' attention was no longer divided. They circled the couch. "Dolores, what were you hoping to accomplish with this?" My mother gripped the fraying upholstery. "Help me understand. You know I would have let you go to Shae's house. Why did you lie? And why did you rope Terpsichore into it?"

My train of thought had taken as many doglegs and detours as the domino tracks we'd built when Terpsichore came over. "You wouldn't get it." I stared into the light on the ceiling until a big dark blotch formed in the center of my vision.

"You never got in trouble before, mija, why now?"

I turned to look at my father. His face was totally eclipsed by the round blob temporarily burned into my retinas.

"Can I go to bed now?" I asked.

Liza Minnelli's voice reverberated through the walls. *What good is sitting alone in your room? Come hear the music play!*"

"Fine." Mom rubbed her forehead. "But this conversation isn't over."

"No, of course not." I rolled toward the coffee table and extracted my body from between the couch cushions.

"You're not through explaining yourself," my father added.

I ignored him and retreated to my bedroom. Even over the sound of Mateo's music, I could hear the rumblings of a tense conversation coming from the kitchen. Mom's voice was lower pitched with a precise, sharp edge like a scalpel. Dad's was higher, exasperated, closer to a dental drill. I lay in my bed listening.

"You leave them alone too much," Dad scolded. "They need their mother."

"They *need* a roof over their heads!" Mom spat. "And I am doing everything in my power to keep paying the rent. Which I wouldn't have to do if you hadn't bought the stupid printing business! I never wanted any of this!"

"Never wanted what?" Dad asked. "A business? A future we can build as a family?"

Even though Mom lowered the volume of her voice, she got louder as she approached the hallway. "I just . . . I can't do this right now."

I pulled my pillow to my chest. I didn't want to think about anything, but I doubted I'd be able to sleep, no matter how exhausted I felt. Normally, I could distract myself by mindlessly scrolling on my phone, but that wasn't an option. Then I remembered my parents had forgotten about my computer.

The laptop was a hand-me-down of a hand-me-down, heavy, clunky, and slow. But it had worked well enough for Terpsichore to look up whatever she'd wanted answers about when she came over to the apartment. *Terpsichore.* Her name made my stomach flip. All I could picture were her amber eyes staring at me, hurt and shocked and deceived. All I wanted was to not think about her, but as I pulled up Instagram, this proved difficult.

A video of Terpsichore being roughly pulled across the Ludens' lawn had made it to two different classmates' profiles already. On one, the caption read "Crazy Lady Drags Kid Out of Party." The second video, shot from a different angle, had a flashing sticker of a cartoon helicopter crashing. That caption read "Helicopter Mom Spins Out." Neither clip was more than ten seconds and both were swiftly bringing in comments from future and current Jackson High students.

I was there the party was boring why be like this
I thought my mom was bad
so embarrassing

I closed the laptop and caught my breath. It was clear my brain wouldn't be able to leave Terpsichore alone. But I didn't want to re-play the night, because I didn't trust myself to remember it as it had actually happened, without the smoke machines and special effects. I closed my eyes. My parents were silent now, but Mateo was still up, shuffling around his bedroom as the music played. He was singing along, softly, under his breath. "*Maybe this time . . . I'll be lucky . . . Maybe this time . . .*"

I opened the laptop again and had a single intrusive thought.

What did Terpsichore look up on this computer?

Looking felt like a violation. Reading through someone's search history was like pulling their diary out from under their pillow. Maybe even worse. It was probably closer to breaking the seal of confession. What happened between someone and the internet was their own business. And who knows? She probably deleted it anyway.

Even as I played through each reasonable argument against peek-ing, my pointer finger ran across the touchpad, dragging the little arrow to the top left corner of my screen. My insides felt like a single, wobbly congealed mass as I opened the search history and scrolled down to see the things that Terpsichore hadn't wanted her mom to know about. They were:

Autism statistics college graduations

Autism statistics employment

Autism statistics independent living

Autism marriage rates

Autism divorce rates

Can people with autism be good parents?

Do teenagers with autism date?

How to be a good friend

How to be a good friend specifics

At this point I felt my eyes start to well up. I clicked on the pages that these searches had offered Terpsichore, some of them written to encourage, but most of them cold, clinical, and unhelpful. The future these pages painted was starkly different from the world that Terpsichore was working so hard to build for herself. I thought back to her casually sitting on the computer during that game night, her face never revealing frustration or fear. And I knew she must have been scared, at least, because that's the way I had felt when the internet offered me my own miserable statistics about IC. Would I be able to manage college? Would I ever hold down a full-time job? Would I ever have a sex life? Could someone really love me if loving me meant extra effort?

"*Maybe this time . . . Maybe this time . . .*"

I knew it wasn't the same thing. Terpsichore had explained that. Autism was not separate from who she was; it was an integral part of her identity. Interstitial cystitis was different. It was like I had a parasite living in my bladder, calling the shots for my whole body, bending me to its will. I thought back to that image of slicing it out of my abdomen. Why wouldn't that be an option? It was extreme, sure, but it was a fix. A real fix, not some smelly oil or funky jewelry.

I typed in the search bar: interstitial cystitis bladder removal cure.

That's when I found out something absolutely ridiculous. Something that should have been funny if it wasn't so devastating. I learned that a total cystectomy, a complete removal of the bladder, had been a treatment for IC once. But it didn't work. In fact, the rates of pain relief after surgery were incredibly low, and for that reason, it was almost impossible to convince a doctor to perform the procedure. No, instead, I discovered that "noninvasive" treatment involved medications with dangerous-sounding side effects or administering lidocaine via catheter or regularly seeing a physical therapist to release the tight muscles of the pelvic floor via the vagina. Then there were injections into the bladder wall or lasering ulcers or implanting electric devices along the spine to shock the pain out.

For the first time since receiving my diagnosis, I started to understand the real implications of words like *lifelong* and *chronic* and *incurable*. Years and years of pain, inconvenience, embarrassment, expense. God, how would I ever be able to afford any of it if I couldn't work? And if I could work, what kind of job would let me take off the insane amount of time I'd need to actively treat my condition? The smug little parasite, all warm and cozy, was not going anywhere. Ever. I would live the entirety of my years in bitter conflict with this small invader, until one day, I would die and it would be stuck to rot inside my corpse with me. My one true companion. *Forever for life.*

Forever is such a very long time to think about when you've only lived fourteen years.

~~~~~~~

Me: So, it starts like this: "Dear Terpsichore . . ."

Priest: Go ahead.

Me: That's it. That's all I've got.

Priest: I see.

Me: It turns out I've never had to apologize for something this big before. I don't even know how to do it. "I'm sorry" doesn't feel like it even comes close. You know, I was reading the spooky saints book, and it talked about penitence. Do you know what that is?

Priest: I'm familiar with the concept.

Me: And it said that in the olden days when you'd done something bad, you would punish yourself for it. Your body, specifically. To show that you're sorry.

Priest: I'm not sure that's entirely—

Me: No, no, it is. It was in the book. With pictures. Fasting, walking long distances barefoot, wearing hair shirts, self-flagellating. "Mortification of the flesh," that's what it's called.

Priest: Well. The saints were . . . Many people through history have taken that path, but—

Me: Told you so.

Priest: But is it your goal to emulate medieval Christians, in sackcloth and ashes? To tell you the truth, I haven't seen any sackcloth in the rectory supply closet. I think we ran out about four hundred years ago.

Me: So, you're saying I skipped breakfast for nothing, then.

Priest: I couldn't say. As usual, child, you've stumbled on one of the big questions. Trespass, it's an unavoidable problem. It's impossible to go through life without your decisions affecting others. Just like how the decisions of others affect you. It's part of the human condition. None of us live in a vacuum.

Me: So, what?

Priest: Exactly.

Me: You're infuriating.

Priest: Can you remember a time when someone genuinely apologized to you? Maybe your aunt, your parents, your brother?

Me: My family doesn't really do apologies. Not that I can remember, anyway. We're more the eye-roll-and-get-on-with-it type. Nothing ever changes. Apologizing would be, I don't know, like telling a lie. It's more honest to just move forward.

Priest: Do you feel like that level of communication works well? For your family?

Me: Okay, I feel like you're expecting me to say no. But my parents are still together. And my brother's stuck around. So obviously, it works to some degree.

Priest: Is it how you want to proceed with your friend?

Me: No. I mean . . . no.

Priest: May I offer you an interesting bit of information?

Me: If you must.

Priest: You mentioned penitence, the act of repenting. Technically, that's what most people who join me in the confessional are here for, although I do enjoy the novelty of our less formal conversations. *Repentance*, it takes the prefix *re*, Latin for "again," or "very much." Then there's the second part of the word, which comes from *paenitere*—"to make sorry."

Me: So very much to make sorry.

Priest: Exactly. You know, for a long time, there was no linguistic distinction between *regret* and *repent*. That's a modern division.

Me: I don't get it.

Priest: It's actually fairly significant.

Me: Sure, I believe you.

Priest: It means that on some level, if you truly feel sorry for something, the pain of regret transforms you. And that transformation teaches you, reconciles you. It turns you around. It brings you back.

Chapter Twenty-Three

Sitting at the kitchen table, I chewed the end of my pencil and glared at the page.

> Dear Terpsichore,
>
> It turns out I don't know how to apologize. It would be nice to blame my family . . .

"Where's your brother?" Mom stormed through the front door in her work uniform. Her eyes were bloodshot. "It's noon, and the door is still locked downstairs." She opened the cupboard under the sink as if Mateo might be hiding there, shirking his familial responsibilities.

"I don't know," I said, setting aside my slobbery pencil. "He left about an hour ago." I neglected to mention that Mateo and I had passed each other in the alley by the stairs as I returned from my chat with the priest this morning. My brother's hair was all shiny, and he was wearing a shirt with buttons, something Vera had given him for his birthday a few years back. I thought I could even smell cologne. All in all, he was dressed way too nicely to have been on his way to the print shop.

"Where are you going?" I'd asked him.

He made a face. "Where have you been?"

I wasn't going to answer that, so I stepped out of his way and watched him disappear around the corner.

Mom went down the hallway to inspect Mateo's vacant bedroom. "Work is the only place he's allowed to go," she called. "He's grounded. Technically."

"I'm not sure he agreed to that."

"Don't be snide, Dolores; it's not a good look for you." Mom seethed as she made her way back to the front door, picking the keys for the shop off the counter. "And if Mateo bothers to come home, let him know that I'm downstairs covering his shift and would very much like to speak to him."

The door slammed closed, and my mother's stomping footfalls seemed to shake the outer wall of the building. I picked up my pencil.

Dear Terpsichore,

It turns out I don't know how to apologize. It would be nice to blame my family, and maybe I can a little bit. I know they for sure didn't teach me. I've racked my brain for the last week and the best example of an apology I ever got was from you. When you came into the print shop and said that you'd put a lot of thought into why the whole thing at the communications workshop made me so upset. And that you really never intended it to be that way, but that didn't mean it didn't hurt me. And that I had your "sincere apology." I'd never had anyone in the world talk to me like that. I didn't know what to say. Maybe I didn't say anything. I can't remember.

I know I told you that I had buckets of experience being a great best friend. That wasn't an intentional lie—I really thought I was good at it. But it turns out that I was a super crappy best friend after all. To you, at least.

I don't know why I got so stuck on Shae. You were right. She was mean. It was crazy to still want to be friends with her after she sent that text. I think maybe I was scared that I'd never have a friend again. That I was a leaky loser and a pee-colored stain on the earth. So, I should really just be grateful anyone was texting me at all, even if it was to say that they didn't want to see me again.

That sounds like I'm trying to pity party my way out of this apology letter. I'm really not. Lots of people have bad bladders and don't ruin their friends' lives by getting them put under permanent house arrest. I could have chosen not to do that. And if I could have a do-over, I never would have lied to you or made you go to that party.

I feel awful, like really awful. Someone with some authority on the subject told me that was a good thing, that feeling pain over hurting someone changes you into the kind of person who doesn't do stupid things like that in the future. And the change is what does more than actually saying the words "I'm sorry."

But I'm going to say them anyway. I'm sorry, Terpsichore. I was really lucky that you chose me to be your friend.

My pencil stopped. I didn't want to admit that I'd read Terpsichore's search history. She didn't have to know that I'd done something so prying. But my journey toward self-betterment demanded honesty, so I continued.

And you are a good friend, if you were ever worried about that. Worried enough to google it, I mean. And if you were scared that you wouldn't get to do all the really amazing things that you say you're going to do, you shouldn't be, no matter what the internet says. Those statistics don't know you. They don't know how talented and passionate and creative you are or how determined you get when you decide on a goal. Or that you know how to add pockets to anything and stop a stain from setting or catch a loose chicken. Or how nice you are to be around or the way people just gravitate toward you in a room. I think all those things mean a lot more than some percentages on a website.

Your friend,
Dolores

I tapped the dull lead of the pencil against the word *friend*. It was presumptuous to think she would still see me as a friend. But *Sincerely* felt too corporate and grown-up, and *Love* wasn't an option. I thought of the way that word had felt so hollow in Shae's message to me. *Love you. Love you. Love you.* After agonizing over the question for several minutes, I finally just erased *Your friend* and replaced it.

Yours,

Dolores

Terpsichore's address was still on the fridge, on the weird magnet that Mrs. Berkenbosch-Jones had given Mateo. I wrote it on an envelope in my best penmanship and created a made-up return address so that Terpsichore's mom wouldn't get suspicious. Hopefully she'd think her daughter received some harmless junk mail from the Southeastern Sewciety of Fiber Artists in Atlanta, Georgia. I was set to walk it down to the mailbox when I realized, rather ironically, that I didn't have a stamp. And there weren't any at the print shop, either.

〜〜〜〜〜〜〜

We didn't go to Tía Vera's house for dinner that Sunday. This should have been the canary in the coal mine, the warning sign of our family's imminent implosion, but it didn't feel that way at the time. I didn't realize the little yellow bird had stopped chirping until it was too late.

My brother came home that evening, his feet rattling the staircase in an even, unbothered rhythm.

"Where have you been?" my dad demanded, as soon as he opened the door. "You didn't show up for work today."

Mateo unbuttoned the collar of his shirt. "I was busy." He slipped off his shiny brown dress shoes.

My father's voice was tinny, metallic. "What could have been so important you left your mother in the lurch?"

"I got a job," Mateo said, stretching his shoulders. "I had an interview this morning, and I got it."

"Doing what?" I asked.

Mateo didn't answer. "I'm just grabbing a change of clothes," he explained, heading toward his room, "and then I'll be out of your hair for the night."

Dad's expression darkened. "You expect to live under this roof and not contribute?"

"Why not?" he called. "You do."

There was a silence that felt like a heart palpitation. Dad's face reddened and his shoulders squared, but as soon as he'd opened his mouth to speak, Mateo continued talking.

"Anyways, I figured that instead of giving you free labor, I could just buy my own groceries and pay rent," my brother said, emerging from the hallway wearing his high school backpack, a pair of jeans draped over his arm like a maître d' with a cloth napkin. "You know, how normal adults do." Mateo opened the front door. "Okay, everyone, have a nice night. I'll see you tomorrow."

I followed my brother down the stairs. "Mateo. Mateo. Mateo!"

"What?" He turned around.

"Uh." I held the metal railing. "Do you have any stamps?"

Mateo scrunched up his face and mimed taking off a hat. "No soap, dollface, and the teletype is gone bust too."

"Can you take me to go get some?" I asked.

Mateo tilted his head, suddenly curious. "What do you need stamps for?"

"I wrote Terpsichore an apology letter," I admitted, pulling the envelope out of my pocket.

My brother sucked his teeth, then looked back at Johann's car, which was still running in the parking lot. "Okay," he said, jumping down the last two stairs. "We can check the grocery store, but if they don't have them, we're not going to keep looking."

"Thank you." I followed him down the alley and slid into the back seat of the car, the letter on my lap.

He shook his head. "Nope. No way. I'm only doing it because I need stuff there anyways. This isn't a favor. Don't get used to it."

Mateo threw his backpack at me. I kicked it to the floor.

"Hallo, Lola." Johann gave a sort of sad smile at me in the rearview mirror. "How are you?"

"Uh." I sank a little remembering the last time Johann and I saw each other. "I'm not thriving."

Johann nodded understandingly and shifted the car out of park.

"Just to the store, then we're taking her back home," Mateo explained, glaring at me over his shoulder as he buckled his seat belt.

"Of course," Johann said. He grinned a little out of the corner of his mouth. My brother was too busy staring out the window to notice.

"A letter. Aren't you worried that's kind of a cop-out?" Mateo asked.

"Yeah," I said, pulling the envelope out of my pocket. "I'd apologize in person, but I don't think Mrs. Berkenbosch-Jones will allow me on their property."

Mateo nodded. "That's probably true."

I watched the sunset reflect off the windows and mirrors of the vehicles next to us. A washed-out yellow-orange swam along the curves of trunks and bumpers and hoods. That's when I noticed the familiar shape of a certain Toyota Corolla. I sat bolt upright. "Wait. Mateo, look!" I tapped aggressively on the glass, like a toddler at an aquarium. "Look! That's Mom's car."

Mateo squinted. "What are you talking about?"

"There, right there," I exclaimed, gesturing to the lane to our left. "That's her car! Oh my God, Mateo, it's Sunday. The eight miles!"

It took Mateo a second to process the gravity of my discovery. "Wait," my brother said, leaning forward to see around Johann's broad shoulders. "I didn't even realize she wasn't at home."

"Me neither." I tried to get a good look at my mother behind the steering wheel, but I could only make out the general shape of her ponytail and sunglasses. "We didn't go to Vera's. I forgot about the 'errands.'"

Johann clicked his right turn signal, ready to pull into the grocery store parking lot.

My brother flicked it back up. "Hold on," he said, chewing his lip.

"Follow her," I begged. "Please, Johann, we have to see where she goes!"

Realizing he was outnumbered, the German dutifully slowed the vehicle and changed lanes so we were two cars behind my mom.

"Not so close," I told him, leaning forward between the front seats. "She'll recognize your car."

"Seat belt," Mateo demanded.

"It hurts my bladder," I said. "Just drive carefully."

"*Seat belt*," he repeated.

I sat back. "Fine. She's turning right."

"Yes," Mateo remarked, "we can see that, thank you."

Johann shot me a sympathetic look in the mirror. He put his hand on my brother's knee and gave it a squeeze as he followed my mom through an intersection. We were on the highway now, passing strip malls and fast food joints. Realistically it couldn't be much farther. My bladder was starting to complain again, but I wiggled my toes in my shoes and tried to ignore it.

"She's got her turn signal on," my brother said. "She's getting off at the next exit. Go now, there's another car behind her."

Johann turned to squint over his shoulder as he changed lanes. The sun was low in the sky behind us. "What is on this side of town?" he asked. "I do not know it."

"Me neither," my brother confessed. "She's going into that parking lot." He put his hand on the wheel. "No, keep going for a second, then flip a U-turn when you can."

"That's a church!" I shouted, craning my neck to see the building we'd just passed.

"Don't be stupid, Dolores," Mateo scoffed, looking back at me.

"I swear, it had that pointy thing on top and everything!"

Mateo raised his unibrow. "You mean a cross?"

Johann turned the car around, and I could see the metal roof poking out above the trees. "No," I said, "a what's-it-called! A steeple! There, look, look, look!"

"She wouldn't." Mateo shook his head as Johann pulled into the parking lot. "She must have made a wrong turn."

"There's her car right out front," I said. "And that is definitely a church."

"Okay." Mateo grabbed his phone and pulled up a map. "This must be a freak occurrence, right? Maybe she had an actual errand or something. This can't be the eight miles."

"How many miles are we from Vera's?" I asked.

"Three and a half, give or take."

"And how far are we from home?"

My brother didn't answer, just stared at his screen. I poked his arm. "How far, Mateo?"

"A little under four miles," he said. "This makes no sense."

"We should go in." I studied the other nine cars in the lot. "We can spy on her. Find out what she's actually up to. I mean, she could be graffitiing the altar or something."

"I've never been inside a church." Mateo sounded genuinely nervous.

"It's not a big deal," I told him, suddenly feeling like an expert by comparison. I opened my door. "Don't worry, you won't burst into flames."

Mateo shifted in his seat. "I'd rather not take any chances."

"I can go with you, Lola." Johann had been silent for a while, perhaps sensing that he was a bit of an interloper in this accidental exploration of family lore. "If you want me to only."

"That's okay," I said, sliding out of the car. "I'll be less conspicuous on my own." I left out the part about having mastered the art of sneaking in and out of a church without being seen. The only thing that gave me pause, though, was how different this building looked from St. Francis of Assisi. The closer I got, the less sure I was that every church had the same layout. Did they have a priest-in-a-box here too? I opened the red front door.

Bathroom #66: St. Monica Episcopal Church. This restroom wins points for front-door accessibility, located mere steps from the entrance to the building. A single-seater, one rests assured that there won't be a surprise intruder to interrupt the flow. Automatic fan, recently emptied trash, and clean sink speak to the general upkeep of the facilities; however, it must be noted that the color of the bathroom is mauve. Exclusively mauve. This fatal design mistake must influence the rating. Three and a half stars.

It turned out, I didn't have to do much investigating at all, as right outside the bathroom there was a printed calendar for July. There was "Brass Band Practice" on Tuesdays at 7:00 p.m. and "Puzzle Club" Thursdays at 4:00 p.m., and two services listed for Sunday morning, an 8:30 and a 10:30. Underneath those, at 8:00 p.m., I found the answer to my family's most enigmatic riddle.

"Did she see you?" Mateo asked when I got back in the car.

"No."

"Well, what did you find out?"

"I don't really know," I answered. "It was on the calendar as 'Support Group for Marital Transitions,' but I don't know what that means."

Johann and Mateo looked at each other. Then Mateo took a long, slow breath and turned to stare out the window. He gritted his teeth, shrank his lips, and exhaled, rubbing his forehead. Then he relaxed and whispered one word into his fingers. "Okay."

"What?" I asked, my stomach feeling like it had gotten in an elevator at the top floor and descended all the way to the basement. "What does that mean?"

"Divorce," Mateo answered finally. "It means divorce."

Twenty minutes later, Mateo paid for my stamps at the grocery store. He didn't say anything snippy, not even when the clerk said that they only sold stamps in books of twenty and he had to pull out thirteen dollars to cover it. He even directed Johann to drive past a mailbox on our way back to the apartment. I thought that meant he might cancel his plans with Johann and come back inside with me, but when we pulled into the alley, I got out and he didn't. I went upstairs alone.

Chapter Twenty-Four

Me: Hey, there. It's me.

Priest: Hello. It's been a while since you've come to talk.

Me: A couple weeks.

Priest: I've been praying for you.

Me: If that's true, it isn't working. Can I be honest with you?

Priest: Of course.

Me: Things are not going well. I am not well. Wellness is not my current status.

Priest: I see.

Me: You know, I've figured out that there's something wrong with me. Like, fundamentally. In my soul . . . God, ugh! I feel so stupid for crying! Like, why should I get to cry when everything is my fault?

Priest: It's okay to cry.

Me: Yeah, you have to say that.

Priest: What do you think is wrong with you?

Me: Maybe everything? At this point, it would be easier to throw it out and scrap the whole thing: my brain, my bladder, my personality, I guess?

Priest: That sounds rather drastic.

Me: Not really. The stuff on the outside—family, friendships—they've completely fallen apart. I keep thinking, and maybe this is stupid and selfish, but I keep thinking, what's the point of learning how to be a better person when everything is broken beyond repair? When you can't fix things? If I could just get rid of everything that's left and start from scratch, I could be good this time.

Priest: If you're looking for reincarnation, you'd have to visit a different house of worship. From a Catholic point of view, it's more "you get what you get," I'm afraid.

Me: Figures . . .

Priest: Well, if you're asking me—which I think is a fair gamble—I don't believe anything is unsalvageable. Hopelessness kind of goes against brand.

Me: I hate myself.

Priest: And God loves you.

Me: Because of me, my parents got into a huge fight, and now they're going to get divorced. I got my brother in trouble, and now he's got a new job and a boyfriend and he doesn't want anything to do with me. My childhood best friend outgrew me, and my current best friend hasn't written me back, because sorry doesn't make things better. It doesn't erase the choices I made. And she's got every right to move on in her life without me, and I can't even be mad at her, because if I could move on without me, I would too. And my stupid bladder just hurts all the time, every day, and I'm just so tired of it.

Priest: And God loves you.

Me: Stop it.

Priest: What is it you want to hear, then?

Me: That you can fix me.

Priest: Ah. Do you believe in that?

Me: I mean, don't you?

Priest: I want to pose a hypothetical question. Let's say God, however you picture God, appeared to you right now and said, "I'm sorry, my child. But I am not going to 'heal' your family, your friendships, or your illness. This is the life and body you get." What would you do?

Me: Yell at him. Spit in his face. Kick him in the balls.

Priest: Okay. And when that didn't change anything?

Me: What are you trying to get me to say?

Priest: I only want to know—

Me: What, that I'd suddenly be okay with it? I'm not okay with it! With any of this! I thought you said you don't do hopelessness!

Priest: It's not—

Me: No, shut up! Shut up! Why do people come to you if you don't change anything? If you don't help anyone? Isn't that your job?

Priest: Daughter—

Me: I'm not your daughter! You must be some kind of creep, sitting here all day listening to how messed up and broken everyone is when you don't do anything to make them better. You're useless! *Useless!*

~~~~~~~~

I stormed out of the confessional, my fingers smacking the top of the polished oak pews and the scratchy red upholstery. There was a statue of a robed monk tucked into a hollow in the wall by the door.

St. Francis, I guessed, since the building was named after him. The man was balding and bearded with various woodland creatures caught mid-scurry around his person: birds, squirrels, a lamb, three little rats chewing on his leather sandals. St. Francis's glassy, downcast eyes watched me storm out of the church with an inebriated apathy.

I swung the front door open, almost taking out my aunt teetering up the steps. "Dolores!" Tía Vera gasped, putting one hand on the railing and the other to her chest. "What on earth are you doing—jumping out of churches, frightening old ladies." She squinted, her shock dissolving into suspicion. "Did your mother put you up to this?"

"No," I answered, wiping my tears on my shirt. "It's nothing, Tía. Sorry I scared you." Turning my face away, I tried to maneuver around her, but I was unsuccessful. The woman was a fortress.

"Have you been coming here on your own?" she asked.

"Of course not." I glanced down at the concrete stairs. My aunt's shadow eclipsed mine completely. "Just leave me alone; I don't want to talk about it."

"Where's your bracelet, mija?" Tía Vera asked. "You promised you'd wear it. Have you even tried the oil I got you?" She started rummaging through her purse.

"I don't want to talk about that either," I insisted. "Please."

Vera ignored me and pulled a vial out of her bag. It was the size of a small glass test tube and full of beige powder. It had a sort of iridescent-looking sticker of the Virgin of Guadalupe wrapped around it. She put the object in my palm, then clasped my hands together.

"It's holy dirt," she said.

I looked out at the street. "Tía—"

"Just listen for one minute." She waited until I'd turned my face back to her. "A long time ago, in the New Mexico mountains, there was a magic stream. Our ancestors, the Pueblo Indians, believed the water contained healing spirits. The water is long gone now, but the dirt"—she pointed to my cupped hands—"the dirt is still there! And so are the miracles. The church there, El Santuario de Chimayo, has a crucifix that moves—"

I clenched the vial in my fist and gritted my teeth. "Tía Vera, stop—"

"Listen to me," she begged. Her voice somehow seemed to both plead and condescend. Or maybe I was just imagining that. "I want to help you, mija. At the church, there's a whole room full of ex votos, offerings of thanks people have left because they were healed. Don't you want to be healed?"

"No, Tía! No more!" I pulled away from my aunt, finally managing to sidestep her. "No more oil, no more amulets, no more magic dirt. It's stupid! You're stupid for believing this crap!"

"Dolores!" Tía Vera followed me down the steps. "What has gotten into you?"

I held up the vial of dirt. "How much money did you pay for this?"

Vera adjusted her glasses. "It's not about the mon—"

"See, that's exactly it." I groaned, "God, you raised six children. How could you be so naïve? This is a scam. It's all a scam. This doesn't help anything! Just stop it, Vera!" I didn't realize that I'd thrown the holy dirt until the side of the little bottle hit the edge of a stair and shattered, sending sand in all directions.

"Mija."

I ignored my aunt's indictment and hurried down the sidewalk toward the print shop, shoving my hands into my pockets, the holy dirt clinging to the soles of my shoes.

My bladder and my conscience had made it difficult to sleep at night. As soon as I got home from my confrontation with Tía Vera, I collapsed into bed. Then I heard a noise. I sat up. My heart raced as I lay there, wondering if the sound had been real or a dream. Although I didn't remember falling asleep, I must have been out for hours. The light from the window had become tinged with the first colors of sunset.

I wiped the drool from my cheek and waited for my pulse to slow down. Then, as soon as I'd convinced myself I'd woken up from a nightmare, I heard the sound again. It was my mother's voice. She was shouting.

"—could you?" I only caught the tail end of what she said.

My father, matching her volume, was easier to understand. "I can't force the woman to pay me!"

"Like hell you can't!"

I swung my legs over the side of my bed, realizing I'd fallen asleep in my sneakers.

"She says she doesn't have the money!" My dad's voice rumbled through the hollow drywall. I followed the sound out to the hallway. "What am I supposed to do? Go into her house? Look under her mattress? Steal her costume jewelry?"

My parents were standing toe to toe by the front door. "She scammed you!" My mother put her hands on her head. "You let her scam you! You, you incompetent—"

I poked my head into my brother's room, hoping this might be one of the rare moments he'd be home. But as usual, Mateo must have been at his new job, or out somewhere with Johann. It was just me here. I was on my own. Hugging the hallway wall, I crept slowly closer to the fight, the full picture coming into view. There was a discarded box on the ground with the swirly pyramid-scheme logo on the sides. It looked like my mother had stomped on it a few times.

Mom grabbed a stack of angry-looking envelopes from the kitchen table. She held them in front of Dad's nose. "Look! Look at this!"

Dad gulped, flushing red. "Yes, well, I was meaning to—"

"Oh, you were meaning to," she repeated, laughing coldly. "Gambling, Diego? I work all hours trying to keep us afloat, and you spend my money on lottery tickets?"

"I've done research! The odds—"

She threw the envelopes at his face. "You've bankrupted us!" my mother shouted. "We're going to lose our home! We have nothing! We have *less* than nothing!" She pulled open the front door. "Get out of here, Diego! *Get out!*"

Dad caught the door with his hand. "Why can't you just believe in me?" His voice was sharp and accusing.

My mother bent at the waist, like she was going to be sick. "Why, why would I do that?" She shook her head. "Look what you've done!"

Dad's knuckles were white. "I've given our kids a future!"

"*You've given them nothing!*" Mom screamed.

"I got the TV."

Four words.

They rolled off my father's tongue as if they were any other statement. Our *couch is old. The laundry is dry.*

I *got the TV.*

But it *wasn't* any other statement. The words were like lightning.

They sent an electric current of white-hot energy through my mother. She snapped upright.

"You got the TV?" she mouthed. She turned around to the cardboard box that had become a fixture in our living room. "You got the TV," she said, loud enough for me to hear it this time. She put her hands on either side of the massive box, crouching slightly. "That's right. The TV. How could I forget the goddamn TV?"

My mother picked up the TV box, that horrible hulking thing, and heaved it the five steps to the entry, navigating it between her and my father and the open door. Her eyes flickered with something deeper than anger in the way that wine is deeper than grape juice. It was anger that had aged, matured, fermented into something new entirely. And my mother was drunk on it.

"Mom!" I shouted, running across the room. I reached the door. "Mom, stop!"

With one guttural scream, she ran out onto the landing and threw her whole weight against the railing. The TV soared from its sheath. Freed from its cardboard cocoon, the colors of the sunset reflected off the plastic screen-protecting sticker that no one had removed. It looked like an oil slick. Like a rainbow prism. Like a great black bird. Watching it, I remembered those first few moments of flight when I too had gone out over the stairs to face the alley below. But there was no well-timed German to break the TV's fall.

The impact was so much softer than I'd expected, so much more contained. I braced for an explosion, for shrapnel ricocheting six feet in the air. But there wasn't any of that. Just a single, sad sort of sound when the screen hit the ground.

Crunch.

My dad stood frozen in the doorway, staring at my mother in disbelief. "Abigail!"

Mom tossed the cardboard box and sank to her knees. "You come one step closer to me, Diego," she warned, "and it'll be you going over the railing next."

"Okay," Dad said, slowly lowering himself to a sitting position. He put his hands up. "Okay. I'm sitting down."

A pair of tattooed faces peeked around the corner of the building. "Hey, uh, you guys cool up there?" Teardrop asked.

Thank God, I thought, hurrying down the staircase.

"You need help?" Spider looked concerned. "We were closing up, and we heard shouting."

"Yes!" I answered. "I need to borrow a phone."

Teardrop pulled his out of the front pocket of his apron. The lock screen was him and the woman with the baby who was always in the shop. They were all on a park bench, snuggled up together. He typed in a password and handed it to me.

Only one phone number came to mind. It was one that had been drilled into my head since I was old enough to repeat it. The number to call in an emergency.

"Who is this? Who's there?"

"Tía, it's Dolores." I glanced sheepishly at Spider and Teardrop, feeling self-conscious explaining the situation in front of them. Picking up on this, they stepped back respectfully and stared at the ground.

"Dad bankrupted us, and Mom threw the TV off the balcony."

"I'll be right there," was all my aunt said. Then she hung up.

I handed the phone back to Teardrop. "Uh, thanks." Mom was

clinging to the flaking green metal railing like a rabid koala while Dad threw increasingly stupid platitudes at her.

"It's not normally like this," I explained, sniffling.

"Yeah, no, we get it," Spider replied. He nodded like this was totally normal. But I could tell by his eyes that this was very much not normal at all. "Families, right?"

"Right," I said. I rocked on my heels and waited for Vera.

"Abigail, come back inside!" my dad begged.

Mom gripped the railing tighter. "Twice a month I go to this support group," she said, "for people in unhappy marriages. And I listen to the others talk about their spouses. They all have these horrible stories of cruelty, violence, infidelity. Our marriage isn't like that." She glanced back at my father. "You've never been like that. So, I'd come home and tell myself that I'd stay and try again. Just for two more weeks. Over and over again. For *years*."

I couldn't see Dad's face. I wondered what his reaction was to finding this out.

"And no one I met that first meeting still comes to that group," Mom continued. "They left their partners and moved on with their lives. They're not stuck in this horrible cycle anymore. And I'm so jealous of them."

Five minutes later, Tía Vera's red car pulled up in front of the print shop, the plastic St. Christopher dancing on the dashboard as she jerked the vehicle into park. Then, with surprising agility, the woman jumped out and ran up the alley in her slippers. Yes, her slippers. As promised, my aunt had come straight here. She had no makeup on, no jewelry. Her thinning hair was tied up in a scarf, and her loose breasts sagged in her nightgown. She grabbed the railing and marched up the stairs.

Mom's face twisted in pain. "I don't want to hear it, Vera!" she said, gasping. "I don't want to hear what a terrible mother I am, letting my daughter see me like this. Letting the whole street see me like this. It doesn't matter anymore." She ran her cheek down one of the metal bars. "We've lost everything."

Snap, snap, snap, Tía Vera's slippers vibrated the stairs. My stomach sank. Why had I called her? What was she going to do? After so many years of tense Sunday dinners and passive-aggressive sparring, how would Vera react to seeing her dueling partner brought so low? What words would she have for my mother now?

"Vera." My mom cowered back as my aunt reached the landing. "Vera, I'm warning you—"

But Tía Vera didn't say anything at all. For the first time in my memory, my aunt went into a situation entirely silent. She lowered herself to sit beside my mother and reached out to hold her. Mom's face disappeared entirely, buried in my aunt's shoulder. Vera patted her back and rocked her—as if my mother was one more of her orphaned siblings. And Vera hummed, just two notes over and over, higher then lower, droned like a mourning dove.

It was as if this pattern knocked something loose in my mother. And she started to sob. She sobbed like a child sobs, with big, long gulps of air and retching coughs and wails.

It scared me. My hands started to shake, and my chest felt how it had when Terpsichore dug her knuckles into my sternum.

"Hey, kid," Spider said gently. "You want to sit inside the ice cream shop?" He looked at the crushed screen. "I mean, whatever's in these new TVs can't be good to breathe in."

I nodded. Spider seemed to make a reasonable argument.

But I couldn't move.

Johann's car pulled around the corner to park in front of the shop. The tires scraped the curb, making a terrible sound. Mateo tumbled out of the driver's side, practically falling over his feet to get to the alley.

"What the hell happened?" he demanded.

"I don't know. I just woke up and they were fighting," I explained. "But not normal fighting. I think we might be homeless?" I hugged my shoulders. "How did you know to come here? I forgot to call you."

My brother didn't answer. He was too busy piecing together the scene, looking up to the top of the stairs, then down at the TV.

Teardrop cleared his throat. "Hey, man, if you want to take your sister and go wait inside," he told Mateo. "Get yourself some ice cream; we can clean up—"

From up on the landing, Vera finally spoke. "I can't believe you would put your family at risk like this, Diego," she said, still rocking my weeping mother.

Dad stepped out from the doorway, looking deflated. "They're the reason I did it all in the first place." He sighed. "All of this was for them."

"No," Tía Vera corrected him harshly. "You wanted this. You've been foolish and selfish. You leave right now and don't bother coming back until you are ready to be a husband and father."

Mateo steered me around before I could see Dad's face. Before I could read a decision in his eyes. "Yeah, uh, ice cream sounds good. Thanks."

Chapter Twenty-Five

A half hour later, I sat staring into a bowl of melted vanilla ice cream while doing little ninety-degree rotations on a barstool. Absentmindedly, Mateo picked up a rag and started wiping down the counters. Neither one of us had spoken about our parents.

"You're cleaning," I said.

"So?"

"You never clean at home." I rested my forehead on the counter.

"I don't get paid to clean at home."

"You don't get paid to clean here—" I paused, glancing up at him in surprise. "Wait, this, this is your job?"

"One of them," Mateo answered. "I'll need at least one or two more, but, you know, it's a start." He peeled me off the counter and ran the rag over the surface in front of me where my oily skin had left a smudge. "You hear anything from Terps?"

"You don't have to pretend to care about that," I scoffed, pushing his hand away.

"I'm not pretending." Mateo's face suddenly reminded me of Mom's, long lines plowed by sleeplessness and concern. "Dolores, I'm not pretending," he repeated.

"I haven't heard anything from her," I said. "It's been weeks, so at this point, I don't think I will."

"Maybe she didn't get the letter," my brother offered.

"Or maybe the damage has been done." I leaned my chin into my hand. "I'm just really sad now. I was so stupid."

"You're a lonely high schooler. Sometimes that turns you into an idiot." Mateo dropped the rag into a bin behind the counter. "I remember what that's like."

"You were never lonely in high school."

"I was."

"Nuh-uh. You were Mr. Popular."

"That doesn't mean I wasn't lonely."

I shook my head. "I don't believe you."

"What, you want proof?" Mateo motioned to a booth in the corner. "Come here. Come sit down, and I'll show you."

I sighed, but was too curious not to follow him. It sounded distracting, and at that moment, I would have given my left butt cheek for a distraction.

Mateo settled on the seat facing me. "So, this all starts a couple of years ago, right? When I saw this news story about a snail named Jeremy that was born with its shell twisted to the left instead of to the right." He made a Fibonacci spiral in the air with his finger. "Like, its whole anatomy was flipped the wrong way. And that's a real problem for snails, because their stabby face genitals are on the right side." He dropped his hand back to the table. "Or they should be, which was Jeremy's issue."

I squinted. "Where is this going?"

"Stop it, just listen. So, this poor little backward snail couldn't have a relationship with any of the other snails, because it was born wrong." Mateo paused. "I mean, not technically wrong, I guess, just different. Rare. Anyway, the news report was calling for people to go

out to their gardens and parks and forests to find another lefty snail."
My brother's voice became hoarse with emotion, and he cleared his
throat. "It was, like, this big, international effort. This race to find love
for Jeremy."

"Are you crying?"

Mateo kicked me in the shin. "Shut up. It resonated."

"Ouch! I'm sorry. Very serious global snail mission. Continue."

"So, picture me, sixteen and stupid drunk at a party when someone pulls out a stick-and-poke kit and asks if anyone wants a free tattoo." Mateo turned to the side and pulled his foot up to his seat. He
started undoing his laces.

"Naturally, I volunteered. The guy asked me what I wanted, and all
of a sudden, I remembered that news report and Jeremy, and so I told
him, 'Give me a snail with a left-twisting shell.' Sinistral is the fancy sci-
ence word. I looked that up later." Mateo winced and held his naked
foot out for inspection. There, covered in sweaty sock lint, just above
my brother's hairy toes, was the goofiest looking snail I'd ever seen.

"Holy . . ."

"I don't want to hear it," Mateo warned. "The kid said he was going
to be a tattoo artist. I think he's studying accounting now."

I held my hand over my mouth to stifle the involuntary laughter.
"Oh my God, Mateo," I whispered. "It's cross-eyed."

My brother pulled back his foot and pouted his lips. "Okay, sharing time is over. You've lost your privileges."

"No, no, it's . . ." I stalled, trying to find an appropriate adjective.
Finally, I settled on, "Sweet," and quickly added, "but I don't totally
get why you're showing it to me. I mean, you've kept it secret for four
years."

"Four years is nothing," Mateo sighed. "When I sobered up the next day and saw it, I was pretty sure I'd have to hide the tattoo for the rest of my life. Be one of those people who has sex with their socks on."

I grimaced. "Ew. Please don't elaborate."

"But it's okay now, I think." He wiped the lint off his foot, examining the lopsided gastropod with an expression not too far off from fondness. "I think I kind of like it. And I remember why I got it in the first place. The meaning."

"There's a meaning to that?"

Mateo nodded and adopted a serious tone, like he was explaining the moral of a fable. "When you're built different from most other snails, it's easy to become bitter and give up," he said. "Or you can keep searching, believing that someday you'll find your snail soulmate. The snail who makes you feel like you make sense in the world. And you'll stab each other with your wrong-sided face genitals and slink off into the sunset."

"Wow." I uncovered my mouth and shook my head. "You should write children's books."

My brother laughed.

"Do you know what happened to the snail in the news story?" I asked. "Jason? Jeffrey?"

"Jeremy." Mateo cleared his throat. "Yeah, I looked it up not that long ago. After that news story, people all over the world went looking, and they found not only one but two other sinistral snails. And they shipped them out to wherever Jeremy was."

"Huh," I said. "That's really kind of nice, actually."

"You'd think so." Mateo grimaced. "But the two lefty snails mated with each other instead. Like a lot. Incessantly." He shrugged. "And eventually, Jeremy died."

My eyes popped open. "Oh my God."

"Yup."

"That. Is. Tragic."

"Oh, I'm well aware of that." Mateo looked at his watch and put his sock back on. "But the scientists studying Jeremy believe the little trooper was responsible for at least some of the snail babies they found in the enclosure. So, not a totally loveless existence for our slimy nonconformist." He paused. "Don't give me that look, Dolores; my tattoo's message of hope and belonging is still relevant."

"If you say so." Something about the purposeful way my brother tied his shoelaces made me nervous. "Mateo?"

"Yeah?" He stood up to clear my ice cream dish.

"Are you leaving?"

"I've got to return Johann's car. I'll be back tomorrow."

"But—"

"Don't worry." He held out his hand and pulled me up. "Vera's got this. She and Mom, they're going to figure something out. Nothing else is going to happen tonight."

"I think we're fighting," I said. "Tía Vera and me."

"Well, I won't take sides here, but if I were you, I might consider a truce." Mateo held the door expectantly. The air outside was hot and damp.

I stopped in the doorway and raised my eyebrows. "Are you going to show Johann your tattoo?"

"Time to go, Dolores."

"He's already seen it, hasn't he? That's the only reason you showed me."

Mateo rolled his eyes and tugged my elbow, pulling me out of the ice cream parlor. Outside, Spider and Teardrop were leaning against the front of the building, as if they'd been reluctant to interrupt us by returning to their establishment.

"Thanks for calling me," Mateo said, shaking their hands. It looked like such a grown-up thing to do. "And handling the mess. Families, right?"

"Right," Spider answered. "You two need anything else, you just come by, okay?"

Mateo forced a smile. "For sure."

Mom and Vera weren't on the landing anymore. I was relieved. As my brother and I walked up the stairs, I looked down over the railing. The TV and its box were gone from the alley. So was my dad's truck.

"Get some sleep, Dolores," Mateo instructed. "It's going to be okay."

I remembered hearing once that if you were in a plane and it hit turbulence, you should look at the flight attendants. If they were acting calm and casual, it meant that the plane wasn't actually going to fall out of the sky, even if it felt like it was. Mateo looked tired, but not scared. And he was still leaving to spend the night playing footsie with Johann, which made me believe we weren't all imminently about to crash and burn. Probably.

Mom and Tía Vera were sitting at the kitchen table, but neither seemed to hear me come in. Mom stared vacantly into a cup of coffee while my aunt opened and organized the multicolored bills, setting them into neat stacks. Without saying anything, I walked past them and retreated to my bedroom.

Chapter Twenty-Six

As much as I wanted to stay in bed all day, I was hungry and had to pee, which meant going out and facing the new shape of my family. Mom and Vera were still sitting at the same spots at the kitchen table. But they hadn't stagnated. Mom was doing research on her laptop while Vera squinted through the bottom of her glasses at a calculator, cleared her throat, then scribbled in one of my half-empty school notebooks.

I went to the kitchen, purposely avoiding eye contact with either woman. It terrified me to have to come up with a greeting. "Good morning" felt like a slap in the face after the night we'd had. I poured some Flaked Corn cereal into a Christmas mug and opened the fridge.

"We're out of milk," Mom said. I turned around to see her looking up at me. Her face was puffy and her eyes were red, but her voice sounded relatively normal. Not quite upbeat, but not hoarse with despair, either. "Sorry," she added.

"That's okay." I closed the fridge and grabbed a plastic spoon from the drawer. Vera typed something else into the calculator, mumbled to herself, and scratched another note. I ate standing up against the stove, chewing the stale flakes into a thick paste.

"I can go get some more today." Mom closed her laptop. "And some other groceries. I know we're down to condiments." Her gaze followed me anxiously, like she was bracing for me to ask any one of the numerous uncomfortable questions that the last twenty-four hours warranted.

I nodded and looked around. Something was different in the apartment, but I couldn't quite place the change. Then I figured it out.

"I forgot how much space we used to have in the living room," I said finally.

Mom exhaled, the corners of her mouth relaxing. "Me too," she replied.

Vera looked up over her glasses, clicked her tongue, and motioned me to the table. "Come here, mija."

I hesitated and set my mug on the counter.

~~~~~~~~~

EXTERIOR ST. FRANCIS OF ASSISI CATHOLIC CHURCH, AFTERNOON, THE DAY PRIOR

DOLORES and TÍA VERA are caught in an escalating physical struggle. Gusts of wind swirl billows of holy dirt all around them as the music becomes increasingly intense. The camera pauses on Tía Vera's expression of unbridled rage. Desperate to escape and filled with righteous indignation, Dolores pushes her aunt down the stairs. The woman shrieks and tumbles—

~~~~~~~~~

No. That wasn't what happened. Vera hadn't been angry on the church steps. The interaction had never come to blows, there were no industrial fans blowing sand, there were no violins.

Tía Vera reached up and grabbed my hand, holding it firmly. She waited until I looked up to meet her gaze. "I love you so much," my aunt said, squeezing my fingers on each word. Like she was reiterating the statement in Morse code.

"I love you too, Tía."

She nodded, satisfied, and released me. "Now, go get another pot of coffee started for your mother," she instructed me, heaving herself up from her chair. "I'm going home."

My terror must have been obvious.

"Ay, niña," Vera sighed. "I'm just going to put on my face and change my clothes, then I'll come back."

"Oh. That's good." I glanced at my mom. "I mean, as long as . . ."

Mom gave a small, wry laugh. "Yes, Dolores, it's good your aunt is coming back."

I relaxed. "Then it's good."

Vera patted my shoulder as she maneuvered around the table to the door. "Coffee," she repeated. Then she kissed my forehead and left.

"Right." I picked the pot off the table and set it back on the hot plate. "Uh, do you want me to just run the same grounds again, or do you need the big guns?"

Mom turned in her chair. "What do you think?" she asked. There was just a touch of her sarcastic wit in her bloodshot eyes. It was encouraging.

The staircase announced my brother's return before he opened the door. "Friends"—Mateo nodded at my mother, then at me—"Romans, countrymen. Lend me your ears!"

Mom shook her head and sighed.

I felt as bitter as the coffee dripping noisily into the pot. "You know," I told Mateo, "you look more cheerful than you've got any right to be."

Mateo came over to me and leaned coolly against the kitchen counter. "Hold on, mopey, wait until you see why before you bite my head off." He pulled a green envelope from his pocket and waved it in front of my nose.

"No." My eyes widened in disbelief.

"Oh yes," he answered. "Found it in the mailbox on my way in."

I snatched it out of his hands and studied the careful cursive along the first line of the return address. *Terpsichore Berkenbosch-Jones.* I flipped it over. "It's opened," I said, shooting an accusing look at my brother.

Mateo frowned in mock surprise and leaned down to look at the envelope. "Really? Huh, I hadn't notic— Ow, Dolores, my spleen!"

I shook out my punching hand and retreated to my bedroom.

Dear Dolores,

I apologize for the lateness of my response. Although your letter reached me some time ago, I am just now putting pen to paper. You've given me much to think about, and I wanted to fully explore those thoughts on my own before sharing them with anyone else. Especially you.

I don't see myself as blameless in my current predicament. Unlike you, I had no experience with friendship. My mother ensured that, and I'm starting to understand why. Friends make one bold and foolish and happy. They influence what direction one goes, what choices one makes. They can lead one into trouble. But I didn't mind the trouble so much when I was with you.

I'm not entirely sure when we'll meet again. My mother has made no mention of returning phone or internet privileges. As I stare down another year of homeschooling, I'll think a lot about the world out there with the knowledge that someday my mother won't be able to stop me from participating in it. But no one's stopping you. If I could give you one piece of friendly advice, it would be to stop holding yourself back. It's incredibly aggravating to watch, which means it's probably ten times worse to live. Get on with it, Dolores. Honestly, what's the alternative?

Fondly,
Terpsichore Berkenbosch-Jones

I laid the letter out on my bedspread. Terpsichore's carefully written words warped in the creases on the page, folded in on themselves. I pressed the paper flat against the mattress and read the whole thing a second time. Then a third.

The floor creaked in front of my bedroom. Mateo leaned on the doorframe watching me.

"Well," I said coldly, holding the paper up. "Since you already know what it says, do you care to weigh in?"

Mateo smirked. "I told you I liked her."

I pulled my legs up toward my body, hugging them to my chest. "So?"

"She's good for you. And I think you're good for her." Mateo wrinkled his nose. "At least you could be. If you get your hot-mess self together."

I glared. "And you're speaking from your wealth of brotherly wisdom?"

Mateo shrugged. "All I know is that someone who can point out your, uh, you know—" He paused, looking for a word that wouldn't set off the hair trigger that currently held my stronger emotions in check.

"Flaws?" I prompted, gritting my teeth.

"Opportunities for growth," Mateo decided, waving his arm. "Anyone who can point those out in a way that doesn't make you want to punch them in the face is someone to keep around."

"I don't think I have the option to keep her around." I folded the letter and put it back in the envelope. "She's in lockdown for the next four years."

"You never know," Mateo said, turning on his heels. "I don't think Terps is as helpless as she thinks she is."

~~~~~~~~~

Me: Hey, sir. I'm back.

Priest: Oh, good. I'm so relieved. When you left—

Me: Yeah. I was not having a good day. It got worse after that, which is impressive, honestly. It got so horrible, it was almost a relief.

Priest: How so?

Me: It's like . . . you spend so much time being afraid of something, of a worst-case scenario, and then it happens. The worst happens, and then the sun comes up the next day, and you put on a pot of coffee and make stupid jokes, and it's all still terrible, but you don't have to worry about how much more terrible it's going to get. Because it's already the worst, you know? That probably makes no sense.

Priest: I think I understand. So, are you still feeling the need to "scrap the whole thing"?

Me: I guess that does sound pretty drastic, doesn't it? No, I don't think I feel that way right now.

Priest: I'm glad.

Me: Hey, the last time I was here, I accidentally dropped a vial of holy dirt on the steps out front. I don't know if that's something I'm supposed to report to someone? Don't worry, I picked up the pieces of broken glass on my way in today, but the dirt is pretty much settled into the concrete at this point.

Priest: Hmm. That's interesting.

Me: It is?

Priest: I guess I should say it's interesting in an etymological sense.

Me: Oh. So, like, not actually interesting.

Priest: (*laughs*) Probably not.

Me: Tell me anyway.

Priest: Well, in Genesis chapter two, God forms a man out of dirt. He breathes into his nostrils, and the man comes to life. God names this man Adam, from the Hebrew word *adamah*. Guess what that word means.

Me: Dirt?

Priest: Exactly.

Me: That's kind of a diss.

Priest: Is it? Many etymologists believe that the word *human* can trace its origin to a Proto-Indo-European language thousands of years old. And that ancient root? It means "earthling" or "from the earth."

Me: Earth like dirt.

Priest: Ashes to ashes. Dust to dust. We come from the soil of this planet, no different than the flowers or the trees.

Me: Just with extra steps.

Priest: Exactly. But that's a very difficult thing to wrap one's head around. Dirt.

Me: Why?

Priest: Because our bodies belong to the natural, cyclical, decaying world. You see, it's easy to hate the things that tie us down, make us baser than the heavenly hosts. Defecation, sexuality, blood, pain, exhaustion, illness, death. But these things are so unique to the physical, the corporeal, that God had to come down and take on a living, breathing, failing form to truly understand the experience. We are immortal souls in mortal flesh. No wonder we're so mixed up inside.

Me: But what if I don't believe in God?

Priest: You believe in atoms? Elements? Energy?

Me: Yeah.

Priest: Think of it this way. Like all things, we're made of immortal building blocks held briefly together, but our consciousness means we understand the brevity. And it frightens us. So we try to put distance between the dirt we are, the dirt we were, and the dirt we'll become.

Me: That's a lot.

Priest: Absolutely. Now, how do we make sense of it?

Me: How?

Priest: I don't know. I was asking you.

Me: So, we're immortal souls stuffed into pooping, bleeding flesh sacks of pain, basically, and someday we die.

Priest: I mean, I feel like my description was a little more poetic, but yes, that is the gist.

Me: And somewhere along the line in this short little life, we're supposed to figure out how to reconcile all of that?

Priest: I don't know about reconcile. That's quite a lofty ambition. My hope is that it's enough to make peace with it. Learn from our dissonance. Use that to connect with and care for each other as best we can. Religion is the route I've taken to reach that destination, because it made sense to me. But I don't think it's the only way.

Me: Let's say I make peace with it all on my own. Does that mean I get a free pass to heaven without ever having to sit through Mass?

Priest: Another very good question.

Me: That you're not going to answer.

Priest: You guessed it.

Me: Hey, I'm sorry I called you useless, by the way. It wasn't really directed at you.

Priest: I know.

Me: You've actually been pretty helpful. As far as disembodied voices in cupboards go.

Priest: I'm happy to hear that.

Me: If it's okay with you, I think I'll keep coming back here. When I need to feel confused.

Priest: I'd be honored.

Chapter Twenty-Seven

Dad texted me every day after he left. Some version of:

> Just wanted to say I love you and miss you!

And I would reply some version of:

> I love you and miss you too!

I didn't hate him. I wasn't even angry at him—Mom, Vera, and Mateo managed that very well on their own. I did love and miss him. I didn't understand why he'd made the choices he had, but then again, he'd been making those choices my whole life. I wasn't surprised by where we'd ended up. When Johann and Mateo dragged that TV up the stairs, it merely ignited a fuse as old as my parents' marriage.

Mom and Vera spent days uncovering the table, shifting and sorting paperwork like they were managing an archeological dig. The week after that they spent on the phone, taking turns waiting on hold as they tried to break through maddening automated loops.

"How's it going?"

Tía Vera pulled the phone away from her mouth. "It's fine, mija, shoo," she muttered quickly, then returned to her conversation with the stubborn robot. "No, I told you already, I need to speak to a person. A human being!"

"What's going to happen?" I leaned over to peek at the long string of numbers she'd written down.

She flipped the notebook and glanced up at me over her glasses. "I told you, everything is fine." She waved me away. "Shoo!"

"Mom?" I asked.

My aunt gestured toward the bathroom. "Yes, that one!" Tía Vera exclaimed into the phone. "Speak to a representative."

My mother had just gotten out of a shower. Her first in a week, probably. She'd put her hair up in a towel and rubbed a thick layer of lotion all over her face, as if that would ward off the early aging brought on by the stress of the last few years. "Don't worry," Mom said. "We're figuring it out."

"*A representative.*"

Mom checked the clock on the stove. "Why don't you go out and do something?"

Because there are limitless extracurricular opportunities for someone with no money and no friends, I thought, rolling my eyes. "What am I supposed to do?"

Mom hung her head upside down and squeezed the towel. "I don't know, Dolores. Toss a ball. Play with a stick. Dig a hole and fill it up."

"How old do you think I am?" I scoffed.

"If you don't find something to do," Mom warned, "I will find something for you to do. And I guarantee you're not going to like it nearly as much."

"Fine," I said, sulking. "I'm going down to the print shop."

"Great." Mom sat up. "Just don't touch the machines! I've got someone coming on Friday to see about buying them."

"REP-RE-SEN-TA-TIVE!"

"Okay, bye!" I shouted, closing the front door behind me.

I sat down on the metal stairs and pulled out my recently returned phone. My lock screen photo was now one of those preset wallpapers, a picture of pine trees on a mountain. I texted Mateo.

> What are you doing later?

> Miss me already loser?

> Just bored. Want to hang out?

> Can't. Scooping ice cream then going to another job interview. What do you think about the fit?

Mateo sent a picture of himself all dressed up in an unfamiliar bathroom—Johann's, I decided. My brother's toiletries were stacked on the counter, and there were two toothbrushes in a mug by the mirror. I couldn't fully judge based on a single photo, but it seemed like Mateo had upgraded from our one-star apartment bathroom to at least a solid three. Maybe three and a half, but I'd have to see the space in person to judge for sure. Another text popped up.

> The tie is Johann's.

> Your toothbrushes are touching. You better start speeding up your fifteen-year plan.

> I think Johann's in looooove.

> Wait

> Is that a thing??

He told me to leave some stuff at his place
"for convenience."

Am I missing something????

DOLORES

I sent the GIF of the green dancing tube man.

"It must be funny, whatever you're looking at on your phone."

Terpsichore was standing at the bottom of the staircase. For a moment I was too stunned to speak. She was *here*, in the alley. In broad daylight. Where anyone could drive past and see her. And people would see her, standing there in a bright orange sundress, her white hair braided down her back.

I scrambled down the stairs. *"What are you doing here?"* I whispered. "Your mom—"

"Thinks I'm at the library," Terpsichore interrupted. "That's where she dropped me off, and that's where she'll pick me up."

I was not at all comforted. "I don't want you to get in trouble," I said, steering Terpsichore into the shadow under the staircase. "What if she drives by and sees you?"

Terpsichore didn't answer my question. "The Southeastern Sewciety of Fiber Artists," she said. "As a name, it's a little over-the-top."

"I was trying to be, I don't know, clever," I stammered, blushing. "I just didn't want your mom to know it was from me."

"You succeeded." Terpsichore tilted her head, her braid swinging to one side. "Interesting to see you use your finely tuned powers of deception for good."

I swallowed. "Okay, that's a fair blow. I deserved that. I am so, so sorry, Terpsichore." I thought about reaching for her hand, but my palms were suddenly sweaty. I stared at the ground. "I've been really stupid."

Terpsichore twisted her ring. "Yes. You have."

"But I'm trying to be a lot less stupid," I explained. "Going forward."

She smiled a little. "We all need something to aspire to."

I still couldn't believe she was here. "Are you okay?" I asked. "What happened after the party?"

The memory seemed to cause Terpsichore pain. Her expression became uncomfortable, and she fluttered her hand over her neck. "It was very overwhelming," she answered. "I couldn't think straight. My dress . . ." She trailed off.

"Yeah. I saw," I said, remembering the way the emerald velvet dragged under Terpsichore's knees as her mom pulled her to the car.

"And there was a lot of yelling," she continued. "Everyone was yelling by the time we got to the street."

"I remember."

"When we got home, I was so angry." Terpsichore took a quick inhale. "I've never been that angry in my life. I couldn't talk for a whole day. I was angry at you, of course. But mostly I was angry at my mother." Terpsichore rubbed her nails together. "Am angry at her."

I thought back to the last time we'd seen each other in front of the Luden mansion. Not mansion. House, Dolores. Large house. "How did your mom find out about the party?" I asked.

Terpsichore pushed her glasses up her nose. "You know, I've thought a lot about that. I think she tracked my phone. But now that's confiscated . . ." The girl gestured to the phone in my hand. "Have you heard anything from Shae?" she asked, buckling her ankles out.

I put my phone in my pocket. "Oh, uh, no. I mean, I wasn't

expecting to. And at this point, I don't think there's anything to say." I could still hear Shae's words from her bedroom: I outgrew you. But they no longer had the same sting.

"We were friends," I said. "We aren't anymore. That happens, I guess." I laughed a little, digging the toe of my sneaker into the asphalt. "It probably would have saved everyone a whole lot of grief if Shae and I could've just had that conversation to begin with."

"You're just now realizing that?"

"Yes, well, I think we've already established my stupidity."

The girl shrugged. "You've proved you can learn things, at least. Maybe there is some hope for you, after all."

"That would be something." I leaned against the exterior brick of the print shop, trying to stretch the unreachable ache in my body, the crushing, twisting pain that never went away.

Terpsichore tilted her head. "How's your bladder?"

"Terrible," I muttered. "But, then again, it's always terrible. So, I guess I could just say average, really." I pulled myself up with a groan. "Chronic pain is so tedious. No one told me that."

Terpsichore was quiet for a moment, thinking. "Well," she said, "you've got quite some time to learn how to manage the tedium."

"I guess that's true." I pursed my lips. "Terpsichore, I—"

"How could you?" The shrill voice shook the metal of the staircase, scared the pigeons off the roof. Mrs. Berkenbosch-Jones marched down the alley. She had her car keys in one hand and Casimir's wrist in the other. The child dragged his feet in protest. It seemed Terpsichore's mother had gotten tired of the kid-in-a-hot-car routine.

"I was afraid I'd find you here," the woman continued, "but I didn't want to believe it."

"What are you doing here?" Terpsichore asked. Her face was entirely unexpressive, blank.

Mrs. Berkenbosch-Jones hiked her purse up her arm. "I'm here because you lied to me. I followed you."

"I'm seeing my friend," Terpsichore explained coldly. "I was going to walk back to the library afterward."

Mrs. Berkenbosch-Jones gripped Casimir's arm as he flopped around defiantly. "Don't pretend you don't understand why this is entirely inappropriate."

The corners of Terpsichore's mouth began to twitch downward. "I wouldn't have to lie if you would just be reasonable."

Casimir stopped struggling and glanced up at me, like he was checking to see if I'd also heard the change in tone. How could I not? It was like a car shifting gears.

"*Reasonable?*" Mrs. Berkenbosch-Jones sneered. "I'm the one being unreasonable? When everything I've done has been in your best interes—"

"There's nothing wrong with me, Mother!" Terpsichore interrupted. "I'm autistic. I'm not broken!" She shook her head. "All the things you told me I couldn't handle, I can!"

"You don't know that!" her mom protested. "You spend one night out, and suddenly you're ready to take on the world, but think about it, Terpsichore!" The woman adopted an expression of pity. "You fall apart if a room is too hot or if a drink is carbonated. And heaven forbid you spill something on your clothes—"

Terpsichore's hands began to tremble. She covered her ears. "Turn it off, Mother!"

Mrs. B-J ignored her, gaining momentum. "You go to one party, sure, but how do you know you're not the butt of some joke? How do you know everyone wasn't laughing at you as soon as you left the room?"

"I said turn it off!" Terpsichore shouted. Mrs. Berkenbosch-Jones froze, stunned. Her mouth hung open, her eyes popped, and her purse straps slid to her elbow.

Terpsichore threw her arms down at her sides. "Nobody laughs at me! Because I laugh first—at me! Me from nowhere, me with no real education, me with no social skills, as you've kept reminding me my whole life." Terpsichore gestured to the center of her chest. "Well, look at me now! Look how I live. Look at my friends. Look where I'm going. I am not staying in my room anymore. I am moving, maybe up, maybe down, but wherever it is, I'm enjoying it.

"Mama, I am having the time of my life"—her voice became gravelly with emotion—"because for the first time it is my life, and I love it. I love every second of it. And I'll be damned if you're going to take it away from me. I am Terpsichore Berkenbosch-Jones," she declared, hugging herself tightly, "and I love her. And if you don't, you clear out right now!"

I watched Terpsichore gasp for air, her shoulder blades rising and falling like restless, vestigial wings. For maybe thirty seconds, none of us spoke, not even Casimir. We felt the shifting tectonic plates reform the foundation of the alley. But we alone knew what was happening. Out on the street, cars sped by, people walked past without a second glance.

Mrs. Berkenbosch-Jones choked on a sob. "Of course I love you," she said.

And as much as I abhorred the woman, I believed her.

I think Terpsichore did too. She swallowed and stared at a spot just in front of her mother's feet. "Mama," she said, "you have got to let go of me."

Mrs. Berkenbosch-Jones stood there, blinking at her daughter. I don't know if it was wheels turning or fuses tripping or connections short-circuiting, but something was happening in the woman's head. "I—" she babbled. "I—" She took a deep breath. "I'll . . . wait for you in the car," she said finally. "Come on, Casimir. We'll get your tablet."

"You might be waiting awhile," Terpsichore said. "I'm not done talking to Dolores."

Her mother scowled, then forced a pleasant look. "Fine," she said, taking her nephew's hand. "Take your time." She gave me a curt nod. "Dolores."

"Mrs. Berkenbosch-Jones," I replied, nodding back.

The woman glanced around the alley, as if checking for some lost item. Then she wiped her eyes, cleared her throat, and walked away.

"That was . . . freaking awesome," I said reverently. "I can't believe—I mean, how the hell did you think of what to say?"

"I didn't." Terpsichore slumped against me. I had to take a step back to keep her upright. "It's from the dressing room scene at the end of *Gypsy*. I changed a word here and there, but only a couple." She frowned and muttered, "Always gets nominated for the Tony, Best Costume Design. Never wins."

"I've never seen *Gypsy*," I confessed.

"Neither has my mother." Terpsichore put her hands on my arms to steady herself. Her fingers were clammy and cold. "It's my favorite."

"You should win a Tony for that performance," I told her.

Terpsichore shook her head emphatically. "It wasn't a performance,

Dolores. I said someone else's lines, but I wasn't acting." She regained her footing and glanced up at me, her amber eyes meeting mine for just a moment before she flicked them back down. "I'm not good at pretending to be someone I'm not," she stated.

"You're amazing, Terpsichore," I said. "Really."

"I feel like my bowels are going to prolapse," she wheezed.

"Well, do you want to come up?" I asked. "Get some water? We've got donuts, too; Johann brought them over yesterday."

She perked up. "What kind?"

"Regular and chocolate sprinkle."

"Okay." She gave me a stern look. "I will come upstairs for a donut, Dolores. But this doesn't mean we're back to the way things were. You've got to earn my trust."

~~~~~~~~~

That night I dreamed I was sitting on the front steps of St. Francis of Assisi Catholic Church. Except it wasn't really St. Francis of Assisi Catholic Church because instead of being downtown, across the street from a vape shop and a brunch place, the building was in the middle of a silent, sprawling meadow. A bubbling spring carved its way through the green undergrowth, and little yellow wildflowers bloomed in clusters along its path. The round leaves of birch trees flapped against each other in the wind like insect wings.

At first, I thought I was alone in the dream. But that quickly changed. All of a sudden, the meadow took on the feeling of a festive garden party, and I looked around to find myself surrounded by a group of freaky-but-familiar figures laughing, talking, and enjoying the lovely weather.

St. Bartholomew stretched out his loose skin suit across the grass as a picnic blanket for St. Cecilia, who sang a beautiful folksy melody in spite of the fact that her head was mostly severed from her body. St. Sebastian pulled an arrow from his side and used it to roast marshmallows over the grill on which St. Lawrence was burning, while the two of them chatted. St. Lucy napped and worked on her tan while her gouged-out eyes read a novel in the grass.

A long-haired, bearded man in a crimson robe materialized to sit on the stair beside me. I recognized him immediately from the bottle of oil that Tía Vera had begged me to use.

"St. Vitalis of Assisi," I said.

The man nodded, setting his scepter against his knee. The two of us looked back out at the group of happy martyrs. Liters of blood poured out of the saints' wounds and drained into the spring, except for some reason, their blood wasn't red. It was yellow, so yellow it turned the babbling brook the color of those marshmallow Easter Peeps.

"Why is everyone having such a good time?" I asked.

St. Vitalis shrugged without looking back at me. "Honestly," he said, "what's the alternative?"

I didn't have an answer, so instead I watched as the yellow rivulet wound down through the meadow. Then it grew, turning first into a stream, then a river. I realized that I'd stopped being a participant in the dream and was suddenly a formless, floating observer, following the progress of the urine-colored river as it flowed out to a choppy, urine-colored sea. Storm clouds gathered above the waves, growing heavy with the evaporated liquid, until they could hold no more.

But when the yellow droplets poured down from the sky, they

didn't fall back to the ocean. Instead, they rained down onto the linoleum floor of Susan B. Anthony Middle School. And there I was, not the me who was watching it, but me Dolores, lying on her back staring upward with a frozen, glassy expression.

The Dolores in the dream presented one hand palm forward, and with the other, she held the scary saints book to her chest. The yellow puddle grew and created an outline around her body. Then the yellow turned to gold.

Gold like a halo.

Gold like a saint.

Epilogue

The final weeks of summer break were different. They felt the way summer is supposed to feel when you're fourteen. The days tumbled by, blending one into the next. It was like the natural rhythm of life had been restored. It was a relief. In early June, just existing between blessed bouts of unconsciousness had felt like a quixotic task.

Quixotic was my newly acquired Scrabble word, thanks to Terpsichore making me watch a bootleg video of *Man of La Mancha*. Movie night with Terpsichore meant her pausing it every few minutes to share a comment on the costuming or a fact about the characters. Or to reiterate that illegally recording a show was wrong, but that the greater wrong was the inaccessibility of professional theater. She also insisted that I turn off my phone and be fully present, because "that's how it is when you go see a performance for real." We worked our way through a dozen bootleg musicals before August was over. Sometimes Casimir watched with us. He especially liked the ones with swear words.

Casimir was going to be a more permanent fixture in the Berkenbosch-Jones house. His mom was planning on settling locally as soon as she got back from her deployment and finished her military contract. I won't lie: I felt a little bad that Casimir was now condemned to a childhood of having Mrs. Berkenbosch-Jones as a babysitter. To be fair, though, Terpsichore's mom wasn't the same as she had been when I met her. The more confident Terpsichore got standing up for herself, the less opportunity her mom had to trample her. By the end of the summer, Mrs. Berkenbosch-Jones had agreed to a number of concessions: Terpsichore would be allowed to use the family computer without direct supervision, she could spend time with me and my family even though we were "bad influences," and she would start at Jackson High in September. It would be her and Casimir's first year at schools with other students—Casimir as a preschooler and Terpsichore as a freshman. This unifying experience cemented Terpsichore's reluctant fondness for her little cousin. She even started bringing him with her when she visited the apartment, though really this was at Tía Vera's request. My aunt had taken a special interest in the hobgoblin, seeing in him a displaced, lonely little boy in need of boundaries, compassion, and food.

Tía Vera had time to spare now that she and my mother had settled our finances. Well, *settled* was a strong word. Things were still a raging dumpster fire, and it took my aunt and my mom weeks to uncover the full scope of Dad's bad decisions. But after getting rid of the machines and giving up the lease to the print shop and the apartment above it, we didn't have to declare bankruptcy, after all. But we did have to move in with Tía Vera. It would probably take Mom over a year to get out of debt, but she was motivated. She'd even talked about going back to school and getting a technical degree, something with a salary and benefits and upward mobility.

Unfortunately, our current budget meant that a moving company was out of the question.

"No, no," Tía Vera directed, "that goes in the dumpster!"

"Yes, ma'am," answered Spider-whose-name-was-Ricky. He and

Teardrop-whose-name-was-Brian maneuvered the coffee table down the stairs.

Vera caught sight of my brother and huffed. "Ándale, Mateo, I see you hiding behind the car. Get moving!"

Standing on the landing, I held up a long piece of yellow serrated plastic. "Hey, someone needs to snake the drain in the bathtub. The water won't go down."

My brother scoffed. "Um. No? Why would that be my job?"

"I wasn't asking you." I smirked. "I was asking Johann."

Johann poked his head up over the car, where he was roping a blanket-wrapped bed frame to the roof rack. "I will snake the drain, Lola."

"Nope!" my brother shouted, bolting up the stairs. "No. I will do it." He glared at me.

"Thanks, roomie." I grinned and passed him the drain snake.

"That's not funny," he said. "I told you. I'm not moving into Vera's house with you guys."

"Not until Johann gets sick of you," I teased. "You know, she pulled out the matching sheet sets. From when we were kids. The safari print."

Mom poked her bandannaed head out the front door. "Is someone going to deal with the bathtub?"

"On it!" Mateo disappeared into the apartment.

"Thank you." Mom squinted behind me at something in the alley. "Is that a—"

I turned to see what she was looking at. "A dog?" Terpsichore and Casimir had come around the corner. The little boy was holding a leash, on the end of which was a very small, very scraggly canine. "When did you get a dog?" I shouted, hopping down the stairs.

"Yesterday," Terpsichore answered. "It wasn't planned."

Up close, I got to appreciate just how strange the little animal looked. She couldn't have weighed more than ten pounds but should have been twice that at least. The dog was emaciated, her little ribs poking through patches of white and beige fur. I could see the outline of her skull, skin pulled tight over bulging, weepy black eyes. But most striking of all, the dog had the longest, saggiest titties I had ever seen—rows of loose pink flaps that dragged on the pavement when she walked.

"Grandma Vera, Grandma Vera! I found a puppy!" Casimir lifted the dog awkwardly, exposing her lewd underbelly for my aunt to inspect. The dog wagged her hairless tail, her back claws clicking on the ground.

Tía Vera hid her shock under an expression of nurturing enthusiasm. "A puppy!" she repeated. "Are you sure, mijito? She looks a little . . . mature for a puppy."

Casimir set the dog back down. She made little grunting, snorting sounds as she circled the boy's feet.

"Who is this?" I asked.

"Her name is Crockpot," Casimir answered, crouching down to scratch the dog's head.

I looked up at Terpsichore, eyebrows raised.

"Some man was trying to sell her on the side of the road," she explained. "He wanted twenty bucks. Casimir was smitten, but Mom told him there was no way we were getting a dog." She lowered her voice. "Then the man said he was going to put her down if no one bought her. Clearly some kind of puppy mill situation. A lot of inbreeding, I suspect."

Crockpot stood on her back legs to lick Casimir's face, and ear, and the inside of his mouth. The boy laughed. "She loves me the most."

My aunt nodded, eyes wide. "Yes, I can see that."

"Can I take Crockpot inside?" Casimir asked.

"No, not right now. We've got to be out of here in . . ." Tía Vera checked her watch. "Dios mio, thirty minutes!" She clapped her hands above her head. "Let's go, everyone!"

Terpsichore straightened her glasses. "You're wearing jeans," she said, studying my outfit. "You never wear jeans."

"Yeah, I know," I groaned. "All my other clothes got washed and packed. I haven't worn these since the beginning of the summer." I hiked the waist up off my bladder. "Believe me, I'm regretting it. Though you'll never guess what I found in the pocket." I pulled out a folded piece of paper and handed it to Terpsichore.

She read the first line of print out loud. "'Rate each statement strongly agree, agree, somewhat agree, unsure, somewhat disagree, disagree, or strongly disagree. I consider myself an effective communicator.' This is from the workshop."

"Yup. Funny, isn't it?"

Terpsichore tilted her head. "Is it? All it means is that you haven't washed your pants."

Mateo jogged down the stairs with a grocery bag full of drain muck and nearly curb stomped the newest member of the Berkenbosch-Jones family. Casimir gave him an impassioned scolding.

"*Dolores,*" my brother whispered after he'd been properly introduced to Crockpot. "*Dolores, the dog has boobies.*"

"Yes, Mateo, we can all see that the dog has boobies." I turned to
Terpsichore. "You should sew her a bra," I said. "Her little nipples are
going to chafe off."

Terpsichore sighed. "I had considered that."

"I mean, it doesn't have to be boring. Make it saucy—1930s bur-
lesque." I put my arms out and shimmied. "Consider it practice for
your *Gypsy* revival."

"Swarovski is so expensive." Terpsichore spun the ring on her
thumb thoughtfully. "But I guess fringe might work."

"Tassels," Mateo offered. "Definitely tassels."

Somehow, we managed it. Spider-whose-name-was-Ricky and
Teardrop-whose-name-was-Brian were the last out of the building,
dragging that awful beige couch down the stairs and out to the dumpster. After Vera had adequately thanked them and promised to bring
by home-cooked meals, the two ice cream shop owners went back next
door. This left me, Mom, Mateo, Johann, Vera, Terpsichore, Casimir,
and Crockpot waiting for the landlord to arrive and pick up the keys.

"Should we say something, maybe?" I asked. "You know, about the
print shop? Something, I don't know, commemorative?"

As if she alone took my words to heart, the dog squatted down
and peed on the lowest stair.

"Ew, gross!" Mateo stood up. "Did she have to do that there?"

"Don't urine-shame Crockpot," I told him. "It's not her fault."

"That's right," Mom said. "I doubt her pelvic floor works after having as many babies as she's probably had."

Mateo gagged. "Please never say 'pelvic floor' ever again."

Johann smirked and pulled my brother close.

"Pelvic floor. Pelvic floor. Pelvic floor," I goaded.

"Yeah, yeah, laugh it up, but at least my bladder works," Mateo said. "Unlike some of you."

There was a momentary intake of breath around me, as Mom and Vera and Johann and Terpsichore all waited to see how I would react to someone poking this ulcerated wound. Mateo's eyes sparkled. Not with malice, I realized, but with genuine curiosity. *Where is the line?* he asked me silently. I asked myself the same question. What story would I tell about my bladder someday? Would I say that it ruined my life? That it corroded my hopes and dreams, stopped me from finding love and meaning? That it was something so awful, so painful, that there would never be any room to laugh about it? *There once was a girl named Dolores* . . .

"A bad bladder is better than a bad tattoo!" I spun around to face my aunt. "Did you know about that, Tía? Mateo has a tattoo!"

"Mateo!" Tía Vera gasped.

My brother stood up. "Dolores, I swear to God—"

"Run, Terpsichore, run!" I shrieked. As we jumped over the bottom stair, I saw the sparkling urine dripping through the punches in the metal to pool on the ground below. Crockpot started to bark, little yelping bleats that sent Casimir into a fit of contagious giggles.

Terpsichore and I ran down the alley and out onto the sidewalk, and then, for whatever reason, we kept going. Still laughing, we dodged pedestrians, ducked around lampposts, sprinted along alleys. Terpsichore's cheeks flushed pink and her hair came loose as she held her glasses on her face with one hand and gripped my arm with the other. Her fingers dug sharp into my skin as she kept hold of me. My heart thumped. My lungs burned. My bladder ached.

All of these sensations, pleasant and unpleasant, coursed through my body and told me that I was alive.

And because of that, all of them were beautiful.

Author's Note

It's common knowledge that most writers draw on their own experiences to create the main characters and conflicts that appear in their books. I'm no different. Like Dolores Mendoza, I was told I had interstitial cystitis as a young teenager. I received my diagnosis not long after I first started showing symptoms, when an exploratory procedure revealed the bleeding on my bladder wall.

A few years later, as my IC became more debilitating, I cut out one of the scope photos the urologist took, framed it, and set it on my bookshelf next to the pictures of friends and family. Being young and sick is a bizarre and frustrating experience. When I felt like I was going crazy, I'd look at the photo on my bookshelf and remind myself that the pain had a visible source. To me, that meant my experiences were valid, and I could hold compassion for myself and my body.

However, there were many other kinds of experiences in my life I'd invalidated because they weren't visible in a photograph. Feelings that had been around for as long as I could remember: anxiety, isolation, overwhelm, ineptitude, otherness. I'd always had a sense that there was something inherently different, and thus wrong, with the way my brain related to the world. In movies and books, I gravitated toward stories of characters who started their story arc on the outside of society, but through some event or relationship, they were able to finally belong. Those who read my first book, *Popular*, will probably recognize that theme. By the end of the book, "Character Maya" seems cured of the differences that kept her separated from her peers. She is fully confident in herself. She has finished her hero's journey.

It wasn't a lie. That's how it felt at the time. But "Character Maya" stayed where I left her on the last page of the book, and my life kept going. The same struggles I'd always had didn't stop once I started high school. Even as I was finishing the final edits on *Popular* my freshman year, I started to feel a nagging fear that following Betty Cornell's advice hadn't fixed me. In fact, Betty had been part of a much larger pattern in my life: meticulously researching a "right" way to exist and testing it with a calculated, scientific approach. I did this because I believed that if I changed enough of my behavior, I could become socially integrated, just like the characters in those movies and books.

I couldn't keep up this act all the time. Most days I would come home from school and completely melt down. But how could I talk about that publicly when I felt like so many people wanted me to be the character at the end of my book? Or the person I pretended to be on TV or in interviews or at book festivals?

Autism wasn't a label I felt comfortable with immediately. My younger sister's intellectual disability had always been lumped in with her autism diagnosis, so I often wrongfully conflated the two. But several years ago, my mother came across a list of characteristics in young girls with autism and, in an unexpected twist, recognized her *oldest* daughter there, not her youngest. She remembered things I couldn't about my behavior as a little kid, things that had always just been quirks of my personality or running family jokes. My inability to make friends or pick up on social cues, my extreme sensory processing issues, my hyperfixations and special interests. Annoying or self-injurious habits we'd worked hard to break suddenly made sense as stims.

I was shocked when my mother first introduced this idea. I told my fiancée, whom I'd just started dating at the time, about this jarring conversation. She said she didn't see anything like that when we hung out. I agreed that my mom was way off base.

After we moved in together, my fiancée changed her mind. Autism had been the right word all along. We just hadn't been close enough for her to see it yet. She didn't love me any less because of it. We spent time together learning about autism in women, and I heard about masking for the first time. Finally, I had a word to explain why I have such a deeply complicated relationship with Popular as an adult.

As a teenager, I learned tools that would become critical for me later in life. Tools that have helped me give presentations in front of hundreds of people, ace job interviews, and blend in at parties. But what I wish I'd learned was that there'd been nothing actually wrong with me that needed changing in the first place. I wish I'd learned that not every person is safe and worthy of my kindness and effort. I wish I'd learned that setting boundaries is critical. I wish I'd learned that fake-it-till-you-make-it just doesn't work for everyone. I wish I'd learned that it is okay for some people not to like me, because there are plenty of people who love me.

So, along came Terpsichore. Terpsichore isn't a perfect or complete representation of autism, because there is no perfect or complete representation. All autistic people are unique, and autism looks different for every individual. So I built an autistic character based on myself. Well, the self I would love to become. Terpsichore shares my special interests, stims, and sense of humor. But she doesn't hate herself. She has unshakable self-worth and self-efficacy. She listens to her body. She says what she thinks. This fourteen-year-old character is who I want to be when I grow up—someone who breaks down societal inequality instead of her own personality.

I knew that featuring an autistic character in *Chronically Dolores* would mean owning my identity as an autistic person. Almost five years after that initial conversation with my mother, I'm ready to share that information with others outside my immediate circle. It's not because I feel like I owe this explanation, but because representation matters, and if I'd seen women like me talk about their own neurodivergence, maybe it would have helped me figure all this out earlier.

Although interstitial cystitis and autism are fundamentally different, they've both been a formative part of my life, teaching me about advocating for myself and for others. When I saw my bladder, I was able to view the experiences I was having with IC as valid, and I knew I needed to take care of my body differently than other people. Now I try to extend that compassion to my brain, mainly by making an effort not to mask in situations where it's safe to do so. In the past, moments of authenticity were always negative, meltdowns brought on by burnout. I'm trying to figure out what the reverse of that is. What happens when I consciously choose to experience the world without editing down my joy or interests or passions for being "too much?" I have no clue. But I'm excited to find out.

Acknowledgments

Chronically Dolores has been a decade in the making, and unfortunately there aren't enough pages in this book to thank all of the friends, family, and readers who have seen me through the last ten years. I owe so much love and gratitude to these supporters, named and unnamed. They are the reason this book exists.

I want to start by thanking my editor, Julie Strauss-Gabel, for investing in me when I was fourteen. She saw potential and gave me the time and space to actualize it. This deep gratitude extends to the rest of the Penguin Random House team, who used their considerable skills in copyediting, translation, design, and publicity to bring Dolores and her family to life.

I owe so much to my agent, Dan Lazar, for believing in me years after I'd stopped believing in myself. It's impossible to express how much his guidance has shaped the writer and person I am now. I hope this book makes him proud.

The unseen, unnamed priest in the book is heavily based on the compassionate, funny, and brilliant Episcopal priests I've had the pleasure of knowing: Joan, Father Charles, Mother Rebecca, Mother Sarah, and Father Trey. Tía Vera takes her name, her culinary expertise, and her taste in home décor from my great-grandmother Vera. I want to thank her and the family who kept her memory alive to share those stories with me.

There were many teachers and professors who read and weighed in on other manuscripts and writing projects that spanned the gap between *Popular* and *Dolores*—including Mr. Law, Professor Sexton, Dr. Pellegrino, and Dr. Griffin. Their feedback and guidance helped me to reach the point where I could write this book. I also want to thank this book's early readers, including Andy, Angela, and Melinda, among others, for helping me refine what this book would be.

I want to spotlight my amazing friends Becca, Jaala, and Kate, who have been around for the entire ordeal that was writing my second book. I also want to express my gratitude to the Cokers for welcoming me into their family and being incredibly supportive of this project. I am eternally thankful for the original Van Clan—my parents, Michael and Monica, and my siblings Brodie, Natalia, and Ariana—as well as Emily and Zina, the brave members who've signed on to join our wacky crew. I owe an added thank-you to Zina for her expertise in religious etymology and spooky saints, and to my mother for always being my first reader and biggest cheerleader.

Additionally, I'd like to thank my therapist for helping me heal my relationship with writing. When things get stressful, I remember that writing is something I do and not who I am. I would be a worthwhile human being deserving of love and happiness even if I never wrote another word.

Finally, this book wouldn't have been possible without my fiancée, Eli. Not only is she an amazing person, she is also a brilliant editor. This skill isn't the reason I fell in love with her, but it's definitely a plus. I must also thank our pets—Mittens, Matilda, Martha, and Eris—for getting me out of bed in the morning. Usually with their persistent screams for breakfast. Words can't describe how much I love our little family and the life we are building together. My heart is full.